DEATH WASHES ASHORE

A DAVE CUBIAK
DOOR COUNTY
MYSTERY

PATRICIA SKALKA

THE UNIVERSITY OF WISCONSIN PRESS

The University of Wisconsin Press
728 State Street, Suite 443
Madison, Wisconsin 53706
uwpress.wisc.edu

Gray's Inn House, 127 Clerkenwell Road
London EC1R 5DB, United Kingdom
eurospanbookstore.com

Printed in the United States of America
This book may be available in a digital edition.

Library of Congress Cataloging-in-Publication Data
Names: Skalka, Patricia, author. | Skalka, Patricia. Dave Cubiak Door County
    mystery.
Title: Death washes ashore / Patricia Skalka.
Description: Madison, Wisconsin : The University of Wisconsin Press, [2021]
    | Series: A Dave Cubiak Door County mystery
Identifiers: LCCN 2020035751 | ISBN 9780299328207 (cloth)
Subjects: LCSH: Sheriffs—Wisconsin—Door County—Fiction. |
Murder—Investigation—Fiction. | Door County (Wis.)—Fiction. |
    LCGFT: Detective and mystery fiction.
Classification: LCC PS3619.K34 D435 2021 | DDC 813/.54—dc23
LC record available at https://lccn.loc.gov/2020035751

Map by Julia Padvoiskis

Door County is real. While I used the peninsula as the framework for the
book, I also altered some details and added others to fit the story. The spirit of
this majestic place remains unchanged.

For Carol,
who was there from the beginning . . .

All the world's a stage.

William Shakespeare, *As You Like It*

DEATH WASHES ASHORE

1 \ STORM DAMAGE

Anoise pierced the predawn silence, and Dave Cubiak woke with a start.

In the eerie half light, nothing looked familiar. The room was oddly shaped, and he didn't recognize either the bed he lay in or the thin cotton blanket that was draped over his legs and chest. Mostly it was the stillness that seemed out of place.

A powerful storm system had stalled over Door County, and for thirty-six hours, howling winds and slashing rain had torn at the soul of the peninsula. But that morning, the world was submerged in a soft quiet. Listening to the stillness, the sheriff realized that the tempest had passed and that he was in the guest room of his own house, unshaven and fully clothed in the same pants and shirt he had on the day before. He had come in around midnight from a grueling day, and rather than disturb his family, he had headed to the back room and immediately fallen asleep.

The noise came again. It was the squeak of the door being pushed farther open. The pit-pat of light footfalls headed toward the bed.

"Dad?"

Cubiak's eight-year-old son, Joey, materialized in the pale ribbon of light along the edge of the window shade. The boy was dressed in his favorite red T-shirt and pajama pants inexplicably decorated with rockets and fish. With Bear, their young black Lab, at his side, he approached.

"Dad?"

The sheriff was parched, exhausted. He wanted water; he needed more sleep. But as his son neared, he pushed up on an elbow.

"What are you doing up so early? What's wrong?" he asked.

"There's something weird out there on the sand." Joey's eyes were heavy with sleep, but he spoke with unusual urgency.

"The lake's been churning up a lot of stuff. Because of the storm." Cubiak kept his voice low, hoping not to rouse Cate, who was in their room across the hall.

"I know."

The boy perched on the edge of the futon and searched for his father's calloused palm. His skin was smooth but no longer baby soft. "This is different."

Cubiak pulled him closer. "I told you not to go outside. It could be dangerous."

"I didn't go anywhere, I just peeked. I couldn't sleep. You gotta come look. Please."

Tugging his father's hand, Joey slipped to his feet. "I think there's a body on the beach," he said.

In the kitchen, Joey knelt by the window. With an arm around the dog, he pointed down the foggy shore.

"There, can you see it? It's near the rocks."

Cubiak crouched alongside his son and followed the line of his thin, suntanned arm to the spot where his fingertip pressed against the glass.

Like a compass dial aimed at true north, Joey targeted a gentle mound atop a low sand dune that had been formed overnight by the rampaging waves. The mysterious hump was long and softly contoured, but the heavy mist obscured any telling details. The sheriff's best guess was that it was a tree trunk that the storm had left half-buried in sand and layered with algae and beach grass. He would have dismissed it except for the two appendages jutting upward near one end. Sticking out the way they did, they looked like arms and gave the mound a grotesque human form, as if someone lay on the shore beseeching the heavens for help.

If there was a body out there, he dreaded to think of the condition

4

it was in. Across the peninsula, lightning had sliced giant trees in half, exposing their secret naked interiors, while the wind-whipped water gouged the shoreline and cattle drowned in rain-swollen creeks. The sheriff had witnessed much of the damage firsthand and could imagine the havoc the powerful storm could inflict on human flesh and bone. He didn't want his son to see such violence.

"I'll go check," Cubiak said.

He stood and pulled on his rubber boots. Then he lifted Joey onto a stool. "Stay here and be quiet. We don't want to wake your mother." He tousled the boy's hair. "Don't worry. I'll find out what it is."

Cubiak shouldered the door open against the pile of damp sand that had blown up against the house. The deck was wet and slick and laced with strands of dislodged beach grass. After nearly losing his footing, he slowed down.

The beach was a junkyard of trash. A tree trunk the length of a telephone pole lay just a few yards from the house with a colony of rocks the size of bowling balls dammed against it. Smaller pieces of driftwood, snarls of barbed wire, an overturned Styrofoam cooler, and the remnants of a one-armed Adirondack chair disfigured the shoreline. The larger mess provided a backdrop for a tangle of detritus: shards of glass, mangled monarchs, dented beer cans, rusty iron spikes. Amid piles of blackened algae, the sheriff came upon a pink plastic pail, a child's toy, which sat incongruously next to a dead salmon lying sightless in the weeds.

All the while he kept his gaze on the odd shape that had attracted Joey's attention. The apparition reclined on a crest of sand near the edge of their beachfront. Cubiak's first guess was correct. It was a massive tree trunk half-buried in the sand. The two armlike appendages were pieces of broken mast clothed in weeds and strips of canvas that waved like jacket sleeves. No wonder the boy had mistaken the form for a body. Cubiak snapped a close-up photo with his phone to show his son. Then he kicked the sticks to the ground so there would be nothing for the boy to come out and investigate amid the rusty nails and worse that littered the beach.

By the time Cubiak got back to the kitchen, Cate was up. She was barefoot like Joey and wrapped in a yellow-checked cotton robe. She had made hot chocolate for the boy and tea for herself and had put on a pot of coffee for him.

"You didn't have to get up," he said.

She rubbed his shoulder. "And miss all the fun?" She smiled, though fatigue showed on her face.

"Everything's okay. It's just a big tree," Cubiak said, opening his phone to the photo. "There's nothing to worry about."

"It looked like a person," Joey said. He pulled his feet up and curled over his knees.

"You're right, it did, but it's not. Everything's fine."

The boy blew on his hot drink and then took a sip. He was tall for his age. Like his father he wore glasses, and like his mother he was artistic. The previous year, he had painted a watercolor of Door County for a school project, and Cate had framed it. Now it hung on the wall behind him. Joey had festooned the peninsula with images of trees, seagulls, ships, and paint palettes. The legend boasted the peninsula's vital statistics: Population: 29,000. Area: 2,370 square miles. Shoreline: 300 miles. State Parks: 5. County Parks: 18.

The sheriff glanced from the whimsical drawing to the harsh scene outside the window. In less than forty-eight hours, the record storm had devastated their pristine beachfront. The rest of the county had not fared any better. Reports of injuries and destruction to roads, barns, houses, and bridges continued to fill his in-box. The damage was especially severe along the shoreline. He and his deputies would be busy for days.

"We better make sure we're current on our tetanus shots," Cubiak said, giving Cate a nuzzle and a quick kiss on the cheek. "Not just us but everyone in the county. Lord only knows what we're going to find out there in all that muck."

While he finished his coffee, the sheriff scanned texts and emails. Then he showered and dressed and headed to work. He was backing out of the garage when the department radio beeped. The call was from the communications center. He had expected to hear from the dispatchers earlier, but he knew that the local residents were doing their best to cope on their own. Anyone dialing 911 had a serious problem.

"Dave." Despite the weariness and fear that masked the female voice on the other end of the transmission, he recognized the caller.

"Lisa, are you all right?" Cubiak said. Three months earlier, his assistant's husband had walked out the door and left her to raise their two young children alone. What was she doing at the 911 center?

"I'm okay. We're fine," she said. "But a man just called from Rosemary Lane. There was a lot of static on the line and the reception was lousy. He kept fading in and out, so I couldn't get his name. But I'm sure he said he'd found a body on the beach."

Cubiak sighed. Was this another mirage, like the one Joey had seen, or was it a genuine emergency? How many more reports like this would the department have to deal with? The National Weather Service had started issuing storm warnings twenty-four hours in advance of the onslaught. His department had broadcast alerts and information. Local radio stations had relayed the forecasts, urging people to seek shelter. Maritime warnings had cautioned boaters. Even the large cargo vessels sailing into the waters of Green Bay and Sturgeon Bay had been rerouted or delayed. Every precaution had been taken to prevent the loss of life. There would be no escaping property damage and human injury as well, but the sheriff had hoped that the county would survive the disaster without fatalities.

"Do you want me to call Doctor Pardy?" Lisa said.

Cubiak was reluctant to disturb the medical examiner unless it was necessary. "Not yet. I'll check it out first. It could be a false alarm."

"I hope so."

"Why are you at the office? Who's got the kids?"

"They're here with me. I picked them up from my mother's yesterday after work, but I couldn't get home because the roads were flooded. I couldn't make it back to my parents either, so I came to the justice center. It was the only place I could think of where I knew we'd be safe. I fed the kids sandwiches and peanuts from the vending machines, and they slept in a couple of empty cells last night. It was great fun for them. Anyway, it's worked out for the best because no one on the communications staff made it in this morning, and I've been taking the calls."

"Well, that's a good thing, I guess." He rubbed his chin, glad for the chance to shave.

"Dave?"

"Yes?"

"We're not the only ones here. Other people came in too. There's about a dozen of us who couldn't get to where we were going. We all slept in the jail. I hope that's okay."

Cubiak laughed. "Only if you promise to post a four-star review about the mattresses. Seriously, though, that's fine. There's a roll or two of quarters in the top drawer of my desk. Let people help themselves to whatever they want."

The storm had been vicious and relentless. Winds gusted to more than sixty-five miles per hour and spattered golf ball–sized hail on Fish Creek. The first night, more than thirteen inches of rain fell on the southern part of the peninsula, breaking a state record. Before the weather finally cleared, the National Weather Service tallied more than two thousand lightning strikes in the county.

Damage was severe and widespread. All along the waterfront, piers were shattered, and boats were torn from their moorings and pitched onto the docks. Even the more sheltered marinas in Sturgeon Bay were hit hard. The entire county lost power for hours. Towns reported broken shop windows, flooded stores, shredded canvas awnings, and twisted street signs. Calls came in about roofs ripped off barns and houses. A farmer claimed one of his cows had been impaled with a hoe. On Highway 57, just south of Sturgeon Bay, a semi had flipped onto its side and slid into a ditch. On Highway 42, north of Sister Bay, neighbors had rescued a pregnant woman trapped in an overturned car.

The lane from the sheriff's house was dotted with deep potholes and blocked with fallen branches. The rest of the drive was no better. Away from the lake, the fog lifted, and as he headed south, Cubiak tallied the storm wreckage. Massive, ancient trees were snapped in half; bushes were uprooted and twined into the barbed-wire fences that rimmed the perimeters of flooded fields. Four houses lost their front porches, and at one farm the domed metal top of a silo lay upside down in what had been a vegetable garden, leaving the open cylinder to stand guard over a gaping hole in the barn roof. A hefty man in overalls slogged through the muddy yard toward the damaged structures.

The sheriff slid onto the shoulder and lowered the window. "Anybody hurt?" he called out.

The man waved. "We're good," he said.

A mile farther, Cubiak swung back toward the water and encountered the mist again. Fog danced in and out of the pine trees that lined the road and snagged on the tips of the branches. The forest was like a laundry room that had been draped with ghostly tendrils hung out to dry like lace curtains.

Along Rosemary Lane, an eight-mile span of winding blacktop that skirted the lake, the fog thickened to a gray wall. Cubiak was at the north end of the rustic road; the address Lisa had given him was nearly five miles farther south. The road cut through a stretch of exclusive property, but the large, elegant homes were hidden in the fog. No one should be out in weather like this, but someone had seen the body and made the call. Cubiak hunched over the steering wheel and pinned his eyes to the blacktop. At the first quarter mile, a small white sign appeared on the left. The sign marked a beach access trail—a private footpath to the water for those who lived on the wooded side of the lane. There would be more markers along the way, each one denoting another access point.

Technically, only residents were allowed to use the trails, but curious tourists often stopped their cars and darted down the footpaths to enjoy the view from the exclusive beaches. Kids on bikes came, and because they were kids, they ignored the signs, figuring they had as much right to the peninsula's sand and water as anyone. Otherwise the beach was private. The residents paid dearly for their views and privileged location. Life on Rosemary Lane did not include bodies on the beach.

At the top of a rise, an animal darted into the road. It was brown and low to the ground. A fox. The sheriff hit the brake. The deer would be out too. Forced to hide during the storm, they would be hungry and foraging for food. Cubiak rolled on slowly, unwilling to risk an accident.

When he reached the seventh white sign, he grew more vigilant. At the eighth, he eased onto the shallow shoulder, set the blinkers flashing, and killed the engine. As soon as he opened the door and stuck his head out, mist speckled his lenses, adding another layer to the viscous atmosphere. He wiped the glasses on his damp sleeve and squinted at the sign. Peony Path. He was in the right place.

Fog obscured the lake, but he heard the water sloshing against the shore and walked toward it. At first the footpath was firm and level. Then as the trail sloped upward, the sand softened to mush. When the sheriff reached the place where the high waves had torn away the front of the dune, he pitched forward. Thrown off balance, he skittered down toward the shore and stuttered to a halt alongside a large tire rim that was stuck in the sand near a pile of dead fish and decaying weeds. A sliver of water, gray as the fog, came into view.

"Hello," he said. Nothing. He called again, louder. There was still no answer. Only the sound of his voice echoed through the ghostly landscape.

Cubiak walked north, skirting segments of green garden hose and the driftwood and tree trunks that the lake had belched out. Where did it all come from? How long before another storm carried it back into the lake? One massive log had made the journey from water to land so many times, the color had leached out of the wood and the fibers had separated into long splinters.

This morning's 911 caller had reported a body on the beach. Could someone have seen a beached tree trunk and, in the fog, mistaken it for a body, just as Joey had?

Ahead in the mist, a dog barked. The fog parted and he saw a slender man walking back and forth between the dune and the water. A small black-and-white dog trotted alongside the man. Cubiak braced for the worst and hurried his pace. As he approached, the fog closed in again.

Finally the man saw him. He raised a hand and the sheriff responded.

"There," the man said as he pointed toward a dome-shaped mound.

The hump was too large to be a human and more closely resembled the silhouette of a small beached whale. But it couldn't be a whale. Off the Door County peninsula, Lake Michigan dropped to a depth of 920 feet, too deep for the sun to penetrate. The sheriff had heard stories about giant sturgeons, fish that lived for decades in the cold, night-time pits of water and grew to thousand-pound behemoths in the eternal dark. He didn't know if the stories were true, or if they were tall tales that the locals spun for the likes of him, still considered a newcomer by many of the long-term locals, despite having made Door County his home for fifteen years.

The mist thinned and the mound morphed into a small boat. It was stranded on the beach about ten feet from the water, and it was upside down. The vessel was old and weathered. Layers of white paint had peeled off, exposing strips of graying wood. The sheriff was no expert on boats, but even to his inexperienced eye, this one seemed oddly configured. In length and width, it had the appearance of a rowboat, but instead of a flat bottom, the underside sported a slight keel, which was laid bare to the sky in what struck him as a slightly immodest pose. What was designed to be hidden from view in the water was unexpectedly on full display.

The hatless man waited nearby.

"Tom Johansson," he said after the sheriff introduced himself. "And Pepper." He leaned over to pet the border collie that sat at his feet.

"You made the call?" Cubiak asked, pulling a notebook from his pocket. Everything he'd seen on the beach that morning was etched into his memory, but he had to write down the name to make sure he got the spelling correct.

"I did."

"The message I got mentioned a body on the beach." The fog had retreated farther out over the lake, and Cubiak let his gaze run up and down the stretch of littered sand that had become visible.

Pepper whimpered and Johansson settled a hand between its ears. "Quiet," he said. The dog shook its head but did not make another sound.

"To be precise, I said that I thought there was a body on the beach." The man's formal manner reminded Cubiak of his good friend Evelyn Bathard, the former coroner.

"Where is it then?"

"Under the boat. Look over there, on the other side." Johansson pointed to the battered hull. "Pepper found it," he added. At the sound of its name, the dog pricked its ears and glanced at its owner as if awaiting an order.

As Cubiak moved to the stern, he tried to make out the name of the vessel painted on the hull, but half the letters were missing and those that remained were upside down and difficult to discern. An *M* or *W* followed by several gaps and then an *O*, or maybe two *O*s.

On the port side, he ran his gaze from the stern to the bow. At first all he saw was the jumble of weeds and trash that blanketed the beach. He kicked a dented beer can out of the way and stepped into a pool of decaying algae. A swarm of blackflies rose like a miniature storm cloud and buzzed around his ankles. As he bent down to swat them away, he spotted the hand.

The hand stuck out from under the rim of the boat and lay palm up in a bed of tangled beach grass. The thumb was bent at an unnatural angle, and the other digits splayed out. It was a man's hand, with a thick, roped wrist. Could it be a silly Halloween prop or part of a mannequin? The skin was wrinkled and sickly gray.

Then the flies resettled, and the sheriff knew the hand was real.

2 | INTO THE MIST

Cubiak knelt by the exposed hand and pressed two fingers over the radial artery. The flesh was cold and clammy. He tamped down the growing dread and waited for the throb that would reveal a glimmer of life. But there was nothing.

Johansson stood over him and watched. "He must be dead, whoever he is. You can tell just by looking," he said. "I'm a sculptor," he added, as if his occupation bequeathed him the ability to distinguish the living from the dead. The artist spoke louder than necessary, or perhaps the fog amplified the volume of his voice.

Cubiak nodded and pushed up from the sand.

For a moment, they stood in respectful silence. Then, for the official record, the sheriff took pictures of the hand, the boat, and the surrounding area.

"Did you try to move it?" he said, indicating the vessel.

"Sure, but it wouldn't budge. It's probably burrowed a couple of inches into the sand. The wood looks rotten, and I didn't want to put too much pressure on it. Besides, I have a bad back, and even if I got it loose I couldn't raise if off the ground by myself, so I gave up."

Cubiak didn't blame him. Who knew what he would find underneath? The rest of the arm. More body parts. A bloated body.

"Of course," the sheriff said. He surveyed the shore again. "Was there anyone else on the beach?"

"Not that I was aware of. The fog was real heavy when I got here. I must have been walking around for ten or fifteen minutes before I even noticed the boat. Then I saw the hand. I tried calling nine-one-one, but I couldn't get a signal so I started walking up the beach. I had to go quite a ways before I could use my cell. A woman answered, and when I told her what I'd found, she said I shouldn't leave until someone from the sheriff's office got here. I gave her as much information as I could, and then I turned around and came back. I was just past the footpath when I heard a car door slam on top of the ridge." Johansson pointed toward the dune and the trail that Cubiak had followed to the beach. "I figured anyone up there would come down to the water, so I waited. Whoever it was had a dog because Pepper barked, and then the other dog barked and came racing toward us. It was a big white thing, looked like one of those expensive breeds. He must have pulled loose from his owner because he was trailing his leash. I caught the beast and then shouted up to the guy that I had his dog."

"What happened after that?"

"Well, that's the funny thing. I kept waiting for him to come after the dog but he didn't. The fog lifted a bit and I saw him just standing there at the top of the dune. I called out about the boat and said I thought someone was trapped underneath and asked if he'd help me. He didn't say a word. Instead he whistled for the dog. I wasn't holding the leash, and the damn thing took off and ran back up the hill. Then the guy turned and left. Can you believe it? Just like that. Not a word. Just poof, gone."

"Any idea who it was?"

Johansson shook his head. "In the fog, it could have been anyone. But when the other dog ran off, Pepper took off too and started heading toward the dune until I called her back. If it was a neighbor or someone that I knew, they'd have recognized my dog and come down to help."

"What did you do then?"

"What could I do? I came back and waited for you. I don't understand why I had to stay here. I'd already told the emergency people everything they needed to know."

"It's standard procedure. After a storm like we just had, the emergency center will be swamped with calls from people needing help. We don't need unnecessary calls tying up the line. If you were here and someone else showed up, you'd be able to tell them that you already reported the situation so they don't duplicate your efforts."

Beneath a flock of swirling gulls, Cubiak radioed the station. Given the circumstances, the entire staff was on duty or on call, but that didn't mean anyone was available to help. One deputy had a serious family emergency; others were helping residents and the hundreds of campers who had been forced to find temporary shelter, while the rest were unsnarling traffic so food and water and medical supplies could get through.

Mike Rowe answered and listened as the sheriff explained the situation.

"I need help moving the boat. How quickly can you get here?"

"Twenty, thirty minutes, maybe. I'll do my best."

Cubiak was about to end the call when he remembered Lisa telling him about the people who had been stranded at the justice center. The main roads around Sturgeon Bay were clear and everyone was gone, Rowe said.

"Any identification on the boat?" he asked.

"A few letters, whatever hasn't worn off. There's not much to go on."

As the sheriff and deputy talked, Johansson walked Pepper to a snarl of branches and looped her leash over the edge of a branch.

"Sit," he said, and the dog sat.

"Stay."

The dog whined but didn't move.

"Do you have any idea what kind of boat this is?" the sheriff said when the sculptor returned.

Johansson scanned the wreck. "It looks homemade to me, one of those do-it-yourself kits or maybe a design someone came up with on their own. It's kind of a hybrid, don't you think?"

Cubiak nodded. "Have you ever seen it before?" he asked.

"It doesn't look familiar. Mostly what you see around here are kayaks and canoes and those paddleboards, although how anyone stays up on one of those things I don't understand. A couple of people have small sailboats, and there's a catamaran down the beach. Sometimes we see the charters and the fishing boats go out in the early morning, but they're always a good distance away."

"What brought you out here this morning?" the sheriff said as he kicked a clump of moss aside.

"Pepper needed a good run. We've been cooped up because of the storm. I wanted to stretch my legs, and she was anxious to get out. I think my wife wanted to have a little time to herself as well. She had a headache from the pounding waves and needed a bit of peace and quiet."

"You came from . . ." Cubiak glanced up and down the shore and then toward the road.

The beach along Rosemary Lane was a coveted stretch of lakefront. Years before, a local developer had bought up land on both sides of the windy road and then sold it off lot by lot. The residents who lived on the water could stroll out their front doors to the beach; those who lived on the other side of the road had to cross two lanes of blacktop and then follow one of the access lanes to reach the lake.

Johansson pointed up the shore. "I'm about a quarter mile up that way," he said.

"You walked this far in the fog?"

The sculptor smiled. "I like the fog. And I wanted to take pictures of the beach after the storm. Our daughter lives in Denver, and I figured she'd want to see what it looked like. Apparently, the storm made the news way out there."

"Do you live here year-round?"

"More or less. We have a place in Milwaukee too, but we're here more often than not."

"So you're familiar with the area." Cubiak arched his shoulders to relieve the tension in his upper back. Too much time at the computer.

"Pretty much. I guess you could say that." Johansson took his time answering and a sharp edge had crept into his tone.

"There's something bothering you. What is it?" the sheriff said.

The sculptor hesitated. "You don't think I had anything to do with this, do you? Just because I found the body . . ." He let the notion trail off.

"It was just your unlucky morning, that's all," Cubiak said. In murder cases, the killer was often the first person to report finding the victim. But this wasn't a murder case. He didn't even know if there was a body under the boat. And if someone had died, it was probably the result of an accident or a poor decision. "I'll have to file a report, so I'll need a formal statement from you. If you don't mind coming in this afternoon around two, that would be helpful. Other than that, you're free to go."

Johansson gave Cubiak a polite nod. Then he untied his dog, and the two of them headed up along the shoreline, leaving the sheriff alone.

A heavy silence descended on the cove. The lake had calmed further. The gulls had moved down the shore and joined a vortex of birds swirling above a mound of algae, drawn by the prospect of feeding on the dead fish trapped in the mess. Save for the soft lapping of the waves, the only sound was the sheriff's rhythmic scratching as he clawed at the sand, scooping it away from the hull.

The flies returned in earnest. They lit on his neck and swarmed around his ankles. As Cubiak swatted them away, he scraped his hand against the boat and rammed a sliver into his thumb. Cursing, he squeezed the splinter out and sucked the blood away. Then he grabbed handfuls of sand and tossed them at the pesky insects. His fingers were raw and his pants were soaked at the knees. He wished he had gone back for the shovel he kept in the jeep, but he had nearly completed the trench and it was too late now.

Caught up in the rhythm of the task, Cubiak lost track of time. The sound of a car door slamming startled him. He looked up as a man crested the dune and started toward him. The sheriff lumbered to his feet, relieved to be off his knees. He started to warn off the interloper when he recognized the tall silhouette and loping stride of his deputy. Cubiak waited, marveling at the speed with which the younger man approached.

Close up, Rowe looked exhausted. Rough stubble covered his chin, and dark circles colored the skin under his eyes.

"It looks like you had your share of trouble from this weather," Cubiak said.

Rowe shrugged. "We lost a few shingles on the house, and the garage flooded. Other than that, a couple of good-sized branches came down on the back lot. Nothing major. The problem was the dog. I think the wind kept Maize up most of the night. I woke up twice and found her pacing around, and in the morning she started shaking so bad I thought she was going to have a heart attack. My roommates took turns staying with her while I was at work, but last night when I got in, she was still shaking bad. The only thing that calmed her was me hugging her, so I sat in the corner and held her until the worst of it passed. What about you?"

"We were lucky. We got a mess on the beach and a broken pane of glass but nothing really when you consider how bad it could have been."

Rowe scrutinized the boat. "There's a body underneath?"

"Could be. The only thing visible now is a hand. Take a look on the other side." The sheriff pointed over the hull.

"If we can get a grip under the gunwale, we should be able to pick this thing up and move it away. We just have to be careful we don't drop it on whatever is underneath."

Rowe pulled on brown canvas gloves and gave another pair to Cubiak. "You don't want splinters."

The sheriff gave a small laugh. "Too late," he said.

"I'll take the back, you take the bow," the deputy said as he moved toward the stern.

The bow was the lighter end, but Cubiak didn't object. Rowe lifted weights and was younger by more than twenty years. There was no question that he was the stronger of the two.

The men knelt and worked their hands under the gunwale.

When they were in position, Cubiak began to count. "One, two . . ."

On three they pulled upward but the boat remained cemented in place.

"The damn thing's probably waterlogged. Feels like it's made of concrete, or maybe it's caught on something," Rowe said.

On their second try, they pried the gunwale an inch or two off the ground.

"Let's try clearing away more sand and see if that helps," Cubiak said.

Rowe circled the hull and started digging. "How long do you think this thing's been here?"

"That's hard to say. I'm guessing it landed on the beach sometime during the storm. So a day or so."

Their third attempt failed, but when they tried again, they felt the boat jerk free from whatever had kept it locked in place. As they lifted the side of the boat farther up, the victim's arm came into view. The two men struggled until the vessel was nearly perpendicular to the ground.

Then they looked down to see what they had uncovered.

3 \ THE BODY
ON THE BEACH

For a moment, neither man spoke.

"What the hell," Cubiak said finally. He glanced at Rowe and then back at the spot where the overturned boat had been lodged on the sand. "Tell me I'm hallucinating."

"If you are, so am I. Which means we're both crazy," Rowe said.

The sheriff had dreaded finding body parts under the boat. From the moment he saw the protruding hand, he knew there was a possibility that the vessel hid a dismembered torso. Worst of all, they would find only the hand. Instead, they had uncovered an entire corpse. What lay in front of them was the fully intact body of a dead man.

The corpse was a study in gray: face and beard and eyes that stared sightless into the fog. So too were the metal helmet on his head and the hip-length tunic and the chain-mail vest. Only his leggings and boots were black.

"If we're not nuts, then what we've got is the body of a man dressed in the armor of a medieval knight," Cubiak said.

"It sure looks that way."

The sheriff tugged at his collar. He was breathing hard and his back was wet with sweat.

"We gotta move this farther away," he said, indicating the boat.

They walked the wooden tug several yards down the beach and lowered it to the sand.

"We'll need pictures of this," Cubiak said when they got back to the body.

Rowe already had his phone out.

While the deputy photographed the scene, the sheriff called Emma Pardy.

He explained the situation to her, and when he finished, there was silence on the phone. "I'm not sure I understood all that," she said after a moment.

He repeated himself.

"Right," she said, but he heard the doubt in her voice.

"I know that you're dealing with the aftermath of the storm like everyone else, but as soon as you can get here," the sheriff said.

The medical examiner didn't hesitate. "I'll be out the door in fifteen minutes," she said.

"Thanks, I appreciate it."

Cubiak put the phone away and surveyed the beach again.

"Most likely the boat and the body were washed ashore together, but there's a chance someone saw the body on the sand and then dragged the boat over to cover it. Maybe they were trying to hide it or wanted to shield it from the storm."

"Why didn't they call and report it?"

"Some people don't like to get involved. At any rate, we need to look around for footprints or imprints that might be helpful."

"The beach is covered with junk and weeds from the lake. We're not going to find anything in this mess," Rowe said.

"You're probably right, but let's give it a go."

A careful search revealed nothing other than the sheriff's and Rowe's tracks on the few patches of bare sand around the boat; several paw marks, probably from Pepper; a trail of larger paw prints near the dune, most likely made by the white dog Johansson had mentioned; and the imprints from one more pair of shoes, which Cubiak figured would match those worn by the sculptor.

That done, the sheriff turned his attention to the boat. One of the seats was missing and the other was cracked. Several boards were nearly rotted through. There were no oars, and he saw oarlocks on only one side. With the transom right side up, he got a better look at what remained of the name and snapped a picture of the state registration number. He was about to turn away when he noticed two dark threads snagged on the ragged edge. He pried the filaments loose and took a closer look. The fibers were coarse and charcoal gray, almost black. He put them in a plastic bag and showed them to Rowe.

"What do you think?" he said.

There was a time when the deputy would have given a quick and not well-considered response, but he had learned to be more deliberate. Rowe held the bag up to the dim light.

"These haven't been exposed to the elements. They look fairly new." He glanced toward the body. "They could be from the man's tunic."

"True. And if they're not?"

"It could mean that someone else was in the boat. Not necessarily at the same time as the dead man but recently."

"My thoughts exactly," Cubiak said.

He paced off a wide perimeter around the body and the upright boat, while Rowe followed and drove stakes into the sand. Then they wrapped a long ribbon of yellow police tape around the spikes to mark off the area.

When they were finished, the sheriff knelt by the body and fingered the chain-mail vest. "It looks like the real thing, all right, not some plastic make-believe costume. The whole outfit must be fairly heavy. Why would someone venture out in a storm dressed like that, especially in such a small boat? And how come he wasn't thrown out when the boat flipped over?"

"Maybe his foot got wedged under the seat or his costume snagged on a loose board. That would explain why we initially had so much trouble lifting the boat," Rowe said.

He looked at the upturned vessel. "Or maybe he wasn't in the boat when it reached the shore. Maybe he was on the beach and had a heart attack or was struck by lightning and died instantly where he was standing."

"And then the boat flipped over and landed on top of him?"

"Why not? Given the conditions the last thirty-six hours, anything's possible. The boat's an old tug. If it wasn't properly secured, it could have been sucked out into the lake by the storm. It probably wouldn't have taken much for the waves—big as they were—to carry it to shore, toss it upside down, and then drop it over him." Rowe frowned. "But why would someone be on the beach dressed like a human lightning rod during a storm?"

Cubiak shook his head. "Who knows why people do half the stuff they do." He studied the dead man. The gray beard had brown roots, and the ashen face was unlined. Despite the swollen knuckles, the victim's hands were relatively smooth. "He's not as old as he appears at first glance. In fact, he looks like he's around your age. Any idea who he is?"

"Never saw him before."

The sheriff continued to think aloud. "He could be an actor from a local theater group. We need to contact all of them and see what they've got in production or rehearsals and also find out if they have any medieval knight costumes that have disappeared."

"I can do that," Rowe said. "A few resorts hire seasonal entertainers. Some of them live here but others are from all over the country. I'll check those too. Maybe he was a singing knight or a medieval storyteller, you know, a King Arthur sort telling a noble tale."

"That's pretty poetic for a cop," Cubiak said as he looked around at the half-dozen homes that were visible in the fog. "He could have been hired for a private party on Rosemary Lane. I can't imagine anyone entertaining during the storm, but we'll have to check. At any rate, someone could have seen or heard something. We can't rule anything out, not with him dressed like that."

The sheriff pushed up from the sand and flexed his right knee, trying to work out the kinks. He would like to blame the stiffness on the weather but knew that was only part of the problem. He was nearly fifty-seven and feeling it.

"Did you get a close-up of the victim's face?"

"Yeah, several from different angles," Rowe replied.

Cubiak wiped his glasses with his sleeve.

"Good, send those to me and then you better go and start asking around. Check the immediate vicinity first. Get one of the other deputies to help, if anyone's free. I'll have Lisa start looking for missing persons reports. When Emma's done here, I'll try to track down the owner of the boat. We'll find a lead somewhere. This guy didn't just drop from the sky."

Emma Pardy sidestepped the debris on the beach with the ease of a kid playing an old-fashioned game of hopscotch on a sidewalk. She was a distance runner, and Cubiak wondered if the daily workouts were the secret to her agility. He also wondered if it was too late for him to start a new exercise routine. He had shrapnel in his left shoulder from his soldier days and a wonky knee from a bad fall on the ice the previous winter, which made weight lifting undoable and his running days history. Cate had suggested swimming. She loved swimming, but Cubiak didn't like to get water in his ears. His wife had also mentioned yoga. He said he would think about it.

Watching Pardy's easy advance, he promised himself that he would come up with a plan.

When the medical examiner finally high-stepped over the yellow caution tape, she wasn't even out of breath. Maybe it wasn't just the exercise; maybe she had been blessed with good genes too.

"Well, this is certainly different," she said as she studied the figure lying on the sand. Then she looked past the sheriff to the derelict boat.

"That thing was on top of him?"

"Yes."

"Any theories about how the poor guy got here?"

"Several, but none that add up, given the storm, unless he was trying to kill himself. I assume he drowned, but he could have been struck by lightning if he was out on the water or standing on the beach before the boat washed ashore."

"If he was killed by lightning, I'll know as soon as I get him on the table. Lightning would have left burn marks on the body. There'd be entrance and exit wounds as well, just like from a gunshot." She paused. "Did you call for an ambulance yet?"

"Rowe took care of that before he left. He's going around the peninsula now, trying to ID the victim."

"Well, he's younger than he looks at first glance. That I can tell you already."

"My thought as well," Cubiak said.

While they talked, the gloom started to lift. Just as Pardy finished pulling on her gloves, the clouds parted and a stream of sunlight shot through the lacy mist of the lingering fog and fell across the dead man. Against the dull detritus that blanketed the sand, his metallic costume glittered like something from a dream.

Pardy glanced back down at the victim. "I feel like I've wandered into an old storybook. I have to say it: King Arthur, Knights of the Round Table, Camelot, search for the Holy Grail, Excalibur. Have I missed anything?"

"Lady Marian?"

"Wrong story. You must mean Guinevere. But what does any of this have to do with Door County?"

"Damned if I know."

Pardy smiled. "But you'll find out."

With that, she knelt next to the dead man, a signal that she wanted to be left alone.

While the medical examiner worked, Cubiak wandered down the shore and searched for clues that could shed light on how and when the man had died. The chance of finding anything useful on the beach was a long shot and he knew it, but it had to be done. As he walked, he tried to imagine the man's final moments.

The sheriff had come close to dying three times. Once from gunfire and twice from drowning. What he remembered was the paralyzing fear, the thought that it couldn't be happening, not then, not to him. And it hadn't. Each time he had been rescued. Most recently by Mike Rowe, who had kept him from sinking into the icy waters of a flooded silo not that far from where he stood now.

The many times that Cubiak had been a witness to death, he had been overwhelmed with despair and helplessness. Most excruciating was when he had knelt on the bloody street beside the still bodies of his wife and daughter, unable to save them or to bring them back.

Wasn't that always the wish of the one left behind? To undo death and rekindle the spirit of the deceased. To do anything, only to realize that nothing could be done.

Where did life go? For weeks after the funeral, he had felt the presence of both Lauren and Alexis in the house. Another time, sitting under a star-studded sky, he was convinced that they had come to comfort him. Had the knight's soul traveled immediately to some distant land, or did it wander the deserted shore, searching for answers, perhaps the same answers Cubiak sought? Had the dead man known fear, or had he faced impending doom with bravado? Had he wished for someone to hold his hand as his life seeped away into the water or into the sand?

"Dave?"

Pardy's voice was sharp, and in the anxious tone he heard echoes of the previous two, or was it three, times that she had called to him.

When he reached the ring of yellow tape, she was on her feet. She had stripped off her gloves and was zipping up her black bag.

"There's not much more I can do here other than confirm the victim's demise. I'll give you a call tomorrow with the preliminary autopsy report."

"How about time of death? That would be helpful."

Pardy sighed. "I know, but under the circumstances it's hard to pinpoint. Exposure to the elements or immersion in water for any length of time would complicate matters. Rigor mortis was setting in, so that's one factor to consider. The opacity of the eyes is another."

"Give me your best guess."

The medical examiner paused. "Based on preliminary observation, I'd say that he's been dead at least twenty-four hours but not more than forty-eight. It's only a guess, mind you, so don't hold me to it."

By the time the ambulance arrived, the fog had moved out over the lake, where it hovered along the horizon like a ridge of mountains. A half-dozen people had gathered near the base of the dune. As they watched the EMTs struggle with the gurney, Cubiak went to query them, hoping to garner bits of information that would help in the investigation. But no one had ventured to the lake during the storm. No one had heard anything unusual; how could they over the roar of the wind and the sound of the waves crashing onshore? Cubiak showed a picture of the victim to the people in the crowd, but no one recognized him.

"What happened?" an elderly man asked.

"That's what I'm trying to find out," Cubiak said.

After the ambulance left with the body, he scoured the area around the boat again in case anything had been missed in the first go-around. But there was nothing. Earlier, in the dim light of the fog-shrouded shore, the ragtag vessel had conveyed a sense of nobility and purpose; in the pale morning light, it looked pathetic, a worn-out relic whose usefulness was long forgotten.

The sheriff was driving north on Rosemary Lane when he called the Department of Natural Resources. From memory, he gave the clerk the spotty information he had gleaned from the boat.

"Lucky for you I came in today," she said. She sounded tired. "I'll do my best."

Five minutes later, she called back.

"You found a record of the boat?"

"Yep, it was last registered to a George Nelson, but that was ten years ago."

"Is there any chance you have an address?"

According to the clerk, Nelson lived ten miles up the shore. A long way for any boat to drift in bad weather.

"Hope he hasn't moved. That's the only lead I've got," she said.

4 THE *WAHOO*

The GPS led Cubiak to the end of Rosemary Lane and then up a county road that turned away from the lake for a mile before it curved back toward the water. The area was heavily forested and lightly populated. The modest frame homes he passed were few and far between. He stopped twice to clear fallen branches that blocked the way and almost missed the fire number that marked the Nelsons' property.

George Nelson was outside when the sheriff pulled up. He was a tall man with gray hair and stooped shoulders. Next to him was a tiny woman with vivid red hair. She had a youthful physique, but when she turned around, her face betrayed her age. The two were supervising a young man who was on the roof replacing shingles that had been damaged or blown off, probably during the storm.

"Our son," George Nelson said, indicating the worker. "We're lucky he lives nearby. I can get around well enough with the new hip, but I don't trust myself on a ladder."

"You should have had it done sooner," his wife said. She looked at Cubiak. "Men! So stubborn sometimes." She smiled to show that the scolding was gentle and good natured.

After the usual exchanges about the storm, Cubiak held out his phone with a photo of the vessel that had come aground on the beach.

"Is this your boat?" he said.

"Well, I'll be damned, the *Wahoo*! We sold that thing ages ago. Ten or more, I think," Nelson said.

"Twelve," his wife said.

"Okay, twelve. Why?"

"It's still registered to you."

Nelson frowned. "You know, I told that guy when he bought it that he had to change the registration."

"Who was that? Do you remember?"

"No, sorry." Nelson looked at his wife. "Honey?"

She pursed her mouth and slowly rotated her head from left to right and then back again.

"We put up an ad on the bulletin board at the supermarket in Sister Bay. It was some young guy that wanted it, I remember that much." As she talked, her husband moved toward the house. Cubiak heard him in the background giving instructions to his son. "He paid cash. George insisted. I remember that distinctly. The man said he wanted the boat for fishing and taking his nephews out on the lake. Jake? John? No. It was Larry." She shook her head vigorously. "Sorry, Sheriff. I really don't know."

"You wouldn't happen to have a receipt, would you?" the sheriff said.

"Oh good gracious, no. I'm sure I did at one point. George would have insisted on it." She smiled at her husband, who had circled back to her side.

"Insisted on what?"

"Getting a receipt for the sale of the boat."

"Indeed, of course."

She went on. "But I've been clearing things out, getting rid of stuff we don't need any more. Old clothes. Old papers. You know how that goes. I probably tossed it ages ago."

"What's all this fuss about an old boat, Sheriff? There's storm damage everywhere on the peninsula. You can't be worried about an old boat that ran aground."

"I'm afraid there was a body found beneath it."

Mrs. Nelson blanched and grabbed her husband's arm. "Oh my goodness, I hope it wasn't the guy we sold it to. He seemed like such a nice young man."

Cubiak showed them the victim's photo. "Do you recognize the man in this picture?"

They stared at the image for several moments. Nelson shook his head. His wife did the same. "No."

"You're sure?"

"Absolutely. The guy who bought the boat was young, a kid really, probably no more than eighteen or so. This poor man looks quite old. Of course, it was years back, but he wouldn't have changed that much."

Nelson was still staring at the photo. "Is that the man you found under the boat?"

"It is."

"He drowned?"

"I don't know. The body was just discovered this morning."

"Jeez, do you think he was out in the storm? Out on the water, I mean?"

"I don't know that either."

"The *Wahoo* may be old, but she was always a seaworthy vessel. Still, she couldn't have handled those waves. I don't know any boat, big or small, that could have. If he went out there, he was a fool."

"George!" the missus spoke sharply.

"You think I'm being harsh, but it's the truth," Nelson said as he patted his wife's hand. "That lake's taken down many a man and it will take down many more. It's a shame when it happens, but people need to learn to be careful. They need to learn to respect nature."

The station was eerily quiet when Cubiak finally made it to his office. The deputies were still out. A skeleton crew was on duty in the jail, and two part-time employees were fielding calls at the communications center. Lisa was gone but the sheriff found a note on his desk written in her looping, oversized scrawl: "Took the kids to my mom's. Need to check house. Back soon as possible." A bag of chips lay next to the note, and the edges were decorated with a ribbon of lopsided hearts that her kids had

30

drawn. An arrow pointed to the snack. "Last of the food. Saved for you."

The sheriff chortled and set the chips aside for Joey. His son could eat anything. Like Cubiak always felt he could, until a year ago when Bathard checked his blood pressure and recommended a diet low in salt and fat.

"I eat fish," Cubiak had protested.

"Very good, but from now on you need to eat more of it," the old doctor told him.

Thinking of his friend, Cubiak felt a pang of guilt. He had meant to contact Bathard that morning to see how he had managed in the deluge, but then the call came in about the body. The sheriff was about to text the former coroner when Rowe walked in. The circles under his eyes had darkened and spread. His pants and shirt were spattered with mud.

"What the hell happened to you?" Cubiak said.

"I slipped trying to help push a tourist out of a ditch," Rowe said. He glanced over his shoulder. "Back's okay, I think."

"Just sit, don't worry about the uniform," the sheriff said. He waited a moment. "Any luck?"

"Nothing. Not so far anyway. I got hold of people from three of the theaters, and no one recognized the man in the photo. None of them own costumes for knights. In fact, they don't have anything medieval at all. From what they said, our best chance will be with the Shakespeare troupe, but there wasn't anyone around. I left a message for them, but I haven't heard back."

"What about the resorts?"

"I could only get to a half dozen today, but I left messages at the rest. The folks I talked with didn't sound hopeful. More than one person pointed out that around here I was more likely to find storytellers and comedians who posed as lumberjacks or boat captains, not knights in armor."

Rowe rested his elbows on his knees and leaned forward. "I'll go home and change and then do a house-to-house near the beach."

Cubiak stood. "Hopefully you'll have better luck than I did. A few people showed up when the ambulance arrived, but none of them recognized the victim or had any idea how he ended up onshore. Nobody saw anything, and for two days no one heard anything but the wind and the waves. If our knight sent up a distress signal, it went unnoticed."

The sheriff turned to the window.

"Imagine yourself out there struggling to stay alive in all that. He must have felt like he was in hell."

5 \\ CAUSE OF DEATH

At ten o'clock the next morning, Cubiak drove Joey to the youth theater camp in Peninsula State Park. There was a production planned for the end of the month, and the director had arranged the Saturday session to make up for the rehearsals they had missed because of the storm. During previous summers, Joey had attended camps for baseball, sailing, and art. He had even roughed it on an adventure outing in the Upper Peninsula. Theater was a new interest, and the bug that seemed to have bitten him the hardest.

"The kid's a natural," the director told Cubiak after the first two weeks of the program.

The sheriff assumed he praised all the kids, but as he watched the rehearsal for their production of *Treasure Island*, he understood what the acting coach meant. On stage, his son seemed to step out of himself and effortlessly transform into the young Jim Hawkins.

"You'll be there, won't you?" Joey said. He had been talking about the upcoming production for weeks. The play was the highlight of the session, and Joey had the lead.

"You bet. Your mother and I have had our tickets for weeks," Cubiak said.

"Promise?" The boy quivered with anticipation. He embraced every aspect of his young life with a level of energy and enthusiasm that seemed surreal to his father. Everything was important. "Promise?" he said again.

Cubiak hesitated. Over the years, he had failed to keep his word so many times, and he had learned the hard way that an unkept promise could break a heart or worse. But he also realized how much the commitment meant to his son.

"Yeah, I promise," he said and cringed inside.

As Cubiak drove away, his phone dinged with a text from Pardy. The message was typical of the medical examiner: terse and to the point. *Meet me at the morgue. Important.*

The sheriff understood that by *important*, she meant complications. And complications usually spelled trouble. Pardy didn't say why she needed to see him, but he was sure that she was referring to the autopsy of the body on the shore.

When he had arrived on the beach, Cubiak assumed he was dealing with a simple case of drowning. The victim was an unidentified male, but they would soon find out who he was. Someone would call the station to report a missing person, or Rowe would get a response from his ongoing inquiries. More than two million people traveled to Door County every year, and even with the high volume of visitors, there were relatively few accidents on either the lake or the bay. With the horrific storm that had pummeled the peninsula, he had expected a rash of water-related accidents and mishaps, but there had been only the one call, the one from Johansson about the body.

Pardy was working on her laptop when Cubiak walked into the morgue. She wore an open lab coat over her jeans and T-shirt, but as soon as the sheriff entered, she buttoned up and moved toward the sheet-draped corpse.

As usual, the medical examiner jumped right in.

"The victim didn't drown. If he had, I would have found water in his lungs, but there wasn't any," she said, lowering the sheet to the victim's waist. "He wasn't struck by lightning either. Like I said yesterday, lightning leaves tell-tale scars or marks on the skin."

She showed Cubiak a picture. "They're called Lichtenberg figures and they look like miniature lightning strikes. You can see that there aren't any on the body."

"Then what was the cause of death?"

"Traumatic brain injury. In this instance, the result of a blow to the back of the skull."

Pardy came around the table and lifted the victim's head. "Here, look," she said and pointed to a deep gash that cut from one side of the skull to the other.

"That doesn't make sense. He was wearing his helmet when we found him and there isn't a mark on it, not even a small dent."

Pardy leaned against the wall. "He must not have had it on at the time he was injured."

"Which would mean that someone hit him hard enough to kill him and then slipped the helmet on his head?"

"I don't know what it means. I'm simply relating my findings, and based on the injuries found on the body, I'm afraid that's the only chronology that fits." Pardy crossed her arms across her chest and swallowed a yawn. "I didn't say it made sense."

"What kind of weapon would cause that kind of injury? Any ideas about that?"

"Indications are that he was hit with a flat board, several inches wide, with a fairly sharp edge."

"Could he have fallen in the boat and banged his head on one of the seats?"

"It's possible, but I doubt it. He has other injuries as well."

The medical examiner approached the body again. "There's a slight bruise on his left cheek that indicates he either bumped into something or was hit, but not very hard. The contusions on his arms and legs are different. They would only result from a severe beating. Judging by the degree of discoloration, it appears that the assault occurred well before he sustained the head wound. In fact, I'd say the beating was administered several hours prior to when the victim received the fatal blow."

Cubiak felt the chill of the morgue in his bones, but he resisted the urge to shiver. Pardy had warned him there were complications, but her report was more convoluted than he had expected.

"What else?" he said.

"No ID, as you know, but I'd estimate his age between thirty-five and forty-three. Height, six two. Weight, one eighty-five. The stomach contents indicate that he'd had blueberries, yogurt, and orange juice for breakfast. Nothing after that. His internal organs are all typical of those of a healthy male."

"What about alcohol or drugs?"

"There was no sign of drug use. But his blood alcohol concentration was point-oh-four, so he'd had at least one drink, probably two, earlier that day."

"And his outfit?" Cubiak said, pointing to the costume that was carefully laid out on the back counter.

"That thing! I had a devil of a time getting it off. The chain-mail vest alone weighed twenty pounds. The helmet was another two. I looked it up; it's a cross between a Spangenhelm and a Norman Helm. Sometimes helmets like these have face masks, noseguards, and chain-mail tails that cover the back of the neck, but this one didn't. If you ask me, no sane person would go out in a storm dressed like that, much less in a leaky old boat." She stopped. "Unless he wanted to die."

They were both silent for a moment. Then Pardy turned to the body and looped the conversation back to the gash on the victim's head. "If he fell in the boat and hit his head on the seat or the gunwale, there'd be traces of blood or hair somewhere," she said.

Cubiak agreed. "Theoretically, yes, but if he was out there for long, there's a good chance that the evidence has been washed away. I'll ask the state crime lab to check it out."

He picked up the helmet. "The question remains: could he have accidentally inflicted the fatal blow and then put this back on?"

"It's unlikely but possible. Even with the severity of the wound, the victim may have been able to function normally for a short period of time before feeling the full effects of the injury. A more probable scenario is that he was attacked on land and already dead when he was put in the boat. I have no proof that's what happened, but that's my opinion."

"And whoever killed him assumed the boat would capsize and he'd sink from the weight of the costume."

Cubiak looked at his colleague for confirmation. Despite the grim setting and the nature of the topic, he enjoyed their quick back-and-forth of ideas and information.

Pardy nodded.

The sheriff went on. "What if he was killed on the beach where he was found?"

The medical examiner narrowed her eyes. "A dead man is lying on the beach—we don't know for how long—and then a wave carries an empty boat toward shore, flips it over, and drops it on top of him." She spoke slowly and used her hands to demonstrate how this would have unfolded. "That doesn't sound very plausible either."

"No, but it's a possibility that has to be considered, especially given the severity of the weather. Everything about this situation is off. I mean, what are the odds of finding a man dressed like a medieval knight dead on a Wisconsin beach?"

"Touché. But there you have it, my friend. Despite all the answers, many questions remain. I wish I could tell you something more definitive."

"You haven't said anything yet about time of death."

Pardy slipped her coat on a hook. "I've been wrestling with that issue ever since I saw the body. It's hard to be accurate given the victim's exposure to the elements. However, judging by the stomach contents and taking all the other factors into consideration, my own best estimate for the postmortem interval is one to three days."

"So, it's mostly likely that he died sometime on Wednesday as the storm was approaching or later during the worst of it," the sheriff said.

As Cubiak headed to the justice center, he went over the session with Pardy. Although the medical examiner had eliminated drowning and lightning as causes of death, her findings didn't eliminate the possibility that the man had been suicidal. He could have ventured out in the rickety boat wanting to end it all, or even done so on a dare and then taken an unintentional, fatal fall. The blow to the head also meant that he could have been murdered. If so, by whom and why?

Even more basic: Who was he? How did he end up under a boat on a beach along Rosemary Lane? Why was he wearing a suit of armor?

6 | A PROBLEM WITH THE NEIGHBORS

As Cubiak turned into the lot behind the justice center, a man emerged from the shadows near the rear door. The sprawling complex that housed the sheriff's department was several miles outside Sturgeon Bay and surrounded by farm fields. The back lot was reserved for staff. Visitors to his office, the county court, and the jail were supposed to park out front. The stranger striding across the lot may have missed the sign that said as much, but Cubiak didn't think so. The man had a no-nonsense expression and was heading straight for the sheriff.

His years as a city cop had taught Cubiak to be aware of his surroundings, and despite the idyllic setting, he was suddenly wary. The previous week, a state trooper had been fatally shot during a routine traffic stop near Wausau. He didn't intend to become a county sheriff injured outside his own office. He glanced over his shoulder. There were only a half-dozen vehicles in the lot.

Who was this guy? What did he want? From a distance he looked young, but as he neared, the sheriff saw that his neatly trimmed beard was heavily flecked with gray and that his face had the weathered look of someone with a long history of working outdoors.

Cubiak got out of the jeep and waited.

When the man was an arm's length away, he pulled off his blue cap and held out a leathery hand. "Florian Urbanski," he said.

Urbanski's coveralls were worn and patched, his T-shirt faded to a pale orange. Beneath the heavy scent of Old Spice, he carried an aroma of cattle and the perfume of freshly mowed hay. For a moment, the sheriff wondered if he owned the pasture across the road where the Holsteins grazed.

"From?" Cubiak said.

"Up the peninsula, around North Bay. I don't get down around here often, but I was in town buying fence wire and figured I may as well stop. I wouldn't want to waste fuel making an extra trip to see you."

"It's Saturday. How'd you know I'd be here?"

"I called and someone said you were out. I figured that meant you'd be coming back in."

"You could have left a message."

"I like to look people in the eye when I'm talking to them."

Cubiak nodded toward the entrance. "We can talk in my office."

"If you don't mind, I prefer staying outdoors. This won't take long."

Cubiak took the man's measure. He didn't appear to be armed and didn't come across as dangerous. A bit peculiar, perhaps, but that wasn't a crime.

"What can I do for you?"

Urbanski snorted. "You can get someone from your namby-pamby department to do something about my noisy neighbors, that's what you can do."

Cubiak swore under his breath. He was in the middle of a potential murder investigation and coping with the aftermath of the worst storm of the century. The last thing he needed to deal with was a dispute between neighbors. He was about to tell Urbanski just that, but something in the man's posture gave him pause.

"Go on," he said.

"I farm some three hundred acres, dairy cows mostly, a few sheep, and chickens. Nothing special. I've been there my whole life and never had anything to complain about until now. The problem's my new neighbor, Scott Henley. He's the one to the east of my place. Ever since he bought the property last year, there's been trouble. He's got people coming up every weekend. Not a few, like family or close friends, but dozens

39

of people. They start up Friday evening and go on carousing all weekend, going at it like it's the end of the world. The racket is unbearable. Yelling, shouting, loud music. I figure they got some kind of orgies going on over there. But sometimes I hear what sounds like fireworks or maybe even gunshots. Whatever it is, the noise is real bad. It upsets the cows, and my milk production is down."

Urbanski rubbed his large hands together. "I got nothing against people having a good time, but I'm barely getting by and these shenanigans are hurting my bottom line. I thought maybe this year it would be better but it's worse. Something's got to be done."

"Have you tried talking to this Henley guy?"

The man pulled his shoulders back, and his posture became even more ramrod straight.

"Yeah, and a lot of good that did. The arrogant son of a bitch said it was his land and he could do what he wanted on it. I'm telling you that the guy's got no concept of being a good neighbor. He said that if my cows don't produce enough milk during the five days a week his property isn't being used, then it's my problem and not his."

"Can you keep the cows indoors on the weekend?"

Urbanski snickered. "You don't know much about farming do you, Sheriff? Take it from me, things don't work that way. If I kept the cows indoors, milk production would be even worse. I'm not one of these mechanized industrial farms. I run a small operation. My cows are pastured. When the weather's good, they need to be outside, period. Keep 'em in! My neighbor said the same thing. Ignorant city bastard. It's people like that who are ruining the peninsula."

"How do you know he's from the city?"

"He told me. He said he came up to the peninsula because it was cheaper to operate his business here than in the city. More bang for the buck, he said. He even said I should join the party. Can you believe it? I'm asking him to quiet things down, and he invites me to come over there and help them make more noise."

"Do you have any idea what kind of party he was talking about?"

"I don't know, and I don't care to know. Although come to think of it, he did say something that struck me as odd."

"What do you mean?"

The farmer tugged at his beard. "He said that if I let my beard grow to here"—he pointed to his chest—"I could be Merlin."

"Merlin?"

"Something like that. I don't remember exactly."

An image flashed through the sheriff's mind. It was from a story that he had read as a kid. "Merlin the Magician?"

"Yeah, that was it. Merlin to his King Arthur, that's what he said. Anyway, I thought the guy was crazy as a loon or leading me on and I told him as much. I said he could play whatever games he wanted and go to hell for all I cared, as long as he and his friends stopped making all that damn noise."

Just then a department car drove by. Cubiak recognized the driver as a young woman who had been hired as a part-time traffic officer for the summer. The car stopped and the door opened. Then footsteps came up from behind.

"Hello, Sheriff."

There was concern in her voice. Was anything wrong? Did he need assistance?

"Morning," he said, and signaled for the junior officer to go on in. Once she had walked past, he turned back to Urbanski.

"What was Henley wearing when you saw him?"

"What do you mean, what was he wearing? Just regular clothes. You know, blue jeans and a shirt. He had on some kind of fancy cowboy boots too. They looked like the genuine article, hand-tooled leather and all. Expensive, I'm sure."

Cubiak opened his phone to the headshot of the dead man on the beach.

"Do you recognize this man?" he said.

Urbanski pivoted away from the sun and angled the photo to get a better perspective. As he studied the picture, his eyes narrowed to a hard squint. "He looks kinda peculiar here, but yeah, that's him all right."

"This is your neighbor Scott Henley, the man you came to complain about?"

The farmer nodded.

"You're sure?"

"My eyes aren't as sharp as they used to be, but it's as close to a hundred percent as I can get."

Urbanski looked almost gleeful when he finally passed the phone back to the sheriff.

"Henley must be in trouble for something if you're carrying his picture around. What's he done?"

"Nothing that I'm aware of," Cubiak said.

"I don't understand."

"Where were you on Wednesday, say, between one and six?"

The farmer scoffed. "Sheriff, I got trouble remembering what I ate for breakfast this morning, much less where I was four days ago."

"I'm talking about the period just before and after the storm hit."

"Then you should've said so. That's easy. I was busy taking care of the animals. I didn't have to listen to the weather reports to know that a storm was coming. The animals could sense it. They were acting all skittish, and I knew I had to hurry to get them inside where it was safe."

As he talked, the farmer scuffed his heel on the gravel. "The cows were spooked, and even with old Shep helping to round them up, it took a while. Besides the cattle, I had chickens, a half-dozen sheep, and a herd of goats to get under cover. Not only that, but I had to make sure I had enough feed at the ready for them. Some of these storms can last for days, and I didn't want to take any chances on not being prepared."

"Did you see or talk to anyone during that time?"

Urbanski shook his head. "Except for the jerk next door, my neighbors are all farmers, and they were busy doing the same things I was. I got a man who comes in and helps when I need him, but I live alone. That day it was just me and the animals, like usual. If you were Doctor Doolittle, you could ask them yourself, and they'd give you a full report on my whereabouts," he said, chortling at his joke.

"What about when you were finished with your chores?"

"By then it was near dusk and storming bad. I went inside and fried up some sausage for supper. Then I hunkered down and watched TV until the power went out. After that I went to bed. The storm was a bad one, you know. One of the worst I ever seen, and I've been around a long time."

Urbanski scowled. "Look, Sheriff, I came here with a problem expecting you to help, and instead you're asking me all sorts of questions like I did something wrong. Whatever happened, I ain't got an alibi. The least you can do is tell me what this is about."

"Your neighbor—the man you identified in the photo—was found dead on a beach off Rosemary Lane yesterday morning."

Urbanski took a step back. "Dead! Well, I'll be damned. I thought the man was a menace, but that's no reason to wish that on him. What happened?"

"I'm not sure. Not yet." Cubiak hesitated. "So far you're the first person who's been able to identify the victim."

"I can do better than that," Urbanski said.

He pulled a small card from his bib pocket and ran a rough hand over it as if trying to smooth out the wrinkles. Then he gave it to Cubiak.

"Here you go, Sheriff. Maybe this will help."

7 \ DOOR CAMELOT

The blue business card was printed on high-quality stock and had a soft, velvety finish. A hatching pattern of fine green-and-white parallel lines covered the front. Embossed gold lettering spelled out the name and limited contact information of the issuer:

SCOTT HENLEY, FOUNDER AND PRESIDENT

MYTHWEAVERS LARP PRODUCTIONS LLC

WWW.MYTHWEAVERSLARPCHITOWN.ORG

Mythweavers was self-explanatory. Larp told him nothing. Chitown meant that the dead knight was from Chicago.

Cubiak walked Urbanski to the front lot and watched until his faded brown pickup disappeared down the road. Then he went in. The waiting room was empty and the halls quiet. At his desk, the sheriff pushed aside the reports he had planned to finish up and logged in to his computer. He had barely finished typing *mythweaverslarp* when the website popped up on the screen, followed by a blast of frenzied music and a flashing message: *Updates Coming Soon.*

Momentarily thwarted, the sheriff turned instead to internet searches. Mythweavers Larp Productions was popular. Dozens of the posts described events that the company had hosted. A *Chicago Sun-Times* article about the organization dubbed Scott Henley the Midwest's King of Larping. A sidebar offered a brief glossary of terms for readers unfamiliar with the concept.

Larp Live action role play
Larping A game where the participants physically portray their characters
Larper A word that describes a live action role player or someone who enjoys acting out fantasy adventures

What the hell is this? the sheriff thought.

With a few taps on the keyboard, Cubiak discovered sites for myriad larping events offering games that spanned much of human history and ventured far into the future as well. Neanderthal costumes were sold alongside outfits for space travel. There were larping sites for weapons, games, scripts, rules, associations, and organizations. Several sources claimed that the Dungeons & Dragons tabletop game from the 1970s was the seed that had given rise to the burgeoning universe of role-playing games.

After an hour, the sheriff felt like he had emerged from under a rock into the sunshine of a brave new world. Enough fantasy for one day. He logged off and spun his chair toward the slice of reality visible through his window. It was a narrow slice, limited to the pasture across the road, but it was a scene he had come to appreciate. Little changed in this world where nature tracked the seasons, and the Holsteins' movements marked the hours of the day. A time for the cows to graze, a time to slumber, a time to plod to the barn for milking. Occasionally a time for them to romp through the grass with tails held high.

Cubiak called Cate and asked if she had eaten lunch yet. She hadn't.

"I'll bring sandwiches," he said.

In the sunlit kitchen, Cate surveyed the two giant BLTs on the counter. "What a treat," she said, reaching into the refrigerator for a bowl of carrots.

"I thought you had reports to finish," she said as she set the vegetables in front of him.

"I do."

"So you're playing hooky?"

"I'm thinking. That makes this a working lunch." Cubiak sat down, wishing he had remembered to bring the bag of chips Lisa had left on his desk.

Cate pulled up a stool alongside her husband. "What are you thinking about?"

"Something called larping . . . Live action . . ."

Cate interrupted. "I know what larping is, but why are you thinking about it? Are you looking for a new hobby?"

He shook his head. "This is about the body on the beach. The victim was a larper."

"Well, that explains the costume."

Cubiak grunted. "How come you know about larping?" He looked at her. "Don't tell me you tried it?"

"Not yet," Cate said with a teasing lilt as she leaned against the counter. "I heard about it years ago before we even met. I was on assignment in Norway, photographing the king and queen at the palace in Oslo, when one of the royal grandkids told me about a larping event at a park down the road. I was curious and so I stopped on my way back to the hotel. It was quite interesting."

"Larping or meeting the Norwegian royal family?"

"Both, actually."

"Humph." Cubiak bit into a carrot stick.

"Larping is a much bigger deal in Europe than it is here. It's been popular there for a long time, and they use it in a lot of practical ways. In fact, there's a school in Denmark that bases much of its curriculum on it."

"You're kidding."

"I'm serious. If it's done right, larping helps kids learn by giving them the opportunity to immerse themselves in a situation. For example, they'll re-create a historical event instead of just reading about it, or they'll figure out what would be needed to establish a colony on the moon—it's a hands-on approach to education. If you think about it, playing the part of Henry the Fifth would be a lot more exciting than reading about him in a book."

Cubiak smiled at his wife. "You're a wealth of information, aren't you?"

"It's a big world. There's a lot to know."

"What about here?"

"Do you mean here in the States or here in Door County?" Cate said as she cleared the dishes.

"Both."

"From what I know, it's more popular on the East Coast than anywhere else in the country. I've never heard of larping events on the peninsula, unless . . ." She raised her eyebrows at her husband.

"I'm looking into it," he said and kissed her forehead.

From home, Cubiak headed north. Florian Urbanski's identification of the dead man in the photo might be correct, but the sheriff needed corroboration. If the farmer was mistaken, then Henley was still alive, and the first place to look for him was at the property next to Urbanski's farm.

The wreckage on the north half of the peninsula mirrored that on the south: fields of tall cornstalks nearly flattened, more downed trees than could be counted, sodden rugs draped over porch rails, and boarded-up windows. But there were signs of recovery as well. Tourists wandered the main drag through Fish Creek, and ducks paddled on the gently rippling waters of the namesake stream, which days before had been a raging torrent. Ephraim's waterfront was packed, and the weekly afternoon concert in the town park was in full swing.

As he neared Urbanski's property, Cubiak slowed to a crawl. The old man's farm was a Norman Rockwell painting brought to life: Stately oaks ringed the neat two-story red-brick farmhouse. Fanning out in the adjacent yard were a kitchen garden, a chicken coop, a weathered gray barn, and a tall white garage flanked by the battered pickup and a shiny red tractor that stood on either side like mechanical bookends. A towering pile of brush behind the machine shed was the only sign of the storm. The old farmer had been busy. A herd of Brown Swiss cows grazed placidly in an adjacent pasture. Probably Urbanski's pride and joy.

Half a mile down the road, a pale blue mailbox marked the driveway to Henley's property. The words Door Camelot were painted on the side in large, bright yellow letters. Beneath in smaller script: Mythweavers Larp Productions.

"Ah," Cubiak said out loud, as if the situation had suddenly sorted itself out.

The grounds were neat, like Urbanski's, but there the similarity ended. The original farmhouse was brown frame instead of red brick, and it had been dressed up with a yellow door and new windows. A massive addition off the back had doubled the size of the building. Along one side, a half-dozen cottages stretched out in a curved-wing formation, like raccoon kits trailing behind their mother. Yellow flowers filled the beds that dotted the neatly mowed lawn—three in front of the main house and one in front of each cottage. The color scheme was reflected in the small yellow barn at the far end of the yard. There was a vegetable garden next to the barn but no corncrib or chicken coop. Opposite the house, six black horses faced the wooden fence that marked off their territory. Piles of green brush and debris were scattered around the ground.

Cubiak followed a sign to the small parking lot wedged between the barn and the fenced enclosure and steered the jeep into a spot marked for visitors. As he got out, one of the horses nickered and tossed its mane. The other five steeds watched him cross the yard, their big dark eyes curious and intelligent. They were fine-looking specimens, and although the sheriff didn't know anything about horse breeds, he sensed that these animals were the kind that came with a hefty price tag.

He was nearly to the house when the yellow door flew open and a tall young man strode across the porch and bounded down the wide wooden stairs. He had a powerful build, pale skin, and dark hair that flowed past his shoulders. The rest of his appearance was equally affected: black boots that came up over his knees, black pants, and a white linen shirt with a round collar and long billowy sleeves.

"Greetings, sire. How are you on this fine day?" he called out as he approached.

Cubiak almost turned around to see whom the young man was addressing.

"What business have you here today, if I may be so bold as to inquire?" the greeter went on. By now he had reached Cubiak and saluted him with a half bow.

The sheriff showed his badge. "I'm here to see Scott Henley."

"Alas, sire, Master Henley is absent from the grounds today."

Cubiak had had enough of the pretense. "You can ditch the routine and fast-forward a few centuries, if you don't mind. Where is he?"

The young man let his shoulders sag, and suddenly he had the posture of someone who spent too much time at a computer.

"Sorry, Sheriff. I don't know. I haven't seen Scott for a couple of days. Is this about that jerk next door? Don't tell me he sent you here to tell us to stop annoying his cows?"

"Nothing like that."

"Then what?"

"Let's start by you telling me who you are."

"Sure, no prob. I'm Scott's assistant, Travis Odette. I help run things around here. Trav to everyone."

"You're not concerned about Henley's absence?"

"Scott keeps his own schedule. He often disappears for a day or two at a time. We've gotten used to it."

Along the fence, one of the horses whinnied and pawed the ground.

"Who else is here?" Cubiak said.

"The rest of the troupe. Well, those who didn't take off when we heard the storm prediction. Earlier in the week, there were thirteen, including Scott. Now we're down to five."

"A troupe? You're actors then?"

Travis grinned and looked even younger than he had first appeared. "Not really, though there are some who like to think of themselves as fledgling thespians. What we do here is called live action role play."

"Larping."

The greeter's eyebrows arched in surprise. "Hey, you've heard of it. I'm impressed. The movement is still fairly new in the hinterland."

"And what's the reaction you generally get out here in the hinterland when you mention larping?"

Oblivious to the hint of sarcasm in the sheriff's question, Travis went on cheerfully. "Most people have no idea what I'm talking about. And those who do generally consider it silly fantasy play. They view larpers as adults in costume acting like kids. Maybe on the surface that's what it looks like, but it goes much deeper."

The assistant director studied Cubiak.

"You carry a gun and a badge, Sheriff. Every day you go to work, there's always the chance for adventure."

"Actually, most of my job is rather mundane."

"Even so, there's always the possibility of something different, something unexpected. A challenge, if you will, the opportunity to use your wits to try to outsmart the bad guys. You get to think! Do you know what a luxury that is? For most people, it's the same boring shit day after day. For them, larping is the key to adventure, to something different. It's a way to escape the mundane routine of everyday ordinary existence. Sure, we have our comforts, and I'm not saying anyone wants to give any of that up. But historically people faced life and death challenges all the time—explorers, pioneers, soldiers. It's in our genes, but what do we do? We concoct fancy coffee drinks. We stock shelves with cereal boxes or make widgets. We sit in front of computer screens and let machines do our work. How tedious is that? Larping is a harmless way to be someone else, someone brave or powerful. It's all a game, but maybe in its own way it's a little like therapy, a cure for the ennui of modern life."

As the two talked, they had gravitated toward the horse pen, where Travis tossed handfuls of hay into the trough.

"Where does Mythweavers Larp Productions come into the picture?" Cubiak said.

"That's Scott's company. He started MLP about five years ago. By then he'd had more than ten years' experience as a GM and knew the ropes."

"A what?"

"Game master. That's the guy, well, it's usually a guy but sometimes a woman, who makes the rules and coordinates the action. Basically, there are two kinds of larps, Sheriff. There's Nordic larping, which is more or less a free-form style, meaning they operate without prepared scripts or assigned roles. That style is mostly popular in Europe. And there's our kind, with scripts and designated characters."

"And a game master."

"Exactly. You're a fast study." Travis paused as if he had given Cubiak a cue and was waiting for a response. When none materialized, he went on. "Anyway, early in his larping career, Scott started writing scripts for a small circle of friends. It was just a lark, something he enjoyed doing, but people liked the stories, and once word got out, other larpers asked if they could borrow the stuff. It didn't take Scott long to realize that rather than give away the scripts, he could license the material and sell it for a profit. Just like playwrights do. A couple of years ago, Scott started a publishing company to print and distribute the scripts, and slowly that grew into Mythweavers. You can find the details on the website."

"I looked. The website is down."

"Oh, well, I don't know anything about that."

"What are the scripts about?"

"You name it and Scott writes it. His specialty is medieval fantasy, but he also does space travel, Viking exploration, early caveman stuff. Whatever."

"And he made a living doing this?"

"That and hosting events here as well. All this took time. But eventually he quit his day job and sank everything he had into the company. You see this place?" Travis gestured at the house and the surrounding buildings. "In four years, Scott made enough for the down payment on all this. The income from script sales pays the mortgage, and what comes in from events covers the taxes and upkeep."

"Business must be good."

Travis grinned. "It's better than good. We're booked every weekend through the rest of the year and well into the next. Oh, and we have a waiting list in case of cancellations. But you don't have to believe me. You can talk to Scott. He's got the calendar and the list of reservations."

"I'm afraid that's not going to be possible."

"Why not? I'll call you when he gets back."

Travis was leaning against the fence when Cubiak showed him the photo from the beach, the same one he had shown Urbanski earlier. "Do you recognize this man?"

The young assistant paled and lurched upright. "That's Scott. Where did you get this? This wasn't taken at a larp, was it?" Panic flashed across Travis's face. "Something's wrong. Something's happened to Scott, hasn't it?"

"I'm sorry to have to tell you this, but the man in the photo is dead. His body was discovered yesterday morning on a private beach along Rosemary Lane."

Travis stared at the sheriff. "Scott dead?" He tugged at a handful of hair. "Are you sure?"

"You're the second person to identify him from the photo."

"I don't understand. How did he die?"

"We don't know that yet. I'm investigating the circumstances, but right now there's not much more I can tell you."

"Where's Rosemary Lane?" Travis said. He seemed dazed.

"It's on the lake, northeast of Sturgeon Bay."

"What the hell was Scott doing down there?"

"I was hoping you could tell me that," Cubiak said.

The tallest of the horses nudged Travis's shoulder, but the larper seemed not to notice. "I have no idea."

"Did Scott live here?"

"Yeah, he had one of the cottages. The first one by the main house."

"I'll need to see it, and his office as well."

Travis frowned. Then he half turned toward the horse that stood behind him and rubbed the beast's jaw.

"Okay," he said finally.

Scott's cottage was the largest of the cabins. From the outside it looked small, but inside, the high ceilings and large windows made the rooms feel spacious. There was a kitchenette, an alcove with a table and chairs, a living room, and a bedroom. The furniture was sleek and stylish.

"Midcentury modern," Travis said.

Expensive, Cubiak thought.

Designer jeans and T-shirts filled the closet. Scott wasn't wearing a watch when his body was found, but there was a Rolex on the dresser and a less costly but still pricey Movado in a drawer. The kitchen had been used recently. There were grounds in the French press, an upside-down mug on the drainboard, a handful of protein powders in the cupboard, and a variety of organic drinks in the refrigerator.

"Scott didn't cook?"

"He was on a raw diet."

Raw meat? Raw eggs? Cubiak wasn't sure he wanted to know.

There were no books or magazines. No personal papers in any of the drawers. Even with the upscale furniture, the cottage struck the sheriff as sterile and uninviting.

"Did Scott have a safe or a safety deposit box?"

"I don't think so. Maybe." The assistant furrowed his brow, thinking. "He kept a lot of stuff in his office."

A white stone path led from the cottage to a side entrance at the rear of the main house.

"This used to be the kitchen," Travis said as he mounted the three steps and opened the door. The office ran the width of the house. At one end, there was a desk and small conference table. A treadmill and stationary bike occupied the rest of the space.

"Scott liked to work out," Travis said.

The exercise area and the conference table were as uncluttered as Henley's cottage. But the desk was littered with letters, reservation forms, and file folders. Books were crammed on shelves and piled on the floor.

Cubiak picked up the laptop. "I'll need to take this," he said.

Travis nodded and brushed his hand against the line of sweat that glistened along his upper lip.

"And these." The sheriff pulled a hand-notated calendar and a small black book from the top desk drawer.

"Sure. Anything you need," Travis said.

"What about his phone? Where is it?"

"He would have had it with him. Scott was never without it."

There was no phone on the body or anywhere near it on the beach.

"And his car?" Cubiak asked.

"He must have taken it. It's not here and there's no other way to get around."

"Unless someone gave him a ride."

Travis paused to consider the possibility. "Yeah, but his car's not here." Scott drove a Porsche, a red two-seater convertible, the assistant said. There had been no reports of an abandoned sports car on Rosemary Lane.

When he finished with the room, Cubiak asked Travis to gather the others. "You can tell them I'm here, but don't say anything about Scott. I want to tell them all at the same time."

8 | THE KING IS DEAD

Travis led Cubiak down a wide hall to the front of the main house. "It'll take me a few minutes to find everyone. You can wait here if you like," he said.

As soon as he was alone, the sheriff called the office and issued an all-points bulletin for Henley's Porsche. Then he looked around.

On the way up, Cubiak had passed dozens of farmhouses similar to this one. They shared a patina of sturdy shabbiness that had been earned by decades of sheltering hard-working families. In most of the houses, the activity centered in the old-fashioned kitchens in the rear, while the smaller front rooms—the quaint lace-curtained parlors and dining rooms—were reserved for Sunday company and holiday meals.

When Cubiak saw the main house at Door Camelot, he expected an updated version of the old standard, but the interior had been transformed and shaped to meet the needs of the new owner. Henley's office, for one, had been added. The foyer where Travis left him had been paneled and converted to a combination reception area and waiting room with padded chairs along one wall and a long, honey-colored oak counter opposite. A rack of colorful brochures was located near the chairs. The bottom row contained information about local venues, but the rest of the material featured Door Camelot and MLP.

Cubiak tapped a silver bell on the counter, and while he waited for someone to respond he flipped through several brochures. The Scott Henley who beamed at him from nearly every page had warm eyes and an engaging smile. He came across as a man who made friends, not enemies. But looks could be deceiving.

After several minutes, the sheriff gave up waiting for someone to answer the bell. He pocketed the brochures and wandered through an arched doorway on the east side of the entrance hall into a large pine-scented room with high beamed ceilings from which hung four antlered chandeliers. The room faced the woods, but there was no view to the outside. The windows were narrow horizontal panes about ten feet above the floor. Ribbons of natural light flowed in, but there was no way to see out, no way to be distracted by the world outside. Leather barrel chairs surrounded a half-dozen low, rough-hewn tables. Seating for twenty-four; standing room for twice as many. The focal point of the room was a massive fieldstone fireplace. What went on here? Perhaps a welcome ceremony, an explanation of the rules of the game, an overview of the larping event being hosted that week or weekend.

As a young boy, the sheriff had attended Boy Scout camp in Door County. Along with the other scouts, he was forced to spend his first precious thirty minutes in a room like this. Not as fancy but large and practical. The leader stood up front and took roll, then he assigned tents and reviewed the rules, more rules than any of them could remember. They were a bevy of city kids bored by the long bus ride up from Chicago and eager to get outside and explore their exotic new world.

Were adults on a larping venture any different? The excitement ramping up, the anticipation of being thrust into a completely new environment. What happened when they were finally set free? Did they, like the boys in his troop, rush out the door and yelp with enthusiasm as they scattered around the grounds, yelling as loud as they could, loud enough to scare a farmer's cows several acres away?

The sheriff carried five of the leather chairs to the front and spaced them out in a single row facing the fireplace. Then he waited for the larpers.

. . .

A tall, slender woman arrived first. She had glittery wide eyes and light blond hair that flowed to her shoulders from a straight part in the middle of her head. Like Travis, she was a twenty-something and oddly dressed. Her long, cream-colored frock billowed gently as she floated silently past the tables.

"Amy Baxter," she said in an otherworldly kind of voice that matched her appearance. Then she gave a small bow and slipped into the seat closest to the wall, careful to arrange her dress over her ecru ballet slippers.

She was barely settled when a scowling man appeared in the doorway. He was stooped, mustached, and balding. His face was etched in a frown that made him look twenty years older than both Amy and Travis. He took in the setting and then tromped in, letting his boot heels smack the floor with every step.

"Martin Quilty. Call me Quill, everyone else does. I'm the head groundskeeper," he said, as if eager to set himself apart from the others.

"You're not a larper then?" the sheriff said.

"Not really. One of the regulars broke his leg, so while he's out of commission I put on his costume and stand in for him."

Cubiak motioned to the empty chairs, but Quill remained standing. "What's this about?" he said, jutting his square jaw at the sheriff.

"You'll find out soon."

The groundskeeper dropped into the seat nearest Amy. She didn't look at him and leaned farther away. Quill made a face and then slumped down until his squat neck disappeared into his shoulders.

Almost immediately, a tall, gawkish man and a petite woman appeared on the threshold. They stood so close to each other that the sheriff wondered if they had been holding hands. They entered the room together, exchanging anxious glances and then smiling shyly as if they shared a secret.

The woman shook hands with the sheriff. "I'm Isabelle Redding, the receptionist."

Her companion followed her lead.

"Nick Youngman, videographer."

"Are you both larpers?" Cubiak asked as they claimed the two seats to the right.

Their answers overlapped.

Nick: "Yeah, when I'm not filming."

Isabelle: "Occasionally. I fill in when needed."

As if by unspoken agreement, the middle seat was left vacant for Travis, the last to arrive. He had changed into jeans and a black T-shirt and had tied his flowing hair into a ponytail. The assistant had recovered some of his color but was still remarkably pale. He took the empty chair, planted his feet under, and stared past Cubiak at the stack of unlit logs on the grate.

"Thank you for coming," Cubiak said. "Travis has already told you who I am, but at my request he didn't explain why I am here."

"It's that fucking farmer and his complaints about our noise, isn't it?" Amy said.

The sheriff studied the young woman. Her harsh tone and crude language surprised him. Neither fit her genteel appearance.

"My being here has nothing to do with Florian Urbanski, although he recently came to see me and to file a formal complaint," he said after a moment.

"Then what is it?" Nick said.

"Yesterday a man was found dead on a Lake Michigan beach along Rosemary Lane. He's been tentatively identified as Scott Henley."

Everyone but Travis stared at Cubiak.

Amy fell back in her chair. "Scott? Dead?" she said in a whisper.

The sheriff held up the photo he had shown earlier to Travis.

Quill leapt up and snatched the picture from him. "Let me see that." Then. "Jesus, I don't believe it."

Amy leaned over his arm. "Oh my God, it is him," she said, and began to cry.

The groundskeeper handed the photo to Travis, who passed it over to the videographer and the receptionist.

Isabelle studied the picture and then looked uncomprehendingly at Cubiak. "I don't understand," she said.

With that the questions tumbled out, one on top of another.

"Where's Rosemary Lane?" Nick asked.

"Past Valmy, on the way to Sturgeon Bay."

"What was Scott doing there?" Quill said.

"I don't know."

"When was he found?"

"As I said before, the body was discovered early yesterday morning."

"Who found him?"

"A man walking his dog. The body was on the sand—under a boat."

They gasped.

"A boat?" Travis said.

Cubiak explained.

Amy sobbed.

"How did he die? Did he drown?" Quill demanded.

"As I've already told Travis, we're investigating the situation."

"Situation?" Amy inhaled sharply and pressed a hand to her chest. "What's that supposed to mean? You don't think someone killed Scott, do you?"

"It was probably an accident," Isabelle said quickly, as if to reassure her colleague, but Amy dissolved in tears again.

"Why was he there?" the groundskeeper said, echoing his earlier question.

"I'm hoping one of you might know."

They looked at one another, each of them waiting for someone else to start.

"I realize that this has been a shock, but I'll need to talk with each of you individually after you've had a chance to absorb what I've said. Perhaps someone could make coffee or tea?"

The sheriff looked at Travis, who nodded and then turned toward Isabelle.

The receptionist pushed to her feet.

"Thank you," Travis said.

"If you have a phone, you need to leave it with me," Cubiak said.

She started to object but then sighed and gave him the device.

The other two men moved to follow her, but Cubiak raised a hand to stop them.

"I'd rather you didn't leave the room," he said.

"Why?" Nick said.

Before Cubiak could respond, Travis stood and turned toward his colleagues.

"The sheriff thinks one of us may have had something to do with Scott's death, and he doesn't want us to compare stories," he said.

9 IN THE LAND OF MAKE-BELIEVE

The explanation from Travis subdued the larpers. Cubiak knew that every organization sowed its own brand of discontent and figured that the longer he let them stew, the better. Fear and suspicion would prompt them to open up and share what they each knew about Henley and Door Camelot. While Isabelle was in the kitchen, he called Rowe and asked him to get to the center ASAP.

By the time the deputy arrived, the refreshments were finished, and Cubiak was ready to start the questioning. He introduced Rowe and announced the order for the one-on-one interviews.

"Travis will go first, then Quill, Isabelle, Amy, and Nick. Until you're called, you'll stay here with my deputy and wait your turn."

Quill started to protest, but Cubiak cut him off. "I know you all want to help, and this is important," he said.

For the interviews, the sheriff used an empty office behind the reception area. The space was cramped and utilitarian. A dull metal desk was pushed up under the window alongside a gray file drawer. The walls were bare, and in one corner, cardboard boxes were stacked halfway to the ceiling. Amid the chaos, two scuffed wooden chairs straddled an oval coffee table.

Cubiak took a seat and laid his notebook and pen on the table. Moments later, Travis appeared in the doorway.

When the sheriff waved him in, the assistant moved toward the window.

"Do you mind?" Travis said as he raised the lower sash. "I get claustrophobic and the fresh air helps."

Once Travis was settled, Cubiak began.

"You said you hadn't seen Scott for a couple of days. When was that, do you remember?"

"The morning of the storm, I saw him at breakfast, then I left. I had errands to run and when I got back around eleven, he was gone. I don't know what time he left."

"Did you expect to see him later?"

"Yeah, especially with reports of the weather heading this way. It didn't make sense that he wasn't here."

"What about the others? Has anyone said anything since then to indicate they were concerned about Scott or knew where he was?"

"I don't remember anyone being concerned about him, but they were upset that he wasn't around to help that day. We were all preoccupied with the forecast, battening down the hatches, as it were. It's Scott's property, and we were the ones doing the work to keep it safe. The horses were spooked, and we had to take turns going to the barn to try to calm them down. Normally one of the local farmers would tend to them, but he left to take care of his stock. Besides all that, we had to cook too, because the regular staff all went home."

"You have staff?"

"Besides me and Isabelle and Quill, sure. When there's a large group here, someone's got to make sure everything runs smoothly. A lot of the visiting larpers camp out and do their own cooking, but more and more the groups buy the deluxe package, which means we need a cook onsite to prepare the meals—either that or we cater the food in, depending on the number of guests. Mostly, too, the larpers bring their own costumes, but sometimes they rent our equipment, so then we have to have someone in charge of wardrobe, checking what goes out and making sure everything that's been rented is returned in good condition."

"Anything else?"

"There's maintenance. Quill and another one or two guys who come in part time as needed."

"They were all here that day?"

Travis ran a hand over the top of his head. "I think so, but I don't really remember. There's a lot of ground to cover, and we were scattered around. I can't vouch for where everyone was. All I know for certain is that at the end of the day, there was just the five of us left."

"Did the staff get along with Scott?"

"Mostly, yeah. People were happy for the work, and he wasn't overly demanding. Though he did have to fire a guy last fall. That didn't go very well."

"What happened?"

"We had a construction team working on the cottage roofs, and a couple of visiting larpers accused one of the men of stealing money and phones, stuff like that. I don't remember his name. Bill, I think. Bill something. I told Scott he should call the authorities, but he didn't want any bad publicity, so he took care of things, you know, reimbursing the losses. Then he let the guy go." Travis frowned. "Bill Fury. That's his name. He was really pissed when he left. A couple of hours later, he came back looking for Scott. He was all liquored up by then, but Scott wasn't here. Bill didn't believe me when I told him, and he went around calling him out. Finally he gave up and left."

"Do you know where I can find him?"

"Not really, but I think Quill knows Bill. In fact, he may have recommended him for the job, so he'll know where he lives."

Cubiak jotted down the name. Good jobs were scarce everywhere, and the TV news seemed filled with stories about people out for revenge after they had been fired. There had never been an incident like that in Door County, and the sheriff hoped he wasn't about to discover a first.

"How long have you been a larper?" he asked, switching tactics.

Travis grinned. "I started when I was a kid. Back then I didn't even know it had a name. For me it was getting together with a bunch of my friends and goofing around. We did *Star Wars* reenactments and took turns being Han Solo and Darth Vader. I was thrilled when I found out that there were other people doing the same thing. One of my buddies had a cousin who told him about larping, and once we realized this was for real we started looking for events. Before long I was scouring the internet reading everything I could find about it and scoping out official larp gatherings. One thing led to another, and eventually I found my way to Scott and the big time."

"Do you know how Henley got involved?"

"From what I've heard, he kind of stumbled into it. He worked in real estate, and one of the professional associations that he belonged to hosted a larp at one of their conferences. You know, as a way for members to get acquainted and build trust, that sort of thing. It's not unusual for organizations and companies to do that. Anyway, to hear him tell it, he got hooked right off the bat."

"Scott sold houses?"

Travis shook his head. "He was into the commercial side. Made a bundle, too, enough to retire early and devote his time to his own company."

"He was independently wealthy?"

"More like comfortably well off, and he deserved it. You know, some people do and others don't. Scott got into the business right out of high school and worked his butt off for nearly two decades at his job. I'm glad he did well. He was a good guy."

Henley might have been a prince of a fellow, but that kind of luck often fueled envy in others. "People weren't jealous?" the sheriff said.

Travis shrugged. "I got the feeling that Scott ran with a crowd of highfliers. A few of them came up here once or twice, and it was clear they all did very well. If anything, they thought he was nuts for chucking it in, so I wouldn't say any of his former colleagues were jealous."

But what about the rest of you? Cubiak wondered.

Travis cracked his knuckles. "I know what you're thinking, Sheriff. Before I got this job, I worked at a plastics molding plant making seat trays for airlines. I didn't really enjoy the work, but I was good at it, and if I stayed with it I'd probably get to be a foreman at some point. But it was tedious as hell and after I quit and hired on with Scott, I never looked back. For me, this was the right decision."

"You're happy doing this?"

"No question about it. I like the variety—never a dull moment, as we like to say."

"When did you meet Scott?"

The assistant crossed his legs. "About three years ago. I was the GM on one of his first larps. By then I'd learned to spot the people who could pull their weight and the ones who were laggards. Scott was the best, always willing to go the extra mile. We hit it off right from the get-go. Over the next six months or so, our paths crossed a few times, and then one day I heard that he'd started his own production company. I was curious and went to talk to him. When he asked me to come on board, I didn't hesitate."

"You work full time for the company?"

"Yeah, at least I did. I don't know what happens now. We have signed contracts running through next season, and we're even starting to see winter business. But I don't know how many people are going to stick around Camelot, and I can't run this show myself."

"How did you and Scott get along?"

"Fine." The answer was automatic and smooth. Had it been rehearsed?

"No disagreements with the boss? No misunderstandings or arguments?"

"With Scott, nah," he said, shifting his gaze away from the sheriff.

He's hiding something, Cubiak thought. "Was there any tension between him and the others?"

This time when he answered, Travis looked at the sheriff. "Not at all. The only problem was with that guy Urbanski, who fussed about his cows. Every time he showed up, he got more belligerent."

"Urbanski came here more than once?"

"Are you kidding? The guy was getting to be a regular. And the last time, he had a shotgun perched on the rack in his truck. You can bet he made sure we saw it."

When Cubiak finished with Travis, he asked him to summon Quill. The groundskeeper verified the assistant's statement about Urbanski's frequent visits and his escalating rage.

65

He also seconded what Travis had said earlier about Henley's frequent absences.

"He'd get a text and take off, no explanation given," Quill said.

"But I'm sure you had your suspicions."

Quill smirked. "I always figured it was a woman."

"Why?"

"Why not? A good-looking guy like that. Women go for his kind, don't they?" The groundskeeper frowned. "Maybe he was two-timing one of them and they killed him."

"Did you ever see him with women away from the center?"

Quill shook his head.

"What about Bill Fury?"

Quill grunted. "Trav told you what happened." It was more question than statement. "Bill was here doing some work when a group from Minneapolis showed up for the week. On Friday morning, a couple of the visitors claimed that cameras and wallets had been stolen and Scott blamed Bill."

"Did he have any reason to suspect him?"

"He didn't like the guy, and for Scott that was reason enough. Bill did good work, but he didn't hide the fact that he thought larping was a joke. Besides, blaming him for the missing stuff gave Scott a way to satisfy the visiting larpers without tainting the staff. There wasn't any proof that Bill did anything wrong, but he was an easy target and Scott always looked for quick solutions to problems."

"Did Fury threaten Scott?"

Quill twisted his mouth to one side. "Sort of, I guess."

"What do you mean sort of? Either he did or he didn't."

The groundskeeper shifted in his chair. "He showed up later that afternoon spouting the usual kind of shit that men say when they've had too much to drink. You know: 'I'll get even with that fucker' and other crap like that. Scott wasn't around at the time, and no one took it seriously. I don't think Bill meant anything, just getting it off his chest, you know. I calmed him down and convinced him to leave. Anyway, it turns out that no one stole anything. A couple of weeks later, the Minnesota GM sent an email saying the missing stuff had been left behind in

Minneapolis. It had never even been here."

"Did Scott apologize to Fury?"

Quill huffed. "Are you kidding? Scott never apologized to anyone for anything."

"You have an address for your friend?"

"Bill? Yeah, he lives in a double-wide behind his parents' place just off Fifty-Seven on the way to Green Bay." Quill rattled off the specifics. "And just to be clear: Bill's not a friend. He's someone I know, that's all."

Isabelle, the receptionist, added little to what Quill had said.

She wasn't on the grounds the day Bill Fury was fired and heard about the incident only after the fact.

"I usually only work on weekends and then I'm inside most of the time. Besides checking people in and out, I'm in charge of the inventory for everything that the GLs use. That's what we call the guest larpers, the ones who come in for a weekend or a specific event."

"What about Florian Urbanski?"

Isabelle sighed. "Him I've seen several times. He was always upset and complaining about something, but Scott never really listened to him, which is too bad. My parents have a small dairy farm, so I know that Mister Urbanski had a legitimate complaint. If you want my opinion, I think everyone here could have been more understanding."

"What was it like working for Scott?"

The receptionist squirmed. "If you did what he wanted, you were fine. If you didn't, you were on thin ice."

"And you?"

"I went to Catholic school, Sheriff. I learned to do as I was told."

"And the others? Travis, for example, or Quill?"

"If there were problems between either of them and Scott, I wasn't aware of it. Mostly he was a good boss."

"How often did you take part in the larps?"

"Like I said, I only got involved when they needed a stand-in for one of the roles, like if someone got sick or didn't show. To be honest, I'm not that big a fan, but please, don't tell Trav I said so. I need my job."

. . .

When it was her turn to be questioned, Amy Baxter glided through the open doorway, appearing even more ethereal than before. Once seated, she positioned her feet under the chair and smoothed her dress over her lap before turning a blank, expressionless face to Cubiak.

"I'm curious to know how you got involved in larping," he said.

Amy smiled as if at a secret joke. "It all started at school, if you can believe it. I was a high school senior. It was a small school. There were only forty of us in the graduating class. We had a new principal, who said we needed to 'expand our horizons.'" She put the phrase in air quotes. "For our senior class trip, she arranged a larp at a nearby resort. She saw it as a form of cultural enrichment as well as a teaching tool."

"Really? What was the larp about?"

"You mean the theme? We were supposed to be space travelers establishing the first human colony on Mars."

"You must have enjoyed it."

The young woman shifted her weight in the chair. "Not at all. In fact, I was annoyed that our class wasn't going on the traditional trip to Chicago to visit the Art Institute and attend the symphony. I thought the larp sounded childish and banal."

"And now you're at Door Camelot playing . . . ?"

"I'm Guinevere."

"Ah, I see. And how did all this happen?" Cubiak said, indicating the room and the complex beyond.

Amy clutched her hands in her lap and smiled. "For me, Camelot was the prize at the end of a very long journey. I grew up in central Illinois near one of the Amish communities. There were four families in our cluster, and while we weren't officially part of that group, we embraced many of their beliefs. It was a somber, fundamentalist environment. Fun was frowned upon. Jokes were taboo. I studied the Bible; I read the approved books. There was no radio, no television. Every Saturday, I stood in the communal laundry room and ironed. Our clothes were simple and all cotton, and they had to be pristine at all times because we never knew the day or hour of our reckoning." She spoke in a singsong rhythm as if she were repeating the mantras she had been instructed to memorize and recite as a child.

"A few days after the school larp, I began to feel different about myself, better in a way I can't even describe. After graduation, I got a job at a nursing home in Decatur and started searching for larps within a day's drive. There weren't very many, but each time I participated in one, I came out a slightly changed person. I started to enjoy having fun, and slowly I became more outgoing. I know it sounds trite, but larping gave me a new lease on life. I always considered myself a very dour soul, but through role playing I learned that the dismal facade had been imposed on me. I wasn't the somber young woman in the plain cotton dress. I despised wearing that bonnet that set me aside from everyone else.

"Once I realized that I could be different, I began attending weekend events in Saint Louis and Chicago. The more I participated, the more I liked it and the more I wanted to do. It gets in your blood. You start asking, 'What else can I try, who else can I be?' I mean, some people stick with one theme and that's fine, but I liked experimenting and trying on different roles." She paused. "Of course, everything changed, everything got better, once I met Scott."

"When was that?"

"About five years ago, at one of the Chicago larps. I'd moved there to go to college and had joined a group that used scripted material. We especially liked Scott's work and invited him to lead one of our events. He kept challenging us to try harder and to put more of ourselves into our parts. He was such an amazing role model."

"How old were you then?"

"Twenty-two, I think."

And the worldly, handsome Scott would have been around thirty at the time. The ideal target for a young woman's infatuation. Cubiak kept the thought to himself.

"What happened after that?"

"I'd see him occasionally. Usually at larping events and once at a regional conference. Then my group did a program up here last year, and we reconnected. After that he started to text and email, and I began using my vacation days to come to the center and help out. When Scott offered me the role of Guinevere, he made it clear that he expected me to forsake the other larps and focus on this one, to help build the community, as he put it."

"When was that?"

"About eight months ago. This was after I played a tavern maid and a midwife in a couple of events. One evening, Scott took me aside and explained that the role of Guinevere was open. He said that he'd been watching me and that he thought I had just the right personality to make the character come to life."

She hesitated and looked down at her hands. "I didn't accept right away. I told him I needed to try it out. You really have to feel the part to do it right. Also, I wanted to know what had happened to the previous Guinevere. Scott said she'd moved on. No hard feelings, just that she wanted to do something different. I suspected that the situation was more complicated than that but, well, I liked him and after the first few weekends I knew that I really wanted the role, so I was willing to look the other way."

"Ignoring what exactly?"

Amy blushed and clutched her hands. "I knew that he'd been in a personal relationship with ViVi Kay, the woman who played Guinevere, and that when they broke up Scott asked her to give up the role."

"Who ended the relationship?"

"He did."

Amy squeezed her hands together. "I wasn't here when it happened, but I heard later that she didn't take it well. Then . . ." Amy looked past him toward the window.

"Then what?"

"She showed up the other day and got into an argument with Scott. She was hysterical . . . I heard them yelling at each other. I couldn't make out what either one was saying because they were in his cottage, but there was plenty of shouting and even a few things thrown around. She looked really upset when she left."

"What day was that?"

"Tuesday, the day before the storm."

"Was anyone else here when it happened?"

"Just me and Trav."

"Do you know where I can find her, this ViVi Kay?"

"I think she lives around here, but I'm not exactly sure where."

"She's local then?"

"Maybe, I guess."

Amy slumped into the chair. "I can't believe Scott is gone. Everything about this sounds all wrong." She frowned and sat back up, her posture rigid. "You said that his body was found on a beach?"

"A private beach on the lake."

"That doesn't make any sense."

"Why not?"

She pressed her lips tight.

"If you know something, you have to tell me. It could be helpful."

Amy looked at Cubiak with eyes that were the gray-blue of the lake on a cloudy day. "Scott hated being near water. He nearly drowned when he was a teenager, and he was a lousy swimmer. He could barely stand being near the creek, and he never went to the lake. He wouldn't even sit on the shore. There's no way he'd be on the beach, or anywhere near a boat, especially with a storm coming on."

When he finished talking with Amy, the sheriff went into the hall to stretch his legs. He was still there when Nick arrived. With his round baby face and stocky frame, the videographer struck Cubiak as an unlikely candidate for the role of a knight in King Arthur's court. Try as he might, the sheriff couldn't imagine Nick riding one of the black horses. He was more the portly Friar Tuck type, leading a donkey through Sherwood Forest. Cubiak knew it was the wrong story and the wrong century, but it was the only image that came to him.

Cubiak started with personal questions, and Nick's responses were invariably brief, often one or two words. He was from Chicago, the youngest of four. He had no hobbies. He liked to watch movies: online, in theaters, streaming on TV, even on his phone.

"The world makes more sense through a lens," he said.

"And what sense did you make of Scott and Door Camelot?" Cubiak said.

"Door Camelot's a dream, and Scott's the dream maker."

"Can you be a little more specific?"

Nick settled in and grew expansive. "Sure. Scott wanted to make this place work, and for that he needed people who were willing to pay to host their events here. If they used one of his scripts, all the better because they had to pay for that too. My work, the documentary, was to be used to promote the center, nothing more. It's visual advertising. Scott planned to post it on the website. He wanted me to edit out clips for Facebook and to use as part of a sales pitch for his presentation at some big larping conference next year."

"How long have you known Scott Henley?"

"We met a couple of years ago when I first heard about larping. Lucky for me, his was the first group I tapped into."

"Lucky why?"

"Because he's good. Everything is organized and things go smoothly. There are plenty of larps that disintegrate into complete chaos."

"You're one of the regulars?"

"Pretty much. Since I started filming this past spring, I've been here just about every weekend. The themes vary, depending on the script, which keeps things interesting. For example, one week there might be a group of thirty or so using one of Scott's fantasy scripts, and the next there might be a dozen people enacting an Agatha Christie mystery. And just like that, the center transforms from a futuristic world to an English village. It's pretty cool, and the more footage I get, the more I have to choose from when I start editing. But mostly I focus on the King Arthur programs. Now, who knows? It's all up in the air, isn't it?"

"Tell me about the King Arthur business."

Nick rubbed his hands on his knees. "Now, that was Scott's love. King Arthur and the Round Table. He reserved one weekend a month for that, for Camelot. It was his thing. He was King Arthur, and we took on the other roles. I'm Gawain. Trav is Lancelot. Quill's been playing Galahad and so on."

"There are twelve of you, then," Cubiak said.

"Twelve knights, just like the apostles. That's the core group. But if we're doing a larp that includes a major battle, there might be thirty or more guys in armor running around."

"You know about Florian Urbanski's dispute with Scott?"

"Everyone here knows about that."

"I understand Urbanski had a problem with the noise."

"The noise. The people. The traffic on weekends. The campsite that he claimed was encroaching on his property even though it was well within our side of the fence. Urbanski blamed us, and therefore Scott, for everything that he didn't like about the world. I even have a clip of him ranting about us being a bunch of rich, spoiled brats."

"Larping sounds like an expensive hobby," Cubiak said. He started counting on his fingers. "Travel, food, accommodations, and of course the costumes." He looked up. "What do those run?"

"It depends. Period dresses generally go for a couple hundred, although I've seen some for three times as much. Of course, a lot of the women sew their own costumes. And a few of the men as well. If you're going for authenticity, a knight costume can run a couple thousand, but it doesn't have to. You can make a sword out of cardboard or buy a Styrofoam one for under ten dollars."

"What about Scott?"

"Oh, Scott had the best, of course. His was the real thing—at least it looked real."

"What do you mean?"

"Medieval armor was fashioned from iron and weighed a ton. Even a chain-mail vest might weigh as much as sixty pounds. Today's stuff is made from aluminum or lightweight steel. It's still got plenty of heft but not like the original."

"So one of the vests your guys would wear might come in at, what, twenty pounds or so?" Cubiak said, recalling what Pardy had said at the morgue.

"Yeah, something like that. The main thing is that everything we use here has to look authentic. Scott insisted on that. He even gave everyone a generous costume allowance. There were no expenses spared at Camelot, I'll tell you that much, Sheriff."

Nick sounded envious, and Cubiak wondered what he earned as a documentary filmmaker.

Like the others, Nick had already seen the close-up of Scott on the beach. This time the sheriff showed him the full-length photo.

The videographer frowned. "Wow, that's weird. That's Scott, all right, but that's not his costume. The King Arthur vest, the one he always wears, has a royal crest, and the helmet's different too."

"Whose costume is this?"

"I'm not sure, but it looks like the Lancelot outfit."

"Why would Scott wear Travis's costume?"

"I have no idea."

"Was this something you guys did, grab whatever you felt like from the costume room?"

Nick shook head. "No." He looked at the sheriff. "Scott insisted that we wear our own outfits. Why would he break his own rule?"

10 THE ROYAL CREST

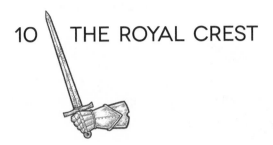

Cubiak found Travis in one of the small offices off the long hall. A green folder lay open on the desk, but he wasn't looking at it. Nor was he looking at the dozens of other green folders that were fanned out around him.

The sheriff knocked. "May I?" he said as he entered.

Travis glanced toward the facing chair. "Take a seat."

"Work?"

"Yeah." The assistant director indicated the papers on the desk. "I hate to admit it, Sheriff, but I'm in way over my head. I'm not sure what to do with any of it," he said, closing the folder.

"Give it time, and you'll figure it out." Cubiak waited a moment. "I need to ask you about Scott's next of kin. Did he have family?"

Travis shook his head. "He was an only child, and his parents died some time ago. He had a couple of cousins, but I don't know their names or how to reach them. Scott never talked about his relatives. Guess I'm not being much help. Sorry."

"There is something else." Cubiak opened his phone to the photo that he had just shown Nick.

"I need you to look at this," Cubiak said as he handed it over.

At first Travis didn't react. Then he blanched and the shock of recognition played out over his face.

"What the hell . . . Is this some kind of sick joke?" he said. "It's Scott, but why's he dressed like that?"

"I was hoping you could tell me that."

Travis thrust the phone toward Cubiak. "This doesn't make any sense. I mean it's crazy. Scott would never . . ."

The acting director fell against the back of his chair. "It's not even his costume."

"How do you know? I thought they were all pretty similar."

"Most of them are, but not Scott's. His has a royal crest, here."

Travis tapped the phone against his left shoulder.

"Do you know whose this is?"

"I'm not sure. Mine has short sleeves like that, but so do a few of the others. There are subtle differences in the chain mail, too, and the design of the vest. We all mark our costumes to keep them straight. I put a notch inside mine, here," he said, pointing to the spot beneath his collarbone.

Cubiak thought back to the garment lying on the morgue counter. Had there been a marking on it? Perhaps one so small he had missed it?

"Why would Scott dress like Lancelot or one of the other knights?"

"I don't know. Scott did what Scott did. But why was he even there? None of this makes any sense." Travis paled and lowered the phone to the desk. "Maybe whoever did this killed the wrong person. Maybe I'm the one who's supposed to be dead."

"Why would anyone want to kill you?" the sheriff asked.

"I have no idea. Why would someone want to kill Scott?" Travis was belligerent, challenging.

Cubiak slipped the phone into his pocket. "Could Scott have had a duplicate costume made, one without the crest?"

"Sure, but why would he?"

"I don't know, but if he did, where would the original be?"

"The costume room." Travis grabbed a set of keys from the desk and stood. "Everyone keeps their stuff there, even Scott."

The Door Camelot costume room was a small brick building tucked away behind the cottages. It was unmarked and nondescript and could have been mistaken for an old-fashioned one-car garage or a large garden shed. A sign over the door read Private.

"Who has keys?" Cubiak asked as they stood on the gravel path outside the windowless structure.

"All the King Arthur larpers," Travis said as he unlocked the door.

He flipped a switch, and two banks of overhead lights flickered on, revealing thirteen open cubicles that lined the walls. One was for Guinevere and the others were for the knights. Each was labeled with the name of a knight. Their suits of armor hung from heavy wooden hangers. Helmets sat on upper shelves, while boots stood on the floor beneath. The place looked like a medieval locker room.

The costume with the royal crest hung in the cubicle marked King Arthur, but Lancelot's space was empty. Travis touched the bare hanger. "It's gone," he said, watching the metal hanger tip back and forth.

As they walked to the front of the house, Cubiak continued questioning the young man.

"Can you think of any reason Scott would wear your costume?"

"I already told you, no," Travis said.

"In the myth, Lancelot betrayed Arthur."

"Lots of things happened in the myth." Travis stiffened. "Are you accusing me of betraying Scott?"

"I'm just thinking out loud. This wouldn't have anything to do with ViVi Kay, would it?"

Travis tossed his hands in the air. "Here we go. In real life, Viv and Scott were an item, okay? In the larp, she was Guinevere to his Arthur. After they broke up and Scott linked up with Amy, I started seeing Viv. Scott didn't want her coming around and told us both as much. I told him that he didn't control my personal life. We went back and forth about it a couple of times, but then he finally let it go. A couple of weeks after that, Viv broke up with me, so it was all a moot point."

"How come you didn't tell me that she was here the other day arguing with Scott?"

"That was about back pay. I didn't think it mattered."

"Everything matters," Cubiak said. "I'll need her number."

Travis snickered. "Can't help you there, Sheriff. I had it on autodial and after she walked on me, I deleted it."

"I understand that she's a local. Do you know where she lives?"

"Not really. We met either here at my cottage or at one of the bars in town."

"You must have her contact information in your files."

"Scott kept all that electronically. I can look on his laptop if you want."

Cubiak had stashed Henley's computer in the jeep. But when Travis checked, all information on ViVi Kay had been deleted.

"Sorry, dead end," he said as he closed the lid on the device. "Are we done now?"

"I'm afraid not. There's one other thing that I need you for," the sheriff said.

"What?"

"I have to ask you to come into town to identify the body."

"Why? I already told you, it's Scott."

"That was from looking at a photo. I need you to do it in person."

It took some coaxing on Cubiak's part, but Travis finally agreed. An hour later, they met at the morgue, and the young larper confirmed that the dead man was Scott Henley.

Ignoring the chill creeping down his back, Cubiak showed Travis the suit of armor that was found on the body.

"Can you check to see if it's yours?" the sheriff said.

Travis picked up the chain-mail vest and pointed to a small notch at the neck. "It's mine all right."

"You understand that we have to hold it as evidence," Cubiak said as he laid the garment down again.

Travis was incredulous. "Do you really think I want it back? Do you think I could ever put that on again? Keep it, Sheriff, and when you're finished doing whatever you need to do with it, bury it with Scott."

11 | PAPER CHASE

When Cubiak joined Cate and Joey for dinner that evening, it was the first time in weeks that they had shared a meal together. The weather was perfect, but the beach reeked of rotting fish and algae, so rather than eat outside they gathered at the kitchen table. Joey talked about the play, and Cate talked about the costumes she was helping sew for the young troupe. Cubiak said little. He was preoccupied with the Henley case, but he didn't want to discuss it in front of the boy. Joey would learn about the underbelly of the world soon enough.

The meal was Cubiak's only break that day. Once they finished, the sheriff settled on the couch and started searching through Henley's laptop and the rest of the material he'd taken from the larper's office, looking for leads into his past. Anything that would shed light on his death.

Henley was a popular guy. Between his personal Twitter account and Facebook page and those for his production company, he had nearly nine thousand followers and friends. There were another hundred or so names in his address book, and every page in his desk calendar was filled with notations about people to meet or call. At first glance, nothing seemed out of line. Henley may have operated in the world of make-believe, but first and foremost he was a businessman.

Cubiak cradled his hands around his neck and leaned back against the sofa cushions. Where to start?

"What's wrong?" Cate asked. A dish towel in her hand, she looked at him from behind the counter that separated the kitchen from the rest of the open floor plan.

"Nothing."

"Then what's all that?" she said, indicating the open laptop and the notebooks that were spread on the coffee table.

"The veritable haystack."

"And you're looking for the needle."

The sheriff massaged his right shoulder. "Correct. Except that I'm not sure there is one, at least not here."

"But you have to start somewhere. Maybe I can help," Cate said.

Cubiak studied his wife. Cate was smart and worldly in a way that he was not. And while he was barely able to fumble his way around the internet, she knew how to zigzag to all the right places.

"Can you run through about a thousand tweets looking for any snarky or negative comments?"

"I can try." She tossed the dish towel onto the counter and then settled in next to him. "What am I after? Complaints and critical remarks?" she said as she pulled the computer onto her lap.

"That and anything that sounds like a threat."

Cubiak gave her Henley's two Twitter handles, and Cate started tapping the keyboard.

He liked sitting near her. During the busy summer season, he spent precious little time at home and wished they had more moments like this. If he could, he would set the computer back on the table and put his arm around her. As if she knew what he was thinking, Cate stopped typing and looked at him.

"Aren't you supposed to be working?"

"I am working," he said and reached for the address book. Flipping through the pages, he recognized the names of a few high rollers and politicians who were often in the news. Did Henley know them personally? Most of the people listed lived in the Milwaukee and Chicago metro areas; several more were in downstate Illinois, a handful in Madison, a half dozen in Los Angeles, and a few in New York City. Henley had international contacts as well: London, Paris, Hong Kong. A smattering of the entries were marked with asterisks, and all of those were in the Midwest.

Henley's personal calendar was a mess. Entries were erased or crossed out and written over. Often one-word notations like *No*, *Yes*, and *Maybe* were scrawled in the margins or printed in microscopic letters. There were no names, only initials, which could refer to individuals, companies, or associations or might represent Henley's private code. Cubiak skimmed through. The entries that he could decipher were designated with one or two letters. Most appeared once or twice. On March 17, the pattern changed. The letters *ALE* popped up, neatly printed in the bottom-right corner of the box that marked the day. March 18 was filled with more scribbled letter combos, but on the nineteenth, *ALE* showed up again. On March 21, the entry was circled in green and marked with an exclamation point. Between March 21 and June 27, the same three letters appeared daily. In early July, the combo disappeared for two days but then returned four times a week through the rest of the month.

Cubiak showed Cate the calendar. "What do you think?" he said, pointing to the three letters.

"It's either a liaison or a running date with his favorite beer," she said.

"Funny. I'll ask Travis if it means anything to him or anyone else at the center." He yawned and stretched. "Have you found anything?"

"Not much, I'm afraid. Most of the reviews for Mythweavers and Great Scott are complimentary, glowing even, and there are a few proposals as well, some of them rather lewd. So far, the only negatives are a couple of complaints about the weather at Door Camelot during a spring larp and one lengthy criticism from a larper who said his dietary request hadn't been honored."

"Nothing serious enough to kill for," Cubiak said.

At ten, Travis emailed that he had asked around and drawn a blank on the mystery letters.

By eleven, Cate had gone to bed. Cubiak worked until midnight and then he gave up. *ALE* remained an enigma, but it was all he had.

12 TIES THAT BIND

The next morning the house was quiet. Joey had another rehearsal to make up for one lost during the storm, and Cate was working on costumes with some of the mothers. Cubiak poured another cup of coffee—it was his third, maybe his fifth, he had lost track—and tried to ignore the stack of reports on the counter. Sunday was his day to catch up on paperwork, but he shouldn't have bothered bringing any home that weekend. Between the storm and the body on the beach, it had been a tough stretch.

The sheriff sighed and reached for the top document. He started to read, but then the sun came out and his attention wandered to the window and the scene beyond. The beach was still a mess. Cate had cleared the storm rubble off the deck and started in on the rest, but there was plenty of debris to deal with. The least he could do was move the heavier pieces of driftwood and bury the dead fish. There would be time for the paperwork later.

He was on the beach digging out one of the larger logs when a car door slammed. Cubiak assumed Cate was home early and kept shoveling.

"Sheriff? Dave?"

He looked up.

"Lisa?"

His assistant had never stopped by without calling ahead. Something was wrong.

"What's happened? What is it?" he said as she picked her way across the sand.

Lisa stopped in front of him and stood arms akimbo.

"What is it?" Her eyes flashed with anger. "Florian Urbanski is my godfather and one of the finest people on the peninsula. I can't believe that you're accusing him of murder," she said.

Cubiak jammed his shovel into the sand. Oh, hell, he'd done it again. He had forgotten about the close ties that linked people in Door County. Many residents had lived in the area for generations and had second and third cousins in common. The resulting network was so complex that only the old-timers could keep track of who was related to whom. He had learned the hard way not to be openly critical of any of the locals for fear that someone in earshot would take umbrage.

He had to tread carefully.

"I haven't accused Mister Urbanski of anything, much less murder. But he had a heated argument with Scott Henley just days before Henley turned up dead, so I had to question him. I had no choice."

It's part of the job, the sheriff wanted to say but didn't.

"Florian wouldn't hurt anyone. He couldn't."

"There's more to it than that, Lisa. Sometimes people know more than they realize. Your godfather had visited Door Camelot several times and may have seen or heard things that could turn out to be important."

She kicked up a puff of sand. "Okay, I get it, it's your job, but you're done now. You're not going to talk to him again, are you?"

Cubiak wiped his face on his sleeve and stepped over the log. "Let's get out of the sun. We need to talk."

On the deck, he pulled two chairs into the shade and sat. Lisa remained standing.

Cubiak planted his elbows on his knees and looked at her. "I hope there isn't a reason for me to talk to your godfather again, but if I have to, I will."

Lisa crossed her arms and stared down at him. But when she spoke, her tone softened and she sounded more like her usual self.

"Please, try to be kind. His wife, my godmother, died two years ago. They'd been married forty-five years, and they'd finally taken a real winter vacation. They were in Arizona when she was killed in a hit-and-run accident. The driver had been drinking . . ."

Lisa stopped talking and caught her breath. "Sorry. I didn't think . . ."

"It's okay," Cubiak said.

It wasn't okay, but that wasn't her fault. Drunk drivers were a national scourge responsible for more than ten thousand deaths every year. The reports landed on the sheriff's desk with sickening regularity; the incidents were reported in the news, mentioned in conversations overheard at the grocery store. Every reference to a fatal DUI hit-and-run took him back to the Chicago street where his first wife and his daughter were mowed down by an inebriated driver in a monstrous green car. Their deaths were a fact of life for him, something he had to deal with.

"Did they catch the guy?" he asked.

"The driver was a woman. She'd been playing bridge with her friends at the country club and enjoying cocktails all afternoon."

Cubiak nodded. He imagined the woman, her manicured hands on the wheel and the radio playing her favorite oldies while she stared vacantly out the windshield, oblivious to the two tons of metal hurtling down the street at her control. Several hours' worth of liquor would have left her tipsy, slurred her speech, compromised her judgment.

"I'm sorry," he said. Then he added, "I didn't realize you knew Mister Urbanski."

"I know half the people on the peninsula and am related to a whole slew of them too."

So, in addition to her job, her responsibilities for her kids, and her concerns about her hopefully soon-to-be ex-husband, Lisa had to worry about the ornery old farmer as well.

"The farm is all he has left. The only things he cares about are me, my kids, and his cows. That's why he's so angry with the people at the larping place. All the noise and activity upset the cows."

She looked Cubiak in the eye. "I don't expect you to understand this, but there are farmers who genuinely care about the stock they raise. Florian does them one better. He loves his animals. When my brothers and I were kids, he let us put halters on the calves and walk them around the yard. Those animals were like pets to us too."

Cubiak had spent most of his life in the city where people lavished attention and love on cats and dogs, the kinds of animals that were common household pets. But cattle? He had always thought of farm animals as commodities that provided food, not comfort or solace. But after watching the Holsteins across the road from his office, he knew different. To his own amazement, he had grown fond of the cows and missed them when they weren't in the pasture. He even had a favorite. And so, he thought he might understand, at least a little.

The sheriff nodded again. "Sit down, Lisa. I'll get some iced tea."

She sat and he stood.

Inside he washed up and pulled on a clean shirt. When he got back from the kitchen, he was relieved to see her still in the chair. She even smiled when he set the tray with the tea and a plate of cookies on the table between them.

"Thank you."

"De nada." Cubiak reclaimed his chair and then asked her about her kids. He checked again about how she had fared through the storm.

"Are you still satisfied with the job, working for me?"

"Oh yes. Absolutely. I love it. Mostly," she said and smiled.

Finally, he brought the conversation back to Urbanski. "Tell me about your godfather," he said, as gently as he could.

Lisa exhaled. "Florian's old school, gruff on the outside but otherwise a real softie. I know he has a temper and sometimes comes across as a hard nut, but he was always gentle with his wife and my mom and really good to us kids. My dad worked two jobs and had little time for us. Not Florian—he always made time when he could. There's a creek that runs through the back of the farm, and after church on Sundays he'd sometimes take us fishing there. He taught me to bait a hook, tie a square knot, and drive a tractor, three things I still know how to do."

She laughed. "You don't have to look so surprised."

"Just impressed," Cubiak said and emptied his glass. "How long has Florian had the farm?"

"Forever, it seems. His great-grandparents bought the property after the trees were logged out and were the first to farm the land. It's been passed down through the family ever since. And now it's his."

"He grew up there?"

"Yep, and he's lived there his whole life. Other than that one vacation and a few trips to Green Bay for a Packers game, I don't think he spends much time away. The things tourists come here for? The festivals and the resorts and stuff, he's oblivious to all that."

Lisa set her glass on the table. "Scott Henley, the man who was found on the beach, where's he from?"

"He worked in Chicago, but I don't know if he's from there. Why?"

"The name sounds familiar. There used to be a Henley Resort up north, somewhere around Ellison Bay. It was one of the bigger resorts back then. My dad worked there when he was a teenager, but it's been gone for years."

"Is the family still here?"

"I don't think so."

Lisa helped herself to a cookie. "Florian told me that his new neighbors ran around in costumes. When we were kids, he used to tease us a lot, so at first I thought he was joking. But then you said that Henley was dressed like a knight when his body was found. What was that all about?"

Cubiak explained what he had learned about larping and Henley's team of knights.

"Henley bought the property next to Urbanski's to give his core group a permanent home for their events. Hence the name Door Camelot."

"King Arthur and the Knights of the Round Table. Sounds like guy stuff."

Cubiak grinned. "I admit I read the stories when I was a kid, but it isn't all guy stuff. Sometimes women take on the roles of the knights. And there's Guinevere too. For a while, a local woman named Vivi Kay played the part, but I'm told she's moved on to new worlds."

Lisa sat up. "I went to school with a ViVi Kay—anyway that's what she called herself freshman year. Her real name was Veronica Vivian Kaiser, but she thought that was too dull. She was a couple of years younger than me, so our paths didn't cross much. It has to be her, doesn't it?"

Cubiak hesitated. The summer that Joey was four, Cate curated a countywide photo installation and to free her afternoons, she had hired a local teenager named Veronica Kaiser to watch Joey while she worked in her studio. The girl was usually gone by the time Cubiak was home, but a couple of times Cate needed her to stay longer and he had driven her back to her parents' house. If Lisa was right, their summer baby-sitter and ViVi Kay were the same person, and if Amy and Travis had told the truth, she might have been one of the last people to see Scott Henley alive.

"Possibly," he said finally. "Tell me, what was she like in school?"

"Veronica was one of the jock girls. Seriously into athletics."

"You weren't?"

"I was more interested in theater." Lisa took a sip of tea. "I'm the one who should have gone into larping, not Veronica."

"Do you know what she's doing now?"

"Not really. I think she worked in Green Bay for a while, but I'm not sure. You don't think she knows anything about what happened to Henley, do you?"

Cubiak pictured the blond teenager who had ridden shotgun in the jeep on the short ride through the countryside. He knew little about her other than her name and the fact that she always tidied up after Joey and even washed the dishes after she had fixed a snack for him. She was quiet, almost shy, but weren't most adolescents in the presence of adults?

He couldn't imagine her being involved in a murder investigation. He was about to say as much when he realized that he would be echoing Lisa's arguments about her godfather.

"Probably not, but I'd like to talk to her. Do you think you can track her down?"

After Lisa went home to start making calls, Cubiak abandoned the tree trunk on the beach and the paperwork on the counter and instead searched the internet for leads on a Veronica or Vivian Kaiser. He found obituaries for two women with similar names, one in Seattle who died at eighty-two and another in Connecticut who lived to be ninety-four. A handful of images popped up as well. One was a photo of a retired lawyer in Atlanta, another of an elementary school teacher in Portland, Oregon. The third was a cookbook author who lived on Cape Cod. The three were middle aged or older and conventionally sedate. The fourth photo was different. It depicted a young woman in heavy makeup and included a link to a website where the same photo appeared along with a one-line bio: "Vivi Kay: Killer instincts wrapped in silk." There was no location or email address, only a contact link on the page.

The vampy ViVi Kay didn't have a social media presence, but the Veronica Kaiser from Door County did. Cubiak opened the page and saw the clean-cut teenager he remembered, the girl with a face full of freckles and a toothy grin who had babysat young Joey. There were photos of her with her pet hedgehog; several in her varsity volleyball uniform; one of her wearing a bathing suit and holding a trophy, grinning wildly; and one of her climbing the old fire tower at Peninsula State Park.

Which one was the real Ms. Kaiser, or were they equal parts of the same person?

It was a few minutes after twelve when Lisa called. According to her informal network, Veronica Kaiser lived in Valmy with her parents and worked part time at the Liberty Grove General Store.

"I phoned and talked to Irma Zubek, the owner. Veronica's there today until six," Lisa said.

Cubiak headed out immediately. When he reached the shop, Veronica was sitting on a bench in the side yard, eating a sandwich and studying her phone. A bottle of water and a brown paper bag sat next to her. Suddenly, she threw down the device.

"Hey, careful or you'll break it," Cubiak said as he approached.

"Yeah, well . . . ," she started and frowned. Then she recognized him, and the expression morphed into a smile. "Sheriff, nice to see you. How's Joey? And Cate? It's been ages. Everything all right at your house?"

"We're fine, thanks. And you?"

"Good. I was gone for a couple of years, living in Manitowoc, but here I am again."

Veronica beamed up at him with the face of a midwestern angel. There was no hint of makeup, no sign of a darker side.

"I'm glad I ran into you. I need to talk to you about something. Do you mind if I join you for a few minutes?"

She picked up the phone and checked the time. "Sure, no problem. What is it?" she said, setting the cell aside again.

The sheriff sat down. "I need your help understanding something. It's about larping. I've heard that you know a bit about it."

"Yeah." She appended an *a* to the word and stretched it out into two syllables. "Oh God, don't tell me you want to get into larping. I don't believe it!"

Cubiak grinned. "No, not at all. It's just that I recently heard about Door Camelot, you know, the larping center near North Bay, not that far from here actually. When I stopped in to see what it was all about, the people there were very helpful explaining things, but I'm still having a difficult time grasping the concept and figuring out the appeal. Everyone I talked to was from out of town, and when I asked if anyone local ever took part in the events, they mentioned your name."

"I see." She seemed to be weighing what he said, separating truth from fiction.

"You're a larper, aren't you?"

"I was, but not anymore."

"But you liked it once. Can you tell me why?"

Veronica exhaled and waved her hand vaguely at the surroundings. "Look around you, Sheriff. What do you see? A two-lane road that leads to what? A few antique shops, a couple of bars, a couple of restaurants, a gallery or two, a park, the beach. That's it, right? That's it all over the peninsula. Tourists come here because it's beautiful and quiet. They stay awhile, and when they're shopped out and all rested up they go back to their exciting lives somewhere else. The rest of us are stuck here. For us it's the same old same old. Other than the new coffee shops and brew pubs, not much has changed since my mother was my age. When I attended my first larp, it was like walking into another world. It was a way to escape."

"Into make-believe?"

"Sure, but what's wrong with that? At Halloween, people dress up in costumes and pretend to be something they're not; larping expands the concept. It gives you the chance to live a different life for a few hours or a couple of days. There's no harm in that. Plus you meet interesting people."

"Like Scott Henley?"

Veronica colored. She tried to keep her voice light but failed. "Yeah, like him," she said.

"If larping was so exciting, why did you quit?"

She looked at her hands. "Personal reasons."

He waited.

Veronica bit at a fingernail and then curled her hand into a ball. "Okay, I'm sure the blabbermouths at Camelot told you the whole story about how I was Guinevere to Scott's King Arthur. We were an 'item,'" she said, putting the word in air quotes. "When the relationship ended, I decided to move on to something else." Her tone took on a sad, hard edge.

"Tell me about Scott," Cubiak said.

Veronica picked at a loose thread along the edge of her cardigan. "I thought he was Prince Charming, a knight in shining armor who'd ridden in on a white horse to rescue me from my boring existence."

The sheriff nodded. He could see it happening. The smooth, good-looking guy from the big city meets the lonely, restless girl from the country. He has charm, money, a fast car. He's been to many of the places she's dreamed of. He feeds her a good line and she believes everything he says.

"You were swept off your feet." Cubiak spoke softly and kindly, trying to imagine Alexis at Veronica's age, going through the heartbreak of a failed first romance.

"Pretty naive, huh?" Veronica said.

Cubiak gave a half smile. "It happens, and to guys as well. I wouldn't be too hard on myself if I were you."

"Yeah, thanks."

"How did things unwind?" He knew one version but wanted to hear hers.

"With Scott? He cheated on me with that bitch Amy. I'm still not sure who was more to blame, him or her, but it didn't matter because she was the new Guinevere and I was back to being Cinderella again. 'We can be friends,' he said when he dumped me. What a joke."

"When was the last time you saw him?"

Veronica frowned and found another loose string to worry. "A couple of months ago. I don't remember exactly."

"You were at Door Camelot last week. Several people heard you arguing with Scott."

"Oh that! I designed the covers for a couple of his scripts and hadn't been paid yet. I wanted my money, that's all. I don't consider that 'seeing' him," she said.

"What about last Wednesday, the day the storm hit? Did you see him then? Maybe not at the center?"

"No!" Her voice was sharp, guarded. "I was at work and then home with my parents. Why?"

Cubiak took his time responding.

"I'm afraid I have sad news for you. Scott died sometime during the storm. His body was found Friday morning on a beach along Rosemary Lane."

Veronica gaped. Her eyes widened and her pink cheeks paled. "That was Scott? No!" she said, scrunching her features in disbelief. Then *no* again, as if her insistent denial could alter what he had said.

A single tear ran down to her chin. "Scottie," she said, as if she were trying to conjure up Henley from an alchemy of memory and thin air.

She looked at Cubiak, puzzled. "There must be some mistake. He can't be dead." Her voice was strained and croaky.

"Why not?"

Veronica hugged herself and rocked back and forth. "I don't know. He just can't be, that's all."

Was she in shock over the news, or did she know more than she was telling him?

The young woman stared straight ahead and seemed uncertain how to go on. "You're sure?" she said finally.

"Travis Odette made a positive ID. I thought you should know before we released the name to the news media."

Veronica bit her lip and nodded in thanks.

"But how did he die? I don't understand," she said.

Before Cubiak could answer, she crumpled over and started to weep.

There was nothing the sheriff could do but let her cry. He wished there was someone who could comfort her, but that was not a role he could take on.

Finally Veronica pulled herself upright and exhaled deeply. She snatched a tissue from her pocket and dabbed at her swollen eyes.

"He is—was—a wonderful guy," she said, sniffling. "I know I said awful things about him, but Scott really was special. He was so different from the schmucks I meet around here. That's why it hurt so much when we broke up. His intelligence, his kindness, his wit. I missed everything about him, missed it all so much. If you watch Nick's film, you'll understand."

"I haven't seen the documentary yet. I understand he's still working on it."

The young woman shook her head, fluffing her short hair. "Not that, I mean the other stuff."

"What other stuff?"

Veronica pulled back, as if suddenly aware that she was in uncharted territory. "All that footage he shot of Scott. Nick was always real secretive about his work, but I used to watch him when he worked, and it was obvious that he spent way more time filming Scott than he did any of the larping stuff. I couldn't help wondering what he was up to."

"Isn't that what filmmakers do? Shoot way more than they need?"

"I guess, but it was really over the top. To me, Nick seemed obsessed with Scott. Sometimes I wondered if he didn't have a crush on him. Well, why not? Almost everyone else did."

"Did you ask Nick about it?"

"Once, but he said I was imagining things."

And perhaps she was, the sheriff thought. Just then a car came around the curve, and they both watched it roar past and disappear in the distance.

Cubiak stood and touched Veronica's shoulder. "You're going to be all right," he said.

"I know." She looked at him and tried to smile. "I always liked bab-ysitting Joey. I'm glad it was you and not someone else who told me about Scott."

The sheriff hesitated, uncertain if he should share more of the details. Word of the boat and the protruding hand would get around—word always got around—but it seemed cruel to leave her with that image. She would find out eventually.

Instead, he offered her a ride home.

She shook her head. "Thanks, but I have my car, and besides I have to finish my shift. There isn't anyone who can sub for me."

As he drove off, Veronica still hadn't moved from the bench. She sat sideways and hugged her knees while the afternoon sun bounced off the soft helmet of her shiny blond hair.

13  FIRE IN THE NIGHT

For the second time in four days, Cubiak jolted awake in the dark. Something had shaken him from his dreamless sleep. Was it Joey again? Or the dog? Or Cate fighting a nightmare? He felt a tug on the blanket as she rolled onto her side. Then the phone buzzed, and he realized that was the sound that had shattered his slumber.

He reached to the nightstand and groped for his cell.

The call was from the 911 center. "Yeah?" he said, casting off the scrim of sleep.

"Sorry to wake you, sir, but there's a fire at Scott Henley's place and I thought . . ."

The sheriff bolted upright. "How bad?"

"Not sure yet. The trucks are headed there now."

"I'm on my way," he said, stumbling out of bed.

As he reached for his clothes, Cate woke and switched on the light.

"What's wrong? Where are you going?" she said.

"Camelot's burning." Cubiak held socks in one hand, shoes in the other.

It took her a moment. "Oh no. Do you want coffee? I'll . . ." She aimed her feet toward the floor, but he was already at the door to the hall.

"It's okay, go back to sleep. I'm fine. I'll call later."

. . .

The sheriff dressed in the kitchen and yanked a thin jacket off the hook by the side door as he headed out into the dark. The deck was slick with dew and the air cool, an early hint of the fall that was still more than a month distant. The clock on the dash read 3:21.

On the road he drove fast, willing the deer to stay in the woods and praying he could stop in time if any ventured into his path.

As he crossed the still landscape, fatigue welled up, and for a moment he wished for a cup of Cate's coffee. He lowered the window and let the cold air slap his face and fill his lungs. In a world made unfamiliar by the dark, he passed shadowy farmhouses and barns that seemed more mirage than real. Unable to read the terrain, he nearly missed the last turn from one country road to another.

He was a mile from the larping center when he smelled smoke. The acrid stench intensified quickly and came at him like a heavy dose of cheap perfume. From a rise, he spotted a red smudge in the distance. Then the road dipped and the smudge disappeared. As he raced through the undulating countryside, the neon blur danced in and out of his view. When he finally reached Door Camelot, the streaks of flame were shooting up above the tree line.

"Fuck," Cubiak said as he spun onto the entry lane. Cars and pickups lined the narrow road, leaving barely enough room for him to get through. The small yard was overwhelmed with equipment: fire trucks from Sister Bay, Egg Harbor, and Ellison Bay, as well as two mobile water tanks. Ironically, on a peninsula surrounded by a Great Lake and a large bay, the mobile tanks provided the only water available to the firefighters who were manning the hoses.

Under the glare of klieg lights, a scene of controlled chaos unfolded, almost like something from a movie set. For the time it took him to blink, Cubiak wondered if he had fallen back asleep into a nightmare. Except he knew that the inferno was real. He felt the heat and inhaled the sulfurous smoke. He heard the crackle of burning wood, the snap of falling timbers, and urgent shouts of the crew.

The communications officer had said that the fire was bad; it was worse than that.

The main house blazed. All that remained of Scott Henley's adjacent cottage was a skeleton of studs and charred window frames. One group of firefighters drenched the smoldering ruins to keep sparks from igniting the costume shed and the other cottages, while a second squadron battled the flames at the burning building to stop the inferno from invading the surrounding woods. Thank goodness for the storm earlier that week, Cubiak thought. Two days of heavy rain had dampened the trees and bushes and given them a chance to withstand the onslaught.

The sheriff exchanged half a dozen words with the fire chief—enough to learn that the volunteer firefighters were winning. For now, that was all he needed to know.

At the far end of the yard, the larpers had formed an old-fashioned fire brigade. The line began at the well with Travis and snaked behind the cottages to the costume shed. As quickly as Travis filled a bucket with water, Quill grabbed it and handed it to Amy, who ran it over to Isabelle, who carried it to Nick. The videographer tossed one bucketful at the costume shack and the next at the cottage nearest the fire. Each time the larpers handed off a full bucket, they grabbed an empty coming from the other direction and sent it back toward the well to be refilled.

"Was anyone hurt?" Cubiak asked Travis. He had to shout to be heard over the noise of the truck pumps and the voice of the fire chief, who was yelling orders to his crew.

"We're all okay," the assistant director said. His face was streaked with soot and sweat. He was barefoot.

"You need shoes," Cubiak said as he took his place in line and reached for a bucket.

"I'm okay. I run like this. It's nothing."

"What happened?"

"I'm not sure. Someone yelled fire around three, and when I got outside, Scott's cottage and the main house were burning. I turned one of the garden hoses on his house, but it was useless. We could hear the fire trucks coming, but by the time they arrived it was too late to save the buildings." He pumped as he talked. The muscles in his arms pulsed with the up-and-down movement of the handle, and the words came in spurts.

There was nothing more to say, only buckets to be passed, those filled with water in one direction and those that were empty in the other.

It seemed an eternity before Cubiak looked up again. By then the eastern sky was a pale blue and the firefighters were rolling up the hoses.

"The fire's out," the sheriff said. He was wet with sweat, and his back and shoulders ached.

The buckets went full circle one more time. Then Travis let go of the pump handle and fell back from the well.

The exhausted larpers gathered around him and stared at the ruins. The heat had died with the fire and they shivered in the morning chill.

"I'll need to talk to each of you again," the sheriff said.

"Don't waste your time with us. Find the fucker who did this," Quill said.

His colleagues murmured their assent.

"It could have been an accident," Cubiak said.

"Yeah, right. Sure. Scott's dead, maybe murdered, and now this?"

The sheriff knew that Quill was right. The groundskeeper was scared and suspicious. They all were, and he didn't blame them.

"Take a break for a few minutes. Then I'll be back."

While the crew packed up, Cubiak buttonholed the fire chief.

"Your men did a good job."

"Thanks, I'll pass along the compliment." The chief then chuckled and pulled at his chin. "You couldn't tell in those outfits, but nearly half the 'men' are women. Times change, Sheriff."

Women as knights. Women fighting fires. "And for the better," Cubiak said, remembering how Cate liked to remind him that women held up half the sky.

"Any thoughts on how this got started?" he went on, indicating the scarred scene before them.

"I can't say anything for certain."

"But if you had to guess?"

"As wet as everything was and as fast as this took off, I'd say it was a fire of suspicious origin. One probably started with an accelerant."

"Somebody torched the place?"

The fire chief unclipped his heavy coat. Fatigue showed in his eyes. "It looks that way, but I'll know better tomorrow after the investigators start combing through the muck."

The larpers had gathered in Travis's cottage. He was in the kitchen making coffee; the others crammed the miniature living room. Nick sprawled on the floor, snoring. Amy and Isabelle nestled against each other on the tiny sofa, an afghan over their knees and their eyes closed. Quill dozed in the rocker. The place reeked of smoke. Cubiak held up his sleeve and took a whiff. No wonder. They all carried the odor in their clothes, skin, and hair.

The sheriff texted Cate to tell her that the fire was out and that he wouldn't be home until later. Then he joined Travis. "Do you have any food?" he asked.

"There's cheese and sausage in the fridge. Crackers are up there." He pointed his chin at a cupboard.

While they organized the impromptu breakfast, Cubiak questioned Travis.

"Where were you when the fire broke out?"

"Here, in my room, asleep."

"Was anyone with you?"

"No, I was alone."

"Who alerted you to the fire?"

"I heard the bell, the one outside in the yard. We ring it to signal the end of weekend events and to warn people about pending storms when they're out in the field or spending the night in the campground."

"Who rang it?"

"I don't know. When I got outside, everyone was already there. Quill called nine-one-one I got the hose and the others ran to the horse barn for buckets. We all knew the drill. Scott made us go through it every few months. He worried about the animals and insisted we know what to do in case of fire."

Travis swiped at his forehead. "Thank God it wasn't the horse barn."

"Scott worried about fire?"

"Not especially. He worried about everything. The liability insurance on an operation like this is insane; he didn't want anything to happen that would jack up the cost even more."

Travis leaned against the refrigerator. "Now what? The end of a dream?"

"I don't know what's going to become of this place, but we have to find out what happened. Did you see anyone here earlier in the day?"

"No, just the five of us."

"Were there any visitors?"

Travis shook his head.

"Did you notice anything unusual? A car slowing down, someone tossing trash out the car window?"

"No."

"Were there any calls?"

"To the center? I don't know. I was outside all day. You'd have to check the phone for messages." He frowned. "But I guess you can't, can you? Not that it really matters. No one calls anymore. Everything's done by email."

"What about surveillance cameras?"

"There aren't any." Travis pulled at his jaw. "Can we get this over with? I need to get some sleep. We all do."

The other larpers gave similar answers. Other than Isabelle, who had gotten up for a drink of water and seen the fire and then rung the bell, no one had seen anything. No one had heard anything. No one knew anything.

"Is it safe for us to stay here?" Amy said.

"You'll be fine. I'm sure that whoever did this won't come back and try anything else, but just in case, I'm posting a deputy on the premises."

She hesitated. "Would it be okay if I took the Guinevere costume from the shed? It belongs to the center, but I'd feel better having it close by. Maybe I can air it out too."

She had directed the question to Cubiak, but it was Travis who answered and told her it was fine.

Cubiak was on the phone with Mike Rowe when Amy crossed the yard holding the gown in her arms. There was nothing exceptional about the young woman. In her jeans and sooty T-shirt, she could be anyone.

In the dress, she became a woman of royal rank, the wife of a legendary king.

"Clothes make the woman. Or man. Clothes dictate the roles they play," the sheriff muttered. Who are you? he wondered. Not just Amy, but all of them. He knew the roles they assumed in the Camelot tale, but all he knew about their real identities was what they had told him. What if there were double layers of role playing going on and the larpers weren't who they said they were?

By now it was nearly eight thirty, and Lisa would be in. Cubiak called and gave her the list of names. "I need background checks on these people."

"How soon? Never mind. I know. Yesterday would do nicely," she said mimicking his gravelly voice.

She asked when he would be in.

"Not sure. I have to finish up here first," he said.

Cubiak disliked the deception, but he couldn't tell her that he was on his way to quiz her beloved godfather about the fire.

14 OLD FRIENDS

At Urbanski's place, the battered brown pickup and shiny red tractor hadn't moved from their positions alongside the garage. Seeing them, Cubiak assumed that the farmer was home. There was no answer at the house, so the sheriff crossed the yard to the barn. The herd of Brown Swiss lingered in the adjacent field. Their massive heads bobbed gently as they tore at the grass with their giant teeth. Unseen insects buzzed and whirred in the tall weeds along the fence. The chickens clucked in their pen. A plump calico cat slipped out from under a bush and skirted around the sheriff. As quickly as it appeared, it vanished into the shadow of a nearby shed, like a dream.

Cubiak had been up for hours, and in the tranquil quiet, fatigue caressed him like a soft cloak. If he could just sit in the shade with the cat and shut his eyes for a few minutes. He took a deep breath and shook off the temptation. Then he continued toward the huge barn.

Inside, the air was soft and the light dim. A single low-watt bulb at the far end of the long center aisle lit the cavernous, cob-webbed space. At first the barn appeared empty, but as the sheriff's eyes adjusted to the light, Urbanski came into focus. The old farmer sat on a bale of straw in a small pen, his back half-turned to the door. If he was aware of Cubiak walking toward him, he gave no notice. His attention was focused on the newborn lamb that was cradled in the crook of his arm.

"They're usually born in spring. We breed 'em that way to give them the summer to eat grass and grow and get ready for the slaughter," he said as if in answer to an unasked question.

"It's all about cost-effectiveness and feed—that's what they tell you in the books on good farming. But this little gal had her own schedule. She also needs a little help." Urbanski looked up, straightening his shoulders while the lamb pulled greedily at the bottle he held to its puckered mouth.

"You wanna try?" he asked the sheriff, offering up the fragile animal.

"No thanks," Cubiak said, although he felt a rush of envy for the easy comfort the other man seemed to draw from the simple task.

Urbanski resettled the lamb. "You smell like a chimney. What the hell's going on?"

"You know exactly what's going on and why I'm here."

The lamb squirmed and Urbanski pulled the bottle away. Then he tightened his hold. "Gently now, it's okay," he said as he pushed the nipple back toward its mouth.

"I got nothing to do with that fire, if that's what you're thinking," he said, raising his voice and glaring at the sheriff.

"You had plenty of motive to burn the place down."

"You saying it wasn't an accident?"

"I'm not saying anything except that you had reason to want it to burn."

"I want them gone, and I don't make no bones about that. But I didn't try to burn them out. Fire's a nasty thing you don't wish on anyone, not even your worst enemy. Besides, I wouldn't want to take a chance on it spreading here."

"Where were you last evening?"

Urbanski snickered. "Here we go again. I got no alibi, just like the last time you started asking questions. I was home all night. Didn't see another soul, just the animals. Gave this little one a bottle around midnight, but she can't talk and tell you that, now can she?"

"Then what?"

"Then I went to bed, slept until two or so, and then got up for the next feeding. Been that way since 'cause she needs nourishment every couple hours."

Urbanski set the lamb down. Both men watched it wobble on its stick legs and fight to find its balance. Then it took a few tentative steps toward the straw and plopped unceremoniously onto the dry bedding.

"Nap time," the farmer said cheerfully. He gripped the steel railing that separated him from the sheriff and heaved himself up to his feet. "Damn arthritis. Get stiff sitting too long," he said.

It was a good act or maybe he really was hurting. Cubiak couldn't be sure.

"What time was that? When you went back to the house."

"Half past or thereabouts. It usually takes about thirty minutes to feed one of them."

"And you went right to bed?"

Urbanski unlatched the gate and sidled into the aisle. "Usually I do but not last night. For some reason I stayed up. Opened a bottle of beer and sat at the kitchen table to drink it. That's where I was when the first fire truck came by."

"Do you remember when that was?"

"Three ten a.m."

"That's very precise."

The farmer started toward the door. "There's not much else to look at in the kitchen but the clock. I was staring right at it when I heard the siren. Nights here are awfully quiet, so a noise like that gets your attention. A few minutes later, the second truck flew by. By the time I got outside, it seemed like the whole damn sky was lit up. Plenty of racket, too, with the third truck and then the ambulance racing down the road. Bad luck, I guess, for them."

"But not for you."

Urbanski shrugged. "How much of the place burned?" There was a hopeful note in the question.

"The main building and one of the cottages were destroyed."

They reached the exit and Urbanski pulled the door shut. "Better than nothing," he muttered as he blinked at the bright sunshine. "I know I shouldn't say things like that, but I'm not going to pretend I feel otherwise."

The farmer paused. "No one was hurt?" This time his question was laced with caution.

"No."

"Well, that's good."

"I believe you mean that."

Urbanski took his time considering the comment before he replied. "I do," he said with a solemn nod.

Was the old farmer switching roles from angry protestor to concerned neighbor? If he didn't want anyone to die in the fire, then how could he be suspected of killing Scott Henley? Is that what he wanted Cubiak to think?

"But you don't shy from the occasional slugfest," the sheriff said.

"Now, what the hell do you mean by that?" They had made it to the house, where Urbanski slowly mounted the porch stairs. On level ground, he was tall enough to stand eye to eye with Cubiak. From this vantage point, he glared down at the sheriff.

Cubiak took the first step to lessen the distance. "I have witnesses that claim you nearly got into a fight with Scott on your last visit to the center."

"People got good imaginations."

"The encounter was caught on film."

The old man stifled a grin. "Was it now? Well, I guess if truth be told, that fella got my dander up."

"Scott Henley."

"The same."

"There was someone else with you. Who was he?"

"Was there?" Urbanski scratched the back of his head. "I can't recall, Sheriff."

"There's a clear shot of him on the video. He's about your height but thinner."

Urbanski yawned. "It must have been George Tinsel. He stopped by for fresh eggs that morning and we got to talking. He said he'd heard something in town that I was having trouble with one of my neighbors, so I gave him the rundown on who they were and what they did, but I'm not sure he paid much attention. Man's got plenty of troubles of his own."

The calico cat slipped between Cubiak's feet and rubbed its head against Urbanski's boots. The cat waited for him to settle into the old wooden rocker, and then it jumped into his lap. The farmer focused his attention on the feline for a moment and then abruptly returned to the conversation with Cubiak.

"Life's hard for him, especially these last three years since his wife died. I told him he should get out more, but he says he can't, and I guess that's true enough. He's home most of the time. Has to be, I imagine. I was surprised when he said he'd go over there with me if I wanted the company. Only reason I said yes was I thought we'd catch some of them in their costumes, and I wanted George to see what kind of crazy fool people I got running around next door and upsetting my cows."

"Where can I find Tinsel?"

Urbanski waved a hand over his shoulder. "Oh, his place is way the hell south."

He made it sound like his friend lived near Sheboygan.

"Where exactly?"

"Near Clark Lake."

Cubiak pushed away from the banister. "What did you say it was that kept him at home so much?"

"I didn't say." The old man narrowed his eyes and looked out toward the barn. "Man's got responsibilities, Sheriff."

Cubiak made it to George Tinsel's place in twenty minutes. The farmstead was a sorry, rundown operation, as neglected as Urbanski's was well tended. Whatever kept the man tied to his plot of land, it wasn't a dedication to farming. The pasture and surrounding fields were ringed by tilting fence posts and sagging barbed wire. There was no sign of any animals or crops. The barn roof caved in at one end, and the door on the chicken coop hung from its hinges. No chickens pecked the ground nearby. There was little grass left on what had once been a lawn, and only a handful of scraggly daisies peeked up through the weeds that overran the large flowerbed at the edge of the yard.

Amid the disrepair, the modest white frame house stood out. The pale yellow trim was freshly painted, and new tiles had been carefully fitted to the far corner of the roof. Shades were pulled in all but the corner window, where lace curtains hung behind the glass panes. A wooden rocking chair sat in the far corner of the porch, and a windchime of seashells hung from the ceiling. Two of the porch steps looked new, and there was a long section of freshly varnished wood on the railing of the wooden ramp that ran from the house to a concrete pad at the edge of the gravel drive. A brown van with a handicap parking permit on the dash was parked near the ramp. A pale, lanky man in baggy pants and a faded checked shirt stood nearby. He didn't look pleased to see Cubiak. Urbanski must have called ahead.

"You're here about those idiots next door to Florian's place," Tinsel said as Cubiak approached. No hello or polite chitchat, which were the norm on the peninsula.

The sheriff introduced himself. Tinsel did the same.

"There's been some trouble at the center, and I'm talking to everyone who's been there lately." Cubiak paused. This was the moment when most people would raise objections and declare their innocence, but Tinsel said nothing. The sheriff went on. "Maybe you saw something that would help my investigation."

Tinsel turned his dark, deep-set eyes on the sheriff. "I was only there the one time, and the only reason I went was to make sure Florian didn't get too hotheaded. He's mad as hell at those people, and to be honest I had trouble believing what he told me about them and wanted to see for myself what the fuss was all about."

They had been facing the house, and while he talked Tinsel pivoted toward the dilapidated barn, forcing Cubiak to do the same.

"You know what they say about seeing is believing? Well, I saw enough that day to realize that he wasn't exaggerating. Grown men and women running around in costumes like a bunch of kindergartners putting on a show for their parents. Florian was all fired up that morning, and after what I saw, I could hardly blame him. The man's worked hard all his life for what he's got, and now it's threatened by these pampered city kids with nothing better to do than play dress-up. They've got no respect for anyone living nearby. Shooting off cannons, for Chrissake. Fucking waste of time and money, if you ask me. I want nothing to do with people like that."

"What did you know about the center before you went there with Florian?"

"Not much. He'd talked about it once before, but I never paid that much heed to what he said. What'd they call it, Door Camelot?" he said with a sneer.

"There was a fire there last night. A couple of buildings burned."

"You won't get no sympathy from me. Probably not from Florian either."

"Do you think he's capable of doing something like that?"

"Burning down other people's property? Hell no. He may not like that bunch, but there's no way he'd do that. Florian's the old-fashioned kind. He's got too much respect for things to destroy them."

"Where were you last night?"

"Me? You think I torched the place, as a favor to my friend?" Tinsel scraped his foot against the ground. "Sorry, Sheriff, but that ain't my style either."

"You haven't answered my question."

Tinsel gave Cubiak a hard stare. "That's because I resent the implication. But if you must know, I was here all day, all evening, and all night."

"Can anyone confirm that?"

"No, sir. No one."

"Do you know of anyone else who shares Urbanski's sentiments about the larpers? Someone upset enough to take matters into their own hands?"

Tinsel shook his head. "Besides stopping in on Florian once in a while, I don't mix much with other folks up there."

Cubiak studied the ramp. Why did the man keep it in such good repair?

"I'm sorry about your wife. Florian told me."

Tinsel looked down. "It's been two months now that she's gone. Things haven't been easy, but then I guess you know all about that."

So, he knew about Cubiak's past; everyone knew, the sheriff realized. He nodded, and the two men were silent for as long as it took each of them to unwrap from the memory of a life that had slipped away.

With little else to discuss, they exchanged comments about the storm, and then the sheriff gave Tinsel his card with instructions to call if anything came to mind. Cubiak was ten minutes away when he realized the discrepancy between what Tinsel had said about his wife's death and what Urbanski had told him earlier. The sheriff knew the time down to the minute when Lauren and Alexis had breathed their last breath. Surely a man remembered the date his spouse died. Why would Tinsel say his wife had passed two months ago and his friend Florian say she had been dead for three years? Perhaps Urbanski was getting senile or had been thinking of his own situation.

The sheriff stopped in town and pulled out his phone to search the internet for the obituary. Sylvie Tinsel had a soft smile, curly hair, and sad eyes. She had died three years ago, just as Lisa's godfather had said. It was Tinsel and not Urbanski who was confused or caught up in his own version of magical thinking or sinking into dementia. Given the sorry state of the property, it was a possible scenario. Or had he deliberately lied? And if so, why?

Cubiak was still sitting on the shoulder when the phone rang. The call was coming from Sister Bay, and when he answered, the fire chief's voice boomed out.

"The fire at Camelot was arson." The commander made the announcement as if he were shouting orders to a crew at a fire site.

"You're sure?"

"Absolutely. I'd stake my reputation on it. Whoever did this used an accelerant to ignite the blaze. I told you last night that I suspected as much, given how fast the fire spread. Also the fact that the young man who called it in said that he saw flames in a couple of different locations at the same time. Those two things always add up to the same thing."

"Can you identify the accelerant?"

"Not without further testing. But if I had to guess, I'd put my money on gasoline or diesel fuel. Unfortunately both are readily available."

And impossible to track, Cubiak thought.

"Guess this doesn't help you much." The fire chief hesitated, and when he spoke again, his voice had modulated. "Lucky there wasn't much of a wind, or the whole place might have gone up in flames."

15 \ TRUE IDENTITIES

By midafternoon Cubiak had lost count of the amount of coffee he had consumed since morning. Despite the caffeine pulsating through his veins, he was still tired. One more cup wouldn't hurt and might help. As he stood in the break room, a full mug in hand, the light bounced off the glass front of a vending machine and reflected his twin back at him. The clone looked startlingly haggard. His brow was deeply lined, his hair was gray, and his shoulders slouched as if weighted with a heavy burden. The sheriff frowned and rubbed his stubbled chin. Then he straightened.

"Go to hell," he said. "I'll be fine after a good night's sleep."

He had been gone from his office only a few minutes, but when he returned, a spate of bright-yellow folders waited on his desk. They were fanned out in alphabetical order, evidence of Lisa at her most efficient. Cubiak set his coffee down and lowered himself to his chair, determined to ignore the twinge in his right knee.

Maybe he was getting too old for the job. All around him, reports were whizzing unseen from one office to another, appearing with the push of a button on the department's up-to-date pixelated computer screens. With a pang of guilt, Cubiak thought of the stack of unread reports on his kitchen counter. Although he had grown accustomed to using email and appreciated the information he could garner from the internet, when it came to reading and writing reports, he preferred having things in print, a stone-age preference that made him the butt of departmental jokes.

Well, so be it, he thought as he reached for the folder on Amy Baxter, aka Lady Guinevere. A quick glance indicated that Lisa had peeked under every rock in the young woman's past and unearthed no red flags. Everything the larper had told the sheriff about her sheltered early life and her subsequent move to the city checked out. Amy was one of the good girls, as innocent in real life as she was in Henley's fantasy world of King Arthur.

The sheriff picked up the second folder. The profile of Travis Odette, the sometime Lancelot who served as Door Camelot's assistant director, was similarly unblemished. After high school, Travis enrolled in community college. Midway through the second semester, he dropped out and took the job at the manufacturing plant, where he worked until he joined the staff at Door Camelot. Not so much as a bounced check or a speeding ticket in his record.

The sheriff shifted his weight and reached for his coffee. He picked up the mug and then he set it back down. He couldn't drink any more. Even the aroma was off-putting. He nudged the cup aside and opened the third folder to the known details of the life of one Martin Quilty, groundskeeper. Quill was divorced with two children, ages eight and ten. He had a mediocre credit rating and a sketchy patchwork of past employment but no red flags and no run-ins with the law.

The file on Isabelle Redding, receptionist, portrayed her as a hometown girl from Fish Creek who had left the peninsula to attend college in Whitewater but returned to the county after one semester. She was married at twenty-three and widowed at twenty-five, when her husband was killed in the crash of a military helicopter in the Mediterranean, a cold hard fact that explained both her disdain for larping and her need to keep her job.

Except for Isabelle's loss, the real lives of the members of Camelot's inner circle were exceptional only in their ordinariness. Nothing stood out. Cubiak found nothing unusual until he came to the file on Nick Youngman, filmmaker. The folder was empty, save for a note from Lisa.

"There's no record of anyone by this name in Milwaukee or anywhere else in the state. I tried every variation I could think of for Nicholas, including Nicolas, Niccolo, Niklas, Nickolai, Nick, and Niki, with different combinations of the surname—Youngman, Youngmen, and even Youngmann—and came up with nothing." She added a postscript: "I found a Nicholas Youngman in Florida, age 89; and another in Arizona, age 94. They didn't seem relevant."

Indeed. Nick the videographer and sometime Gawain looked like a man who hadn't yet reached his prime.

The sheriff tossed the folder back on the desk. There were many possible explanations for Nick's deception—he was an investigative reporter working on an exposé, or he had been hired by a competitor to spy on Scott Henley's operation. Neither explanation excused him from revealing the truth to Cubiak. But if he had a personal vendetta against Henley—if he had come to Door County to harm him and to destroy Camelot—now there was reason enough to lie.

Cubiak leaned back in his chair and closed his eyes.

Every murder case was a puzzle, but this one was especially tangled. He was convinced that Henley's death and the fire at Door Camelot were connected, but he had no proof. He had a feeling that the letters *ALE* found in Henley's calendar were important, but he didn't know what they signified—possibly initials? He'd have to ask Lisa. Maybe they'd mean something to her.

Then there were the suspects. It seemed that every time he turned around, he stumbled on another person who had a grudge against Henley.

He had started the day with three: First, there was the laborer Bill Fury, whom Henley had fired after wrongfully accusing him of being a thief. The sheriff's department still hadn't tracked him down to ask where he was on the day the larper disappeared.

Veronica Kaiser, the infatuated former girlfriend, was second on the list. She had pinned her hopes for a more exciting life to Henley and was left sitting on the sidelines.

Third was Florian Urbanski, the next-door neighbor who claimed that Door Camelot threatened his livelihood. The aging farmer had a temper, and he readily admitted that he despised Henley and wanted the larpers driven off the land.

Now Cubiak had a fourth candidate, Nick Youngman. Who was he and why had he concealed his identity, unless he had something to hide?

The sheriff could even add a fifth name to the docket. George Tinsel wasn't a solid suspect, but there were elements to his story that didn't add up: For one, his mistake or deliberate lie about the date of his wife's death. For another, he had been unduly agitated when they talked, ostensibly defending his friend Florian while holding a magnifying glass to the old man's flaws. And there was the matter of the ramp that he kept in such good repair for no apparent reason. These were small details, but the sheriff found it hard to let go of them.

Late that evening, Cubiak stood in the shadowy silence of his deck. The wood was cool and damp under his feet, the air still. After the upheaval of the storm, the lake rested while a billion pricks of light sparkled overhead.

The serenity mocked the tumult in Cubiak's head. He needed order. He needed for the puzzle pieces to fall into place. When that happened, he would know the killer.

16 A SUSPECT WITH
A SECRET

On Tuesday, four days after Scott Henley's body was found on the beach and one day after the fire, Cubiak returned to Door Camelot. A thick cloud layer blanketed the peninsula, trapping the stench of smoke and charred wood close to the ground, and the gray sky heightened the sense of gloom that hung over the ravaged complex. The main house had burned through its bones and into the depths of its soul. Absent the roof and great sections of the walls, it was defenseless against the birds and forest creatures that invaded. Without windows, it stood sightless before those who came to gawk. The wind kissed its bare ribs and toyed with the yellow ribbons that wrapped the perimeter like garlands around a gift. Amid the lush greenery of the peninsula, this piece of the past was reduced to memory and ash.

Dodging the pools of mud and water that remained from the futile struggle to save the house, Cubiak crossed the lawn. Travis advanced toward him.

"What do you want?" the young man said. He had changed his clothes, but the dark circles from the previous day still rimmed his eyes. His greeting came out a harsh bark. Gone were the cheerful demeanor and the phony accent he had used the first time they met.

"I came to check and make sure everyone is okay."

Travis emitted a bitter guffaw. "Okay? The center is a wreck, we're scared shitless that something else is going to happen, and every day a few more cancellations come in. Everything's just fine."

He kicked at the ground. "I hope that bastard Urbanski is happy."

"You think he set the fire?"

"Yeah, and it's not just me. We all blame him. He said he wouldn't rest until we were gone."

"I wouldn't jump to conclusions if I were you."

"Who else then?" Travis didn't wait for an answer. "In fact, I'd like to know why you haven't arrested him yet? Or does the old man get preferential treatment because he's a local and we're outsiders?"

"It doesn't work that way, not on my watch."

Travis went red and started to say something, then he thought better of it and kicked the ground again.

"You're in charge now?" Cubiak said.

"By default, I guess I am."

"Okay, then I'm holding you responsible for your crew here. "

Travis looked up, alarmed. "Meaning?"

"You know what I mean. There'll be a lot of angry spouting off and talk of revenge and getting even, and all of it will be directed at Urbanski. You have to keep everyone calm."

Cubiak tried to rest a reassuring hand on the young man's shoulder, but Travis pulled back out of his reach.

"I know this is hard, but you'll get through it. Just take care of things here, and let me do my job," the sheriff said.

Travis gave Cubiak another hard stare and then walked away.

The sheriff found Nick Youngman behind the horse barn, spreading hay in the troughs for the animals. Two of the steeds gently bucked their heads at him, and he reached up through the fence to pet them.

The sheriff was several feet away when Nick noticed him. The videographer had the same exhausted look as Travis but not the scowl.

"Hey, man, what's going on?" he said, turning a cheerful face toward Cubiak.

"I could ask you the same thing."

"What do you mean?"

"I know you're not Nick Youngman. So the first question is: who are you? And the second: why the charade?"

The filmmaker's smile faded. As he turned away, one of the horses nudged his shoulder and knocked him off balance. Cubiak caught his elbow, saving him from a fall.

Nick found his footing and squinted into the emerging sun. "What are you talking about?" he said.

"Your name's as much a pretense as the knight you portray. There's no record of a Nick or Nicholas or Nicoli Youngman in the state."

"Then the records are wrong."

The erstwhile filmmaker pulled out his driver's license. "Here, this proves who I am."

Cubiak ignored the document. "Licenses can be forged. I'm investigating murder and arson. If you don't tell me your real identity and explain what you're doing here, I can charge you with obstruction of justice."

Nick looked at the license as if he was deciding on his next move. Finally, he put it back in his pocket and moved away from the fence. He was quiet for a moment, his brow furrowed in concentration.

"My name really is Nick. But it's Nick Shelby. Youngman was my mother's maiden name. But I've got nothing to do with Scott's death or the fire. You have to believe me."

Behind him, the horses had lined up along the trough. As they ate, they shuffled and ground their teeth against the dried grasses.

"It's true that I'm a filmmaker, and it's also true that Scott hired me to make a promo film about Door Camelot." Nick looked around and then lowered his voice. "But there's more to it."

"Go on," Cubiak said.

Nick kept his head down. "Is there somewhere else we can go to talk? Some place not at the center?"

The sheriff took the young man's measure. Cubiak had two options: he could either trust Nick or not.

"There's a coffee shop on the right just as you drive into town. We can meet there. I know the make and model of your car as well as your plate number, so don't even think of trying to take off. If you're not at the café in fifteen minutes, I'll have the bridges raised. You won't get off the peninsula."

Nick made it to the restaurant with three minutes to spare. A good sign. Cubiak was at a table on the deck. He waited until they had their drinks before he sat back. "I want the whole story, from start to finish," he said.

"Okay." Nick sighed and rubbed his forehead as if he was trying to organize his thoughts.

"Okay," he said again. When he was playing Nick Youngman at Camelot, his voice was always tinged with a cheerful lilt, but as the real Nick, he spoke in a somber tone.

"This all goes back a long way."

"I've got time."

"What do you know about real estate investing?" Nick said.

"Not much, other than that you buy a house, live in it for a while, and hope it increases in value before it comes time to sell."

"That's how it works with most people, but not real estate investors. They buy houses for just one reason: to leverage the value so they can continue buying more houses, condos, rental buildings—it doesn't matter. The point is to keep accumulating property until you're worth a shitload of money."

"What's this got to do with you and Scott Henley?"

"I'm getting to it," Nick said. He took another moment. "You know how people dream of getting rich quick? My dad was one of those people. He'd been a working stiff all his life, and his one regret was that he hadn't been able to accumulate much. Jesus, he raised six kids and my mom never worked. He did all right by us but not by his own standards. He worried that he didn't have much of a nest egg to leave us, and after he retired, he spent a lot of time trying to figure out how he could make a bundle. He didn't want the money for himself, but for us kids. 'When

I win the lottery, everything's gonna change,' he'd say. Only instead of buying lottery tickets, he went into real estate investing. He'd seen an ad in the paper for one of those free, all-day seminars, lunch included, that promised expert advice aimed at starting you on the road to wealth and happiness. The ad used a big-name headliner to draw people in, but guess who walked out on the stage and ran the show?"

"Henley."

Nick grimaced. "That's right. Our own super salesman, the dearly departed Scott. He was an expert all right, an expert on separating the gullible from their money. He preyed on their weaknesses and their dreams, tantalizing them with what was possible but never really telling them how to do anything. For that, they needed to sign up for the next level of instruction."

"Which your father did."

Nick nodded. "Over and over. Henley pushed all the right buttons, and my poor dad was hooked. Besides, at five hundred dollars, I'm sure it sounded like a real bargain. Only what he didn't realize was that he was being led down the garden path. Five hundred for that first personal step to wealth, but then five thousand for the personal mentor and a series of private coaching sessions. And always another platform with the promise of 'more to learn' and the reassurance that it was a small price to pay for the great wealth it would generate."

"How long did this go on?"

"Long enough for my old man to drain his savings account. Hell, Scott even encouraged him to increase his credit card limit, so he'd have plenty of funds available to take advantage of that first big deal when it came along, but all that meant was that he could charge the instructional fees once he ran out of cash."

"How much did your father pay out?"

"Overall, some thirty thousand in cash, plus another fifteen on his credit card, which he had no way of paying off. And you know what the real pisser is? It was all perfectly legal."

Nick stopped and stared at his drink.

"At some point, he must have known he'd been taken for a ride because he started drinking really hard. It got to the point where he was drunk most of the time. One night when my father was driving home, he plowed into a viaduct and died instantly. The police called it an accident, but I think he did it out of desperation and shame."

"And you didn't know any of this was going on?" Cubiak said.

Nick shook his head. "We knew something was wrong, but this? My dad kept his important papers in his top dresser drawer. After the funeral we went through them to make sure my mother was in line for his pension and health care and stuff like that. She had no idea what had happened to their savings or why she owed so much on the credit card. Neither did we. Then, about a month later, I started to clean out the garage, and that's when I found the box where he'd stashed all this other stuff. He'd hidden it behind his workbench. On the lid, there was one word: Lottery! I figured that it was full of losing lottery tickets, but when I opened it, I discovered all the crap on real estate investing that he'd bought from Henley. Books, CDs, fancy leather binders filled with instruction manuals, stuff like that. Nothing but junk, the stuff Henley had been peddling."

"How'd you track him down?"

Nick snorted. "Easy. I followed my dad's footsteps and signed up for one of the introductory seminars. Henley was long gone by then, but the guy who ran the show spent half the first session bragging about how his predecessor—Scott himself—had made a pile of dough investing in real estate using 'these very same proven methods,' enough that he was able to retire at age thirty-five and pursue his dream of becoming a writer. I googled Henley's name and found a catalog of his larping scripts and the website for Larper Productions. Some writer, huh?"

As Nick talked, he grew increasingly agitated. Suddenly he stopped and looked away. Then he turned back to Cubiak.

"I searched online for information on real estate investing and discovered that nearly everything Henley was peddling was available on the internet for free. That bastard played people like my father for suckers."

"And you decided to get even."

"Damn right. I used my mother's name and registered for the Door Camelot launch party. Henley gave quite a spiel. He was smooth. He'd already bought the property—no doubt with money he got cheating people like my father—and was selling reservations and time shares for larping weekends and events. The house was here, as well as the horse barn and a few of the other buildings, but nothing else. He had plans for developing the property—the cottages first—and then accommodations for visitors and finally elaborate year-round facilities for larps and other events. And though he never quite said so, he implied that anyone who got in early was buying a piece of the action. All he was doing was making promises, but the way people were cheering and lining up to donate money, you'd think he was handing out deeds to heaven. I'd watched those earlier videos I'd found in the garage, and that night I saw Henley give essentially the same kind of performance. You know what they say: once a scumbag, always a scumbag. I vowed I'd find a way to beat him at his own game."

"And did you?"

"I figured my best option was to join his larping crew and work from the inside. Eventually I wormed my way into his inner circle. Once I showed up with my video camera and proved that I knew what I was doing with it, I was in solid. Henley was an egotist; he practically begged me to film him for what he called his GPT, the Great Promotional Tool. So I filmed him every chance I got. I have clips of him working the crowds, talking about the future of larping in glowing vague terms, hinting at financial windfalls, urging his larping colleagues to dream big. Sometimes I think he half believed his own sales pitch, but he was selling pie in the sky—taking money for things that wouldn't materialize for years, if ever."

"What do you mean?"

"Henley was cooking the books. He routinely skimmed money from the accounts. Sometimes as much as forty percent of every dollar that was paid or donated to Door Camelot went into his own pocket."

"Do you have any proof of this?"

"I installed hidden video cameras in his office and cottage."

"That's illegal."

"Yeah, well, it didn't matter for my purposes. My plan was to reveal Henley as a con artist and a cheat. I was out to crush him."

"You realize you've just given yourself a motive for killing him."

Nick nearly lifted out of his chair. "You got it all wrong, Sheriff. I didn't want to kill him. That would have been letting him off easy. I wanted to ruin him. I wanted to destroy Camelot and make him a laughingstock—publicly with my film. I wanted Scott Henley to suffer the kind of shame he'd brought on my father. I wanted to humiliate him to the point where he'd wish he was dead."

"And the fire?"

"I don't know anything about that. Jesus, all the actual records were destroyed. I'd have to have been nuts to do that."

Or clever. Maybe too clever for his own good. "People have done crazier things than that," Cubiak said, and then he stood to go.

17  A FORGOTTEN TRAGEDY

Cubiak believed the story Nick had told him about his father, for the simple reason that it could be checked out and they both knew it. Henley's money hadn't come from his ace performance as a real estate broker, as he had told Travis, but from scamming the desperate. The King Arthur of Door Camelot defiled the memory of his legendary namesake.

The sheriff mulled over the latest development as he headed to his weekly lunch with Bathard. Since the start of the season, the two men had been sampling the county's new brew pubs and recently settled on the Old Black Dog as a favorite. The food was good, but more importantly it reminded them of the now vanquished Pechta's Tap in Fish Creek where they had initiated the lunch tradition more than a dozen years ago. On some days, they circled around life's larger issues and the vagaries of fate. On others, they either sat in amiable silence or talked about an ongoing case.

Bathard was waiting at an outside table when the sheriff arrived.

"I assumed that with the good weather, we would want to dine al fresco," he said when Cubiak joined him. "You don't mind the heat?"

"Not at all," the sheriff said, rolling up his sleeves. At his age, he preferred being warm to being cold. In the summer, he turned up the temperature in his air-conditioned office and often drove the jeep with the AC off and the windows open to the warm air.

As they studied the list of daily specials, Cubiak surreptitiously assessed his friend's appearance and manner. Bathard was seventy-six, and the last time they had met, he looked drawn and pale. The sheriff worried that the retired physician was ill.

"You are not going to start in again about me selling my house and moving to something smaller, are you? Or getting someone to look in on me?" Bathard said.

Cubiak feigned ignorance.

"I see you scrutinizing me, looking for signs of decline. I know you worry about me, and I appreciate the concern, but trust me, I am fine. When the day comes that I am not, you will know because I will tell you."

"I could call you a stubborn old goat," the sheriff said.

Bathard chuckled. "Maybe I am simply someone who knows his own mind." He lowered his menu. "Now, shall we order?"

While they waited for their food, Cubiak summarized the Henley case and ran through the list of people he had met with up to that point.

When he mentioned George Tinsel, his friend stopped him. "I have not heard that name in decades," Bathard said.

"Do you know him?"

"I did. Years back, George and I were on the advisory board for the county park district. We saw each other at monthly meetings and even served on a few committees together. I always found him to be a thoughtful and thorough man. When George started something, he saw it through, and I admired that about him. There was a time when Cornelia and I were casual friends with him and his wife. She was a lovely woman, as I recall. Now, what was her name?"

"Sylvie."

The elderly doctor brightened. "Sylvie Tinsel. George's late wife. The poor woman was subjected to all manner of friendly teasing because of her name, especially around Christmas, but she took it well. In fact, she often commented that as long as silver tinsel was in fashion, she would never have to worry about a dearth of invitations to holiday parties. A lovely woman," he said, repeating himself. "But an unhappy life. Poor Sylvie. She died several years back."

"Three, according to Urbanski. Which is true because I checked it.

The odd thing is that when I talked to Tinsel, he told me that his wife died two months ago."

"That is odd. But grief can muddle the mind." Bathard left the rest unspoken. They both knew what he meant.

Then the old physician frowned and lowered his cutlery to his plate. "Why are you asking me about Tinsel?" he said.

"He witnessed one of Florian Urbanski's tirades at Door Camelot. Urbanski told me they were friends from their school days, and I wanted to ask Tinsel if he thought Florian was capable of getting violent over the problem with the noise and the cows."

Bathard was quiet for a moment. Then he finally spoke. "You might have been better off going at it the other way around."

Cubiak shoved his plate aside, his lunch forgotten. "What do you mean?"

"Only that you might consider asking Florian about George."

"I don't understand."

Bathard sighed. "The Tinsels and the Henleys have a long history, and not a good one. Nobody has told you the story, have they? Well, why would they? It happened such a long time ago, and probably few people even remember."

Nearby a child squealed with joy. She was at a table behind them, and when the two men turned toward the sound, they discovered a sea of happy faces fanned out around them. For a heartbeat, the weight of their conversation lifted. Then they turned back to each other.

"I take it that Tinsel did not mention his daughter?" Bathard said.

"No."

"She was a beautiful little girl, one of those children who sparkled with an easy intelligence and charm. She was always smiling and cheerful. When she was five or six, she was injured on a carnival ride at the old Henley Resort's annual spring festival. The ride had hanging chairs suspended from overhead bars that radiated out from a center pole. As the center pole rotated, the chairs rose into the air. The faster the speed, the greater the centrifugal force, and the higher the chairs were lifted. You had to be a certain height to be allowed on the ride, and the Tinsels' daughter was just tall enough. The ride had just started when several of the chains snapped and the chairs tilted and collided with each other. The chair that she was in hit several of the others and then careened into the center pole. Several minutes of this horror elapsed before the ride was finally stopped."

The child who sat behind them giggled again, but this time they did not turn around.

"Did she die?" Cubiak said.

Bathard shook his head. "She survived, but the accident left her paralyzed from the chest down. I believe she suffered brain trauma as well."

In the leaden silence that followed, the sheriff went cold.

"I lost touch with George years ago. I don't even know if his daughter is still alive," Bathard said after a moment.

Cubiak barely heard. He pictured Tinsel's home, and everything he had seen there suddenly made sense. The freshly painted ramp. The white lace curtains in the window of the corner room. The man's anxious manner. The sheriff imagined the young girl—no, the young woman—lying in an outsized hospital bed behind the curtains, unable to move, and he remembered the day the doctor told him that if Alexis had lived, she would never have walked again. His beautiful daughter would have faced a similar future.

For years, Cubiak had ached to avenge his child. He had imagined half a dozen ways to kill the DUI who had run down his wife and daughter. At night, he waited for sleep to overtake him and carry him to the place where he would get his revenge. Every morning, he woke up sweat-drenched and exhausted. In the end, he did nothing to the culprit but nearly destroyed himself, taking aim not with a bullet but with a bottle.

"Dave, are you okay?" Bathard's gnarled hand rested on the sheriff's fist.

Cubiak took a breath. "I'm fine." A small lie but it softened the worry in the doctor's eyes. "I imagine that Tinsel took it hard."

"Both he and Sylvie. They sued the company that manufactured the ride and the resort as well. Within a year, the Henleys sold the place and moved away."

"And Scott was their son?"

Bathard dipped his head yes.

"How old was he when this happened?"

"He was quite young, no more than a child. If I had to guess, I would say he was probably about the same age as the girl." Bathard frowned. "I know what you are thinking, and I believe you are wrong. George Tinsel is a decent man, not a killer."

Cubiak's mood remained grim. "We're all capable of doing things we can't even imagine. There was a time when I suspected you of murder."

"I know," Bathard said quietly.

"Given enough reason or driven over the edge of it, even good men can turn bad," the sheriff said as he pushed to his feet.

"Where are you going?"

"I need to talk to George Tinsel again."

"Be easy with him, Dave."

Cubiak dipped his head, but the coroner was unable to fathom whether it was a sign of acquiescence or respect.

18 THE STORY THAT'S NEVER BEEN TOLD

The Tinsel homestead looked deserted. The brown van was nowhere in sight. The barn door was closed, as was the back door to the house. In the corner room, the white lace curtains shimmered like finely woven tiffany layers. The bedraggled flowers drooped in their beds, while the birds hid in the cool upper reaches of the trees. Even the insects had sought refuge from the afternoon torpor. Despite the suffocating stillness, or perhaps because of it, Cubiak felt a sense of expectation. As he headed toward the house, each step on the gravel erupted in a miniature explosion. He took the three stairs lightly.

When he reached the door, he realized that the silence was not complete. Deep inside the house, a fan hummed and music played softly. The melody was soothing, perhaps a piano sonata by Chopin or Schubert. He wondered if the melody emanated from the corner room. After his talk with Bathard, he focused on the task ahead and tried not to imagine the scene behind the lace curtains.

Cubiak knocked, and the music abruptly stopped.

He waited and then he knocked again. The rap was gentle and polite, like that of a guest come calling, not the law beating at the door demanding entry. Several seconds passed and then hurried footsteps approached. The door jerked open and Tinsel glowered across the threshold.

Tinsel was shorter than Cubiak, but with his broad shoulders he filled the doorway, preventing the sheriff from entering and blocking his view to the inside.

"You again," he said. He sounded annoyed, but he pulled himself into check. "Sorry, Sheriff, I wasn't expecting anyone, least of all a visit from the law."

As he talked, he sidled forward, a maneuver that forced Cubiak to retreat toward the railing. Once on the porch, Tinsel pulled the door shut. His manner was smooth and matter-of-fact, and Cubiak wondered if this was his usual reaction to finding an uninvited guest at the door.

Tinsel continued inching forward, wordlessly herding the sheriff away from the house and into the yard. Cubiak didn't protest. When they finally reached the jeep, Tinsel halted.

"Jesus, it's hot," he said as he wiped his brow with a red kerchief. He tucked the cloth into his pocket and then he spoke again. "I already told you that I don't know anything about what happened at that Camelot place," he said.

"But you know Scott Henley. Or you know of him."

A shadow passed over Tinsel's face.

Cubiak went on. "His parents operated the resort where your daughter was injured, some thirty years ago."

Tinsel spat at the ground. "You did your homework," he said.

"I do my job, that's all."

"And this newly attained knowledge suddenly makes you think that I had something to do with the man's death and that I started the fire?" Tinsel's voice remained flat, but it was fueled with anger.

"It means you didn't tell me the whole truth, which is what I came back to hear."

Tinsel regarded the sheriff. "All right," he said with an air of contempt.

Abruptly, he spun on his heels and started around the corner of the house.

Cubiak followed him to an aged picnic table that was nestled beneath the low-hanging branches of a massive elm in the side yard. The table had lost its luster; the wood was dry and peeling, but the structure looked sturdy.

"My wife liked to sit here," Tinsel said. He slid onto the bench on the far side and motioned the sheriff toward the other.

"Sylvie was a master gardener and she treasured her time outdoors, as limited as it was. As you have probably guessed, she rarely ventured far from home. Not even to go grocery shopping. That became my job."

He was making small talk, circling around the tragedy that was the center of his life, figuring out what he would say and how he would say it.

Cubiak didn't rush him.

Tinsel worked his mouth for a long while, moving his lips in and out and wetting them repeatedly. Finally, he pressed his clenched hands against the flaked surface of the table and looked hard into Cubiak's eyes.

"Most folks don't understand, but I know you will."

The sheriff dipped his head. "You've done your homework as well," he said.

Tinsel shrugged and scratched at a flake of paint. "Word gets around." An errant breeze came up, and he paused to listen as the chimes on the porch tinkled. "Who told you?" he said when the sound had faded.

"Evelyn Bathard."

"Ah, the old doc. How's he doing?"

"Fine."

"Give him my regards, will you?"

"I'll do that." Cubiak gave the divergence its due and then went on. "As I understand it, the equipment malfunctioned on a carnival ride at the old Henley Resort."

Tinsel nodded. "That's pretty much what it came down to, and once that was established, it became a matter of assigning fault. The equipment had sat idle all winter and was due for a thorough inspection and major maintenance servicing, which the carnival owners admitted that they hadn't performed, settling for a cursory tune-up instead. They claimed innocence because they weren't given the time they needed. Old man Henley had moved the date of the festival up by two weeks and basically told them either show up or forget the job, not just for that year but for the future as well. We learned a lot about the carnival business as the case went back and forth from one lawyer's office to the other and in and out of the courtroom. Apparently, it's a very cutthroat industry. At any rate, the operators hauled the rides here in time to meet the resort's revamped schedule, and the show went on."

"And Henley?"

"Hah, he pointed the finger of blame at the carnie folks. What else would you expect? To be honest, Sheriff, I never liked the man. He was always a little too smooth for my taste. A handsome guy, and arrogant, too, the kind who struts around like he owns the world. Henley said he had every right to assume that the equipment was up to par and said that the owners had assured him of this. He swore on the Bible that if he'd known of their negligence, he wouldn't have signed the contract. The operators said he was lying and that they'd told him that if they were to meet his schedule, they could only do a cursory inspection and partial tune-up. According to their testimony, Henley felt that was enough and assured them that he would accept all responsibility for any difficulties that might ensue. That's the exact wording they said he used: any difficulties that might ensue."

Tinsel went still. He was reliving the heartless drama of the courtroom, as Cubiak had done so often. The sheriff gave him time.

"According to the carnie folks, Henley said if the rides were running in good form at the end of the last season, they'd be good enough to run for five days at his resort and that they'd have plenty of time to inspect the equipment before their next booking. Of course, Henley maintains he never said that. But someone was lying."

Tinsel frowned and stared past Cubiak toward the house. "Maybe they both were."

A sudden breeze ruffled the branches overhead and both men looked up, as if anticipating a waft of cooling air to descend, but the leaves fluttered back into place, and the air around them remained stifling.

Tinsel splayed his hands on the table. "That's one part of the story. The part that never gets told is what happened just before Wendy got on the ride. We never knew how to bring up that part of the story or what to say."

The sheriff waited. There were times he felt like he spent half his life waiting, but Tinsel had committed himself, and Cubiak knew that he would go on when he was ready.

"The festival opened in the afternoon, but we didn't get there until early evening. I worked in town back then and did a little farming, kept a couple of cows and such, so we couldn't go until after I was home and the chores were done. The sky was slashed pink from the setting sun, and I remember thinking how perfect everything was as we were driving across the peninsula. Wendy was so excited she couldn't stop chattering. And there were no mosquitoes. Everyone talked about that. We got food from the booth that the Henleys had set up. Me and Sylvie had brats. Wendy wanted a hot dog. No mustard, just ketchup." Tinsel's voice broke and he averted his eyes.

Again Cubiak waited.

Tinsel cleared his throat. "Sorry, Sheriff," he said.

Cubiak said nothing, knowing that words were not needed.

"Wendy went on the merry-go-round and then the fun slide. When she got in line for the swing ride, there were a couple of boys in front of her. One was a local kid named Timmy or Tommy or something, and the other was Scott. By the time they got to the front, there were just two empty chairs left, which meant the two kids could have gotten on and sat next to each other and Wendy would have had to wait for the next round. But it didn't turn out that way. The first kid—Timmy or Tommy—hopped on, but Scott held back. His friend started teasing him and calling him a scaredy-cat. The rest of the line was waiting behind him, restless and urging him to get on with it. Finally Scott went ahead and climbed into the empty chair. After a couple of seconds, the attendant came over to lower the safety bar, but before he could, Scott jumped out of the chair and ran away through the crowd. His friend starting hooting and rocking his seat back and forth. 'Scottie's a sissy,' he yelled. He shouted it out over and over in that sing-song way kids have, and the attendant waved Wendy forward and helped her up into the empty seat."

"She took Scott's place," Cubiak said softly.

Tinsel blinked hard. "That's right. Our beautiful little Wendy skipped up the ramp and took the chair that Scott had vacated. She was the last one to get on, and she was crippled for life because that little shit lost his nerve. We stood and watched as the motor cranked up and the chairs started whirling around. With each revolution, they went higher, and Wendy sat there waving and smiling at us. We waved back. 'Have fun!' I shouted. And then the chains snapped. First one, then two, then three. Wendy's chair started shuddering back and forth. She hung in the air at this sickening angle and screamed as she was being thrown around. And all the time I stood there helpless, watching her, and thinking it should be Scott Henley in that chair, not my daughter."

The man's fist hit the table with such force that flecks of loose paint bounced on the surface. "You think I'm being harsh? You think I'm being cruel?"

He leaned forward, his hands clenched tight. "Let me tell you what happened after that godawful night. Our daughter's life was shattered, but as unfair and devastating as that was, it was just the beginning. Sylvie and me wanted a big family—four or five kids. That was our dream, but it never happened. How could we take the chance that another child wouldn't be injured before our eyes? How could we even think of taking time from giving Wendy the care she needed to raise another kid?"

There were no answers to the questions. Tinsel went on brutally.

"But you know the real reason we didn't have another child? Because another kid would have been an escape for us, a sign of disloyalty to the daughter we loved so much. Another child would have been a constant reminder to Wendy of all she didn't have and would never have. That would have been the ultimate cruelty, and we couldn't do that to her."

Tinsel flatted his hands against the table. "We won the lawsuit; the money we got helped with the physical care. There was so much need. Treatments, equipment, around-the-clock nursing for years. But there was all the rest, the stuff of life that can't be bought with money. Initially people were kind. The neighbors asked about Wendy; they prayed for her and came by with flowers and small gifts. The local ladies invited Sylvie out for coffee so she'd get a break.

"But after a while, all that kindness withered away. Maybe people were put off by our sadness or the lack of good news, because everyone was always eager to hear good news. Or perhaps they felt guilty because their children were doing fine—playing sports in school, joining scouts and Four-H and such. Don't get me wrong, Wendy went to school, too, and we cheered her on. But life was harder and more complicated for her.

"The summer after she graduated high school, she had her first stroke. For a while, it was like one every year, and each one left her weaker and more prone to infection. She had a hard time remembering things, and she started to withdraw more and more. Her friends started dating and marrying and having kids of their own. Their parents, people we'd been close to, drifted further away. How could they sit down and share their happy news with us when they knew we had so little to offer in return? So they spared us, which ultimately meant that they ignored us."

He gave a quick bitter laugh. "Honestly, I don't know which was worse, listening to the stories of what we would never experience or being forgotten. I went to work every day, so I had an escape. But Sylvie was here. Even when we had nurses in the house and later for the time Wendy was able to attend school, she was afraid to leave for long in case of an emergency, so she was the one who became more and more isolated."

Tinsel choked up. "And during all this time and trauma, Wendy grew up. She changed from a little girl into a teenager and then a young woman. Ironic, isn't it, that her body kept growing even though it didn't work."

Grief was not a single static entity; it vibrated with stratified energy, and Cubiak knew that despite all that Tinsel had revealed, he had exposed only the topmost layer of his pain. The reservoir was bottomless.

The sheriff kept his gaze unfocused and remained silent. His was now the role of confessor.

Tinsel bowed his head. "During the very worst periods, there were times I wished she'd die."

Having uttered the awful truth, he didn't dare look up as he continued talking.

"I'd tell myself that I was just thinking of her, of putting an end to her struggles, but that's only part of the truth. I thought that if she died first, then we'd have a few years to ourselves before we went too. Instead, Sylvie died and now it's just me. And Wendy."

Cubiak put his hand on Tinsel's arm. "I'm sorry," he said.

Tinsel nodded, and when he finally looked up, his eyes were wet.

"For a while, the computer changed everything. Suddenly she was able to connect with the world on her own terms. I know some people curse technology, but I saw the good it can do too. For years, all Wendy had was TV and the books we read to her or played on tape and CDs. Then, almost magically, she had the power to tap into anything she wanted. She loved YouTube. She lived a little bit of life through it, and for that I was grateful. Eventually it became a curse."

"What happened?"

"Camelot happened." The bitterness returned to Tinsel's voice. "After the accident, the Henleys sold the resort and moved away. We'd never forget them, but at least we didn't have to see their name every time we turned around. Then a few months ago, Florian told me about his trouble with his new neighbors. I didn't care one way or the other until he mentioned Scott Henley. I couldn't believe it was him and told myself it had to be somebody with the same name. How could he have the nerve to come back to Door County? I went there that day with Florian to see for myself. And I swear, Sheriff, it was like being thrown back in time. Scott looked just like his father, and there he was in that silly costume, strutting around and enjoying the carefree life. I would have strangled him with my bare hands, but Florian got to him first. I ended up stopping him, but I swore to myself that I would go back."

"Did you?"

"I never got the chance. Somehow Wendy learned about Door Camelot and the larpers. And unbeknownst to me, she reached out to the bastard online."

"Wendy connected with Scott Henley?"

"Yeah." Tinsel pressed his thick fingers into his forehead. "God help me, but we'd never told her about him. She was too young to remember the circumstances of the accident, and we never went into much detail about it later on. She was so excited waiting in line for her turn, I'm not sure she was aware of Scott standing ahead of her and then of him running away."

"She didn't realize that you blamed him."

"No. She asked him to visit her."

"Here?"

Tinsel snorted. "Where else?"

"And you knew about this?"

"Not until afterward. If I'd known ahead of time, I'd have barred the door and not let him anywhere near her. Later she showed me the email she'd sent him, explaining her circumstances. She told him what she'd learned about the larpers and Door Camelot and said she'd always loved the fairy tales about princesses and brave knights. She said she knew he played King Arthur but that it would be a dream come true if he came to the house dressed like Lancelot. All she wanted was to see him in costume, to have him sit and talk to her for an hour."

Tinsel ran his hands through his hair. "Like I said, I didn't know any of this, and I'd become complacent. About a year ago, I got one of those smartphones, and knowing that she could reach me if she had to, I started venturing farther from the house, running a quick errand into town, doing chores in the barn. As long as she had her computer and I had my phone, I figured we were connected. It was the only bit of independence I could give her, and I convinced myself it was okay, that it was good for her.

"One day last week, I went to the post office. I wasn't gone more than twenty minutes, and when I got back, he was here. Only I didn't know that."

Cubiak felt the tenor of the conversation shift to something deeper and more fraught with menace. He listened carefully. As an officer of the law, he listened for information that could shed light on the murder of Scott Henley. At the same time, he was acutely aware that he had entered the intimate space of a man who was desperate to talk, not to a sheriff but to another human being who might understand his anguish.

"I parked the van at the end of the ramp like I always did, and as I walked toward the house, I heard voices. At first I thought Wendy was watching a movie or one of those YouTube videos that she liked. It took me a minute to realize that there was a man in there with her. I didn't see a car anywhere and figured someone had snuck in. I didn't know what was going on and I panicked. I imagined the worst. Jesus, wouldn't you?"

Of course he would, and although the sheriff remained silent, it was as if he had spoken and Tinsel had heard.

"I had to do something, so I snatched a rope from the barn and ran back to the house with it. I had no real plan beyond figuring that I'd nab the guy and haul him outside. I had this vague notion that I'd tie him to the bumper and drag him down the road. Teach him a lessen he'd never forget. I snuck into the house, and I was halfway through the kitchen when Wendy started laughing."

Tinsel inhaled sharply. "Oh my God, the sweet sound of it. But this pissed me off even more. In all those years, I'd never been able to make her laugh, not like that. And that's when I really lost it. I barged into her room and there he was, sitting on a chair next to the bed and holding her hand, not just some man, some crazy maniac who'd broken in, but the fucker Scott Henley in that ridiculous armor. I went crazy and attacked him, like I wanted to go at his father all those years ago. I threw the rope around his chest and yanked him to the floor. He yelled and thrashed around. Wendy started shouting at me, begging me to stop. She kept screaming all the while I was dragging Henley out of her room and then out the door and into the yard. I don't know where I got the strength to do that, but I didn't stop until I pulled him as far as the van."

Grief and pain radiated from the man. He slumped on the bench. "Sylvie and me, we always tried to avoid upsetting Wendy, and here I was scaring the living daylights out of her. And I didn't care one bit. I wanted to kill that guy. I shoved him face down into the gravel and pressed my foot on his shoulder to hold him there while I tied the rope to the bumper.

"'What are you doing?' he said. 'I didn't do anything to your daughter. I swear. I didn't hurt her. I was just talking to her.' He was pleading, begging, scared. That's when I slugged him. 'Not hurt her?' I yelled and slugged him again. 'She's in that bed because of you.' Henley lay there and gaped at me as if I were mad. 'What are you talking about?' he said. 'The accident!' I screamed. 'I saw you. You ran away because you were scared, and Wendy took your place on the ride. It should have been you in that chair.'"

Tinsel stiffened and took a big breath. "Henley lay there curled up in a ball. And just as I kicked him in the head, he looked up at me and said, 'What accident?'"

19 \ A MAN OF SORROWS

"Scott didn't know," Tinsel said. He dropped his head into his hands and sat still, lost in the past. When he looked up again, he was pale and wide-eyed. He splayed his hands on the table and stared at the fingers that were swollen from the heat. He was silent, and Cubiak was reluctant to break the strange spell that had settled over the yard. Then a rabbit poked its head from under a bush and hopped across the lawn, either oblivious to or unfazed by their presence. Tinsel's gaze followed the rabbit's path. When the bunny disappeared, he swiveled sideways and clumsily swung one foot and then the other over the bench.

"I gotta go check on Wendy," he said.

The previous Christmas, Cate had taken Cubiak to a performance of Handel's *Messiah*, and as he watched Tinsel plod across the lawn, a line from the oratorio came to him: a man of sorrows, and acquainted with grief. There was no escaping the burden cemented to the shoulders of the long-suffering George Tinsel. In school, the nuns had talked about free will. They told the students that they had the power to decide how to live their lives. What had happened to Tinsel's free will? A freak accident had altered the course of his daughter's life and his as well. No one had given him a choice, certainly not God.

Cubiak's shoulders ached from sitting on the bench, but he didn't move. He couldn't risk standing and walking around the yard for fear of spoiling the mood and making Tinsel regret his candor. There was more to the story being told, and Cubiak had to be patient. He checked the time. Nearly ten minutes had passed since Tinsel had excused himself. The longer he stayed away, the more likely he would have a change of heart. What then?

Just as the sheriff was about to go looking for him, Tinsel came around the corner of the house and ambled toward the table with an open beer in one hand and another can in the other.

"I know you're on duty, but this don't count," he said as he set the unopened beer in front of the sheriff.

Cubiak peeled back the pop-top. Given the circumstances, he wasn't going to argue the point.

Tinsel drained his beer in several gulps. Then he flattened the can and slid it to the end of the table. He closed his eyes as if taking a moment for a private conversation, and then he looked at the sheriff and picked up where he had left off, as if there had been no interruption.

"Henley didn't know what I was talking about. I was stunned. All those years I spent blaming him and imagining what I would do to him to get even and make him pay."

A gull screeched overhead, and Tinsel looked up at the bird and the scudding clouds.

"Makes you dizzy, doesn't it, watching them fly around like that? Not a care in the world," he said. Then he continued, "Let me ask you something, Sheriff. Did the man who ran down your wife and daughter have a family?"

"No," Cubiak said, his voice low.

"Would it have made any difference if he had?"

Cubiak didn't hesitate. "We both know the answer."

Tinsel nodded. "But if you'd done anything to him, you would have taken your revenge on a guilty bastard. I came this close to killing an innocent man." He raised his hand, showing an inch between the thumb and index finger.

"I don't know how long I stood there and stared at him. I'm not even sure I realized what I'd plan on doing to him until I starting to pull the rope off the bumper. When I got to untying him, it dawned on me that I had intended to drag him behind the van. What kind of sick fuck would do that? Suddenly the whole situation seemed insane, like something I'd dream about but never do."

"Did Henley say anything?"

"He asked me to tell him what had happened to Wendy. I helped him to his feet and walked him over to this very table. I sat him down right where you are, and then I told him the story, beginning to end. He didn't look at me the whole time, just sat there with his head bowed and listened. Even after I finished, he didn't move. Finally he looked at me. He'd gone pale and there were tears in his eyes. 'I never heard any of this before. I was just a stupid kid. I'm so sorry.'"

"Did you ask him why he got off the ride and ran away?"

"Of course I did." Tinsel looked tired. He folded himself over his arms.

"Henley told me he remembered that night all right, but what stuck in his memory was how frightened he was and how ashamed he was because he'd been afraid to get on the ride. His father had told him that he had to go on all the rides to set a good example. If the other kids saw him, they'd want to go on the rides too and would kick up a fuss until their parents bought tickets. Do it or else, his father warned him. Scott knew that the 'or else' meant a whipping if he didn't obey. There were five rides and he'd gone on the first three just like he'd been told. After the third one, he threw up behind a couple of bushes, and he was still sick to his stomach when he got in line for the next ride, the one with chairs. He knew that if he got sick again, he'd vomit over the crowd and would have hell to pay with his father. But he got on the ride anyway.

"Scott said he was a chubby kid back then, something that always annoyed his dad. When he sat down, he felt the seat shift. He was afraid his father would blame him for breaking it and he didn't know what to do. When his friend began to tease him, he was afraid he'd start to cry and that then his friend would make his life miserable. So he slid off the chair and ran into the woods. He knew the paths and there was enough light yet to the day that he could find his way deep into the forest. Later, when he heard the ambulance, he thought it was the police siren and figured that his parents had called the sheriff to look for him, so he went even farther into the woods. He was cold and hungry but afraid of his father, afraid to go home, so he hid out there all night."

"Then what?"

"The next morning, a neighbor found him wandering around and brought him back to the resort. Scott was sure he was going to be punished, but there were a lot of people around and so much was going on that his parents hardly paid any attention to him. Once they saw he wasn't hurt, his mother took him inside and gave him breakfast and a bath and then put him to bed.

"Scott said he knew something bad had happened, but he was afraid to ask because he was sure it was his fault. People came and went, probably inspectors and insurance reps, but he was ordered to stay in his room and play with his model trains. His parents never told him about the accident. They hid the newspapers, not that he could read them yet, but there'd be pictures, and they kept the radio and TV turned off so he wouldn't hear anything about it. If he walked into a room where the adults were talking, they stopped immediately. All he knew for certain was that the festival had ended. One morning, he asked his mother if his friend Timmy—that was the boy's name—could come over and play, but she said Timmy had the measles. Scott knew nothing. He even asked me if that was true or if his friend had been injured as well."

"Had he?"

Tinsel nodded.

"After a few days, Henley said, he was sent to stay with an aunt in Milwaukee. At first he pestered her with questions, asking her what was going on. She told him there was nothing for him to worry about and that he shouldn't try imagining things. A few months later, his parents showed up. They'd said that they'd sold the resort and that they were going to have a new house and a new life in the city. In the fall, he started school, and it wasn't long before he made new friends and forgot all about living here."

"You believed him?"

"Why wouldn't I? He was a just a kid then, so sure, it made sense. And I'd heard about his father's temper. It wasn't hard to put the two together. On the night of the accident, Henley was a scared little boy hiding from his father in the woods, and kneeling in the gravel in front of me last week, he was still a scared little boy hiding in that ridiculous costume."

Tinsel let out a deep breath. "All the while Henley and I were out here talking, Wendy was crying and calling for me. Eventually I went inside to calm her. By the time I got her settled and came out again, Henley was gone."

"Did you try to follow him?"

"No. For what?"

"You let him go."

"What else could I do?" Tinsel scratched at a flake of paint and made a sound like a laugh, but there was no mirth in it. "The venom disappeared, like dew in the sunlight." He raised his eyes to the sky again. "Maybe it's part of the vapor that's floating around up there in the clouds. I don't know. I'm not sure I know anything anymore."

"What about Wendy?"

"What do you mean?"

"How are you explaining all this?"

"Scott's death? She doesn't know anything about it yet. She gets her news from the computer, and I told her that it was broken and I'd had to send it away to be fixed. I'll tell her eventually but not now. And I don't want you talking to her, not yet anyway. You need to give me that."

Wendy could substantiate certain aspects of Tinsel's story: when and how she'd reached out to Scott and what she'd seen and heard on the day Henley came to the house and her father discovered them together. They both knew this.

"It might be better for you," Cubiak said.

"Doesn't matter. I have so much to make up for. Let me do that first and then I'll tell her. You have my word."

And because of what Bathard had said, Cubiak believed him.

20 \ RED CAR, BLUE CAR

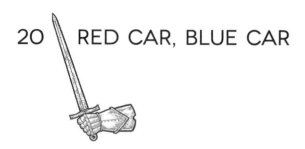

After that, there was nothing left to say. The two men sat for a few minutes, and then they got up at the same time and walked back to the house together. Against the backdrop of the soft piano music, they stood at the base of the stairs and shook hands.

Cubiak was at the jeep when Tinsel called to him from the porch.

"There is one thing, Sheriff," he said. "The reason I didn't know Henley was here that day was because he'd left his car back behind the garage. He must have driven in on the old lane that zigzags through the woods and comes out to my property there. He might've gone out that same way."

It wasn't much, but it was a lead.

The forest was overgrown. The low-hanging branches scraped the jeep's roof while tall grasses and thistle rubbed against the underside. Two parallel lines cut through the heavy brush and showed where another vehicle had passed down the road recently. And if Tinsel's story was correct, it belonged to Scott Henley.

Tinsel had provided a number of facts that could be verified: the accident and the subsequent lawsuit, the sale of the resort, and the Henley family's move from Door County to Milwaukee. Other elements would depend on what others could tell the sheriff: If he could locate Scott Henley's childhood friend Timmy, would he remember the events of that day? Would he admit to the teasing that had spurred Scott to quit the ride and run away? What of the nameless man who had stumbled on the frightened, hungry boy the next morning while out with his dog, a bookend to how the adult Scott was found dead on the beach?

And what would he find at the end of the old road?

From the woods, the lane ran along a fallow field. Then it swerved a second time and entered another patch of trees. More time passed and Cubiak wondered if he had been sent on a wild goose chase. Suddenly the forest thinned, and the trail emerged alongside a county road outside Jacksonport. The unincorporated community wasn't far from where Cubiak lived. It sat on the lake and boasted fewer than nine hundred year-round residents.

The sheriff stopped in the shade and tried to imagine Henley's next move. After the encounter with Wendy and Tinsel, he would have been both emotionally distraught and physically battered. Cubiak thought it unlikely that he would head back to Camelot and chance running into the other larpers, who would question his appearance and demeanor. Most probably he would want to be alone for a while. The lake offered solitude and it was only a couple of miles away. The sheriff turned toward town and the water.

He drove slowly, as he imagined Henley had that day. How did Henley feel after meeting the young paralyzed woman and hearing Tinsel's accusation that it should have been him? He must have wondered what would have happened if he had told his father about the loose seat. If the old man had heeded the warning and ordered the ride stopped, the accident would have been averted. But with the tickets already sold and the excited children waiting for their turns, would his father have taken the prudent path? Probably not.

According to what Scott had told Tinsel, the elder Henley had pressured the carnival to push up its schedule so he could get a jump on the competition. If he needed the festival proceeds to keep the business open through the slow spring season, he would have ignored the boy's concerns; he might even have thought his son was lying to avoid going on the ride.

Cubiak was near town when he spotted a set of tire tracks that had swerved off the road and onto the shoulder. He imagined Henley dizzy from Tinsel's kick in the head and needing to stop, to pull himself together. The landscape was dominated by tractors and pickups. If Henley had stopped there, his red sports car would be noticed. Someone would remember seeing it.

The sheriff turned into the first driveway he came to and pulled up to the house. It was a small ranch surrounded on three sides by a neatly mowed lawn and on the fourth by a garden that was laid out in long, precise rows of flowers and vegetables. A middle-aged woman answered his knock. She was friendly and happy to see a fresh face at the door. She had just returned from a two-week stay in Chicago and was eager to share the details of the wedding she had attended, the plays she had seen, the restaurants where she had dined.

"A red car?" she said when he posed the question. "No, sorry. My grandson used to have a red car . . ."

The sheriff's luck was no better at the next farm. The family had been working in the back fields all week, moving from the kitchen door at the rear of the house to the machine shed and then down the dirt road through the pasture to reach the crops in the back forty that needed to be harvested. No one had paid attention to the paved county road out front. No one had seen a sports car of any color since a silver Jaguar had flown past earlier that summer. That one they all remembered seeing from the front porch.

Cubiak inquired at two more houses without luck. Finally, he reached the auto repair shop on the edge of the village. An old sedan with four flat tires was parked out front. Inside, the air smelled of oil and dust. The floor was swept clean, but cobwebs laced the rafters. When the door closed behind the sheriff, a man on a metal creeper rolled out from under a dusty white pickup.

"Help you?" he said, looking up at the sheriff.

When Cubiak showed his badge, the gearhead lumbered to his feet. He was wiry and tattooed and reeked of cigarette smoke.

"You must mean the Porsche nine-one-one. Oh, right, yeah. Sure, I seen it. In fact, I seen it before it stopped."

The mechanic wiped his hands on a greasy towel. "He was just crawling, going so slow I figured he was having car trouble. I waited for him to make it this far, but he pulled off instead. Then I waited for him to hoof it over here to ask for help. We don't get many of those babies around here, and I couldn't wait to get my hands on it, but he never showed."

"How'd you know the driver was a man?" Cubiak said.

"I didn't, just figured it had to be. You know, a man with his midlife-crisis car. You see a lot of that around here, especially with the summer people. Guy hits his fifties and suddenly he feels the need to reclaim his youth. What does he do? He buys a sports car to tool around in. Thinks it makes him cool, and of course if he's one of the summer folks, he's got the money for it."

"You're telling me the driver was middle aged?"

"Well, I didn't see him up close, but from here he looked all silver haired, if you know what I mean. The top was down, and the sun reflected off his head like a beacon."

The helmet.

"Do you remember what time it was when you first saw the car?"

"Yep, coffee break time. That's when I go outside for my afternoon smoke."

"And that would be?"

"Three, or there about."

"Did you see anyone get out of the car?" He almost asked if the man had seen a knight in shining armor but decided that the mechanic would think he was making a joke at the worker's expense.

"Nope, nada. Not a one. The driver just sat there."

"For how long, do you remember?"

"That I can't say. I got busy in here fixing a flat tire for the lady who owns the café down the road a piece. Then the Lutheran minister came in with an oil leak. The next time I looked out the window, the driver was gone. I figured he must have called someone and gotten picked up when I wasn't looking."

"What about the car?"

"Oh, it was still there."

"You're sure?"

The mechanic smirked. "You can't miss something like that. I closed up a little after six, and the car hadn't moved."

"What about the next morning?"

"I wouldn't know. We didn't bother to open, what with the storm and all. I finally made it in around nine on Friday—the creek by my house flooded a couple of the roads and I had to detour around half the county to get to the garage. Anyway, when I got here, the car was gone. I figure someone came back at some point and got it running, or maybe there wasn't anything wrong with it, maybe the sucker just ran out of gas and whoever came for it poured in some fuel and then drove away."

He looked around the shop. "If there's nothing else, I gotta get back to work. The minister needs his car today."

The local tavern was the only other establishment between the garage and the lake. The one-room pub was empty except for a man behind the bar and a trio of regulars at the end of it. When the sheriff asked if any of them had seen a man dressed in costume on the day of the storm, the bartender and two of the customers scoffed.

"What about you?" Cubiak asked the third man, who had remained silent.

The man stroked his beard. Then he signaled for a shot, downed it, and slid off his stool.

"Sheriff, you just made my day," he said as he reached out to shake Cubiak's hand.

The man went on to regale his buddies with the story of how he had just left to go home that day when he saw an honest-to-god knight heading to the beach. He thought he had lost his mind, like the wife said he would if he didn't stop drinking, and he was so distraught that he came back in for another whiskey, for old time's sake. Then he went home and swore off the sauce. Now he didn't have to, did he?

The witness didn't remember what time it was when he saw Henley, but the rain hadn't started yet.

"Anything else, even if it doesn't seem important?"

The man scratched his beard. "Nah."

"You didn't see anything on your way home?"

"Well, there was a car."

"What kind?"

"I don't know. Blue. Small."

"Did you see the driver?"

"Yep, it was a young girl."

"Which direction was she headed?"

"That way," he said, pointing to the beach.

It was easy enough to connect the dots that tracked Henley's trail from George Tinsel's house to the corner tavern in the quiet hamlet of Jacksonport. The beach was another city block away, and if Cubiak was right about Henley's destination, the trajectory would explain how he ended up at the lakefront, although not how his body washed ashore south along Rosemary Lane nor how his car had vanished. A red Porsche would be easy to spot, yet there had been no reports of it yet.

The blue car complicated the scenario. Especially a car driven by a young woman who appeared to be following Henley's trail.

21 \ DEATH'S DOOR

The next morning, Cubiak was up early. He had already started the coffee and was thinking about the blue car the witness had seen outside the tavern when he heard Joey and Bear in the living room. The boy sprawled on the floor alongside the dog. A bowl of cereal sat near his elbow, and the local paper was spread out before him.

Looking at his son, the sheriff remembered the hours he had spent lolling on the floor as a kid and felt a stab of nostalgia. He also felt a surge of pride. At a time when many adults were abandoning print copy for electronic news, his son read the weekly paper.

"Anything good?" Cubiak said.

"Yeah."

Joey was a boy of few words.

The sheriff poured a cup of coffee. "Like what?" he said as he leaned on the counter.

"Huh?"

"What are you reading? You seem quite intent on something."

"It's about the people swimming across Death's Door."

"That's today?" Cubiak had known about the event at Porte des Morts for several weeks but had lost track of the date.

"Yep. Cool, isn't it?" Joey said.

"And dangerous." Cate appeared in the hall, pulling her robe closed and tightening the sash. Cubiak gave her a kiss. Then she detoured to the living room, picked up the empty cereal bowl from the floor, and looked down over her son's shoulder. "In fact, very dangerous."

Joey shrugged, as only a kid could while propped on his elbows.

"It says that it's been done a couple of times before and that no one's drowned or been hurt. Besides," he said as he half turned and looked at his parents, "there are spotters in kayaks rowing across with them. If the swimmers get in trouble, the people in the boats will help them out."

"That doesn't make it any less perilous. The water is extremely cold and deep," Cate said.

"And the currents are strong. To say nothing of the boat traffic," Cubiak said.

Commercial and pleasure boats would have to be told ahead of time, or the swimmers would risk disaster.

Joey flipped back toward the paper. "Six people are signed up. Maybe I can do it when I'm older."

"Maybe not," Cate and Cubiak said simultaneously.

"Why not? My old babysitter's one of the swimmers."

"You're kidding! Who?" Cate said.

"Veronica. You know, she was the one I liked best." Joey scooped up the paper and carried it into the kitchen.

"Look, here she is," he said. He spread the Door County *Herald* on the table and pointed to the photo of Veronica Vivian Kaiser. The image in the paper was her high school graduation picture, the one Cubiak had seen online just days before. Beneath the picture was a brief bio, which Joey read out loud.

"The Door County native holds two state records for the eight-hundred-meter freestyle race and led her high school team to victory in the relay race. She also won the state championship twice for distance swims. While in school, her swimming talents won her the nickname 'Fish.'"

"Let me see that paper, will you?" Cubiak said.

"I'm not finished."

"I'll give it back after you feed Bear."

While Joey tended to the dog, the sheriff skimmed the page. Photos of the other swimmers accompanied the article. In one, two middle-aged women beamed at the camera from under skull-hugging swim caps. In another, a muscular older man leaned confidently against the gunwale of a beached rowboat. The final two swimmers were boys home from college for the summer who looked equally trim and toned.

"Can a girl jock beat the rest?" Cubiak said.

"What are you talking about?" Cate peered over his shoulder.

"Something Lisa said. She knew Veronica in high school and says she was quite the athlete."

The story ended with a quote from one of the unofficial organizers of the event. "The Death's Door swim requires exceptional strength and training. It isn't a race, but if it was and I was a betting man, I'd put my money on 'the Fish' to be the first one across the strait."

The Fish: aka ViVi Kay, formerly Guinevere and Henley's one-time girlfriend. The woman who had argued with him the day before he disappeared.

The sheriff's reverie was broken by the sound of running water and Joey's loud insistent tone. "Can we, huh?" the boy said as he held Bear's water dish under the faucet.

"Can we what?" Cubiak said.

"You guys never listen to me," the boy wailed.

"That's not true."

Cate picked up the two empty mugs and gave her husband a knowing look. "Joey's been asking if we could go to Northport to watch the swimmers come in. I have the afternoon free, so I can take him."

While Joey whooped and splashed water on the floor, Cubiak turned back to the paper.

There were more pictures on the next page, including one of Veronica standing next to a blue car.

22 VENGEANCE

When Cubiak walked into the Liberty Grove General Store later that morning, Irma Zubek was at her usual post behind the front counter.

"Cuppa joe, Sheriff? I got a fresh pot on." Irma had kept the store running for nearly thirty years, time enough for the pot of fresh coffee to become a local tradition.

"Sounds tempting but I've got a three-cup limit and I'm over it already. Thanks, anyway." He stopped at a display of watches.

"Shopping?" she said hopefully.

For information, yes. Even if he had to feign ignorance to get it. "Sorry, Irma, not today. Actually, I was hoping to talk to Veronica," he said.

"That girl! I've got her working Wednesday through Sunday, five days a week through the season. She's supposed to start at ten, but she almost never gets here before eleven. I let it slide because we're rarely busy that early and once she comes in, she works hard. Anyway, you wouldn't find her here today. In fact, you won't find her anywhere on land. She's doing the swim." Apparently, Irma felt that no additional explanation was necessary.

When he didn't react, the shopkeeper huffed. "The swim across Death's Door."

"That's right, I read something about it in the *Herald*. I must have forgotten that it was today. But if it weren't for the swim, Veronica would be in?"

"Well, she should be here, but you know how that goes."

"I'm not sure I do," he said.

"Veronica likes her time off, so she's not always in the store when I want her here. Other obligations, she says. I don't mind so much early in the season if we're slow . . ."

"But this is the busy season."

Irma took her hands off her hips and moved a display of candy nearer the register. "You got that right, and I have to tell you I was a bit put out last Wednesday when she said she needed the afternoon off. At one point, I had a half-dozen people in here stocking up before the storm, and I could have used an extra hand, that's for sure. I don't get around as well as I used to. Bad hip." She reached down and hoisted a cane for him to see.

"But what could I say, her mother needed a ride to the doctor's. The person who'd promised to take her had their own emergency and Veronica's father doesn't drive anymore. I'm not a heartless woman, Sheriff. I try to be understanding; it's just hard sometimes. I suggested that maybe a neighbor could do the good deed, but no, Veronica said there wasn't anyone else and it had to be her."

As she talked, Irma shifted the candy display back to its original spot. "Of course, today is different. Today's time off has been on the calendar for months." She gave a small smile. "You might not believe it to look at me, but I swam the strait once. Did it on a dare with some friends—'course that was years back when I was young and foolish. Never did tell anyone about it, not 'til it was over."

She pinched her mouth tight. "Scared the living daylights out of me, to be honest. Would never do it again. But you're not here to listen to me reminisce. You wanted to talk to Veronica, didn't you? I'll bet it's about the body on the beach. She knew him, you know."

"Scott Henley?"

Irma scoffed. "You mean Mister Big Shot?" she said and then crossed herself. "I know I shouldn't speak ill of the dead, but I never much cared for him. He came in here once about a year ago. All puffed up and full of himself, asking if he could leave some brochures about this Door Camelot of his. Said he was related to the Henleys who used to have the resort. As soon as I saw that fancy red car of his, I knew he was trouble. I didn't care for the man, didn't like his attitude, but sure, I said, leave whatever you want. Unless it's something illegal, I gotta say yes to everyone promoting business on the peninsula. We all depend on each other, whether we want to admit it or not."

She pointed to the rack by the door. "If there's any left, you'll find them over there." She shifted from one foot to the other. "Veronica was working that day. She's an awfully pretty girl, and I hate to say it, Sheriff, but I think this is where they first met. 'Course it didn't end well for her. And I guess not for him either."

From the store, Cubiak made his way down the peninsula to Veronica's parents' house. The first day Veronica had babysat, Doris and Stan Kaiser had come with her and introduced themselves to him and Cate. But Cubiak hadn't seen them since. The few times he drove Veronica home, they weren't around.

Like most of the homes in the area, the house was modest, but seeing it again after all that time, Cubiak was startled by the run-down condition. The porch dipped toward one end; the paint was peeling; the screen door stood half open, the lower panel missing altogether. Trusting his weight to the edges of the worn steps, he climbed the four stairs to the door and knocked.

A man shouted from inside. "Door's open! Come on in."

Veronica's father was in the living room, encased in a sunken brown-and-yellow plaid couch, a laptop propped up on the coffee table in front of him, and his belly spilling over his knees as he leaned into it. He recognized Cubiak immediately.

"Hey, Sheriff, come on in and have a look-see. Amazing stuff this is. Some guy's filming the swim and streaming it live on YouTube."

Cubiak dodged a shelf of bric-a-brac and angled in alongside the sofa for a sideways look at the screen. All he saw was water, rough water at that. Then a spot of red appeared between two waves.

"See that? It's Veronica in the red swim cap. That's my girl, ahead of the pack. As usual."

The red dot vanished and then popped back into view.

"What's up?" the man said, as if an unannounced visit from the sheriff meant nothing.

"I was just in the neighborhood and thought I'd stop by and see how the missus is doing. I heard she was ill."

Stan Kaiser snorted. "Doris ill? Whoever told you that?" As he talked, he kept his eyes pinned to the monitor that was only inches from his face. "The woman's as healthy as a horse. She's out back somewhere, painting a chair or whatever. Now, if you want to ask about someone in a world of hurt, that would be me. Eyes are failing me, Sheriff. Can't even drive no more."

So at least that much of what Irma Zubek had told him was true.

"Sorry to hear that. But as long as I'm here, I may as well say hello to her too."

"Yeah, go on, just through there." Stan tossed a hand over his shoulder and pointed toward the rear of the house.

The living room led to a narrow alcove where a battered drop-leaf table was pushed up alongside one wall. The table and space beneath were stacked with cookbooks. The walls on both sides were lined with shelves of dusty knickknacks. The kitchen was even more cluttered. Piles of *Gourmet* magazines littered the only counter. Top issue dated May 1999. Canning jars filled the rest of the small work area and surrounded the chipped sink. The smell of bacon hung in the humid air, and the linoleum floor tried to attach itself to his feet.

The sheriff was at the back door when Stan reported on the swim event. "She's halfway across," he announced, loud enough for his neighbors to hear.

Outside Cubiak took a deep breath of fresh air.

Like the house, the yard was a victim of neglect. A listless row of shaggy hedges drooped under the weight of the overgrown branches. Weeds towered over the few vegetable plants that poked through the ground in the garden patch and overran the border into the listless lawn.

The strands on the clothesline hung nearly to the ground. It was a far cry from the well-manicured grounds at Door Camelot.

Doris Kaiser was slopping paint on a picket fence that bordered the far side of the yard. She knelt facing the house, and when the screen door banged shut, she glanced up. Then she quickly lowered her head and continued working.

She didn't look up again until Cubiak stood before her and started to identify himself. She silenced him with a wave of the brush.

"I know who you are," she said.

Doris swept the brush up one of the boards and then laid it on the paint can lid and stood. She was as thin as her husband was stocky. Her face was weathered, her eyes narrowed and worried.

"If you've got bad news, just out with it," she said.

It took a moment for Cubiak to realize that she thought he had come about the Death's Door swim. "No, it's not that. No bad news," he said.

Doris exhaled sharply and planted a hand on her flat chest. "Oh, thank God. I can't watch, not like him."

She pointed to the house. "I can't bear thinking of Veronica in the water with those currents and the ghosts of all those lost souls roaming the lakebed, anxious for more to join them."

"Your daughter's a strong swimmer."

"It doesn't matter. Not out there." She shook her head.

"But there's no talking sense into her." Doris rubbed at a splotch of paint on her hand. "So if it's not about the race, what are you doing here?"

"I forgot that the race was today and thought maybe Veronica would be around."

"What do you want with her?"

"Just routine questions about Scott Henley."

"Him!" Doris spat the word out. "Henley was a class A-one shit. That bastard broke the poor girl's heart. I tried to warn her. He's too slick for his own good, I said, but did she listen? Of course not. Girls never listen to their mothers until it's too late."

A shadow of regret washed over her face, but she shook it off.

"I know I sound harsh, but hearing her cry herself to sleep night after night just about broke my heart too. I'm sorry the man's dead, but I'm not sorry that he won't be coming around here anymore and dragging her off to la-la land."

"You didn't approve of larping and Door Camelot?"

Veronica's mother raised her sunken eyes to Cubiak. "There's no prince charming, Sheriff," she said with a mix of derision and sadness.

At that moment, Stan called out from the house.

Doris made a face. "Time for his tea. Tea for me, that is, and beer for him. If I object, he tells me that it's five o'clock somewhere and that means it's time to belly up to the bar." She swiped her hands on her pants. "You may as well come with. If we stand out here talking, he'll just sit there and holler until I come in."

Without looking to see if he was following, she turned and trudged toward the house.

"Man's gotta have his beer," she said, as if reciting a familiar mantra.

By the time Cubiak was inside, Doris was already at the refrigerator. "Beer?" she said over her shoulder as she pulled a can from the top shelf.

"I'll pass."

She popped the top. "Have a seat, then." She closed the refrigerator door with her foot and disappeared through the doorway.

The mumble of voices from the living room was followed by the creak of the floor, and then Doris was opening the refrigerator once again. This time she pulled out a tall plastic pitcher and without asking filled two glasses.

"Iced tea," she said as she set the drinks on the table. She emptied half her glass, collapsed into a chair, and motioned for him to sit.

"You got any kids, Sheriff?"

The question was a swift kick to the gut. He knew that by now he should be able to respond with equanimity, but it always caught him unawares and left him spinning between the past and the present and grasping for an answer.

"I had a daughter. She'd be twenty-one this year," he said finally, leaving the rest unsaid. "Now I have a son. He's nearly nine."

"Sorry about that, Sheriff," Doris said.

Cubiak hoped she would move on to a different topic, but subtlety wasn't her strong suit. "How old was your girl when she died?"

He took another moment. "She was four and a half, just a little thing."

"Our son was sixteen, but then you wouldn't know what happened to him. You weren't here yet. Anyway, that's when Stan started drinking hard."

Cubiak bowed his head, and in the steamy kitchen the two mourners drank the cold tea in a silence that was broken only by the ticking of a garish wall clock.

After several seconds passed, Doris smiled, and in that smile was a hint of her younger self. "We'd give anything to have them back, wouldn't we?"

The question didn't require more than a simple nod in response, and that's what Cubiak gave.

Doris carried the glasses to the sink. "But we've both been blessed a second time," she said, her back to him.

Cubiak nodded again. He regretted what he had to say next, but it had to be done. He waited until she turned around.

"It must be especially nice for you to have Veronica so close and able to help out as much as she does."

"Hah!" Doris's sharp exclamation reverberated through the kitchen. "Theoretically that's true, but that girl is always busy. Promises made but seldom kept, I'm afraid. Like last Wednesday, she was supposed to come home early and take me to the doctor, but by the time she got here, it was too late. And those?"

She pointed to a stack of boxes in a small side room that might once have been a pantry. "See those? I've been waiting a month for her to get those into the shed for me, but somehow it never gets done," Doris said as she dried her hands in a gray dishcloth.

"Something always comes up with her, although it's not as bad as when she was involved with him. And now this week." She snapped the towel at the table. "Well, it's the big swim. Those boxes will be here until Thanksgiving at this rate."

Cubiak got up from the table. "I'll take them out for you."

"Are you sure?" The words said *no* but her tone was saying *yes, please, thank you.*

"No problem."

The sheriff lifted two cartons off the pile and followed Doris out the door and across the yard to a large metal Quonset hut.

"It used to be a machine shed, but that was when we had machines. Couple of tractors, a combine. Farm equipment," Doris said wistfully as she unlocked the door. "Just back there in that corner would be fine."

The interior was dim and dusty. Cubiak made his way between stacks of crates and boxes and set the cartons down where he had been told to. Walking back, he noticed a large overhead door near the opposite corner. There was something in front of it covered with a tarp. On this ramshackle homestead, what was so valuable that it had to be hidden from sight?

The sheriff made four more trips with the rest of the cartons. Each time he grew more curious about what was under the canvas sheet, but with Doris watching him, he had no chance to look.

As he settled the last carton into place, he motioned toward the tarp.

"Does Stan collect antique cars?" he asked.

"Oh, that. Heavens no." Doris moved toward the exit and waited for him to follow. Once outside, she glanced back in.

"He used to race stock cars, but once his eyes went, he sold them off. That's just something Veronica is storing for a friend."

And with that, she pulled the door shut.

23 \ A CHARMED LIFE

From the Kaisers, Cubiak headed to the ferry dock at Northport. Traffic was heavy and by the time he arrived, a small crowd lined the rocky shore, waiting for the swimmers. The sheriff hung back, but after a few minutes Joey spotted him and ran over.

"Dad! You came. Veronica's in the lead," the boy said, his pride of association obvious.

"Good for her, but it's not really a race."

"I know, but still, it's something. Maybe I can get her to teach me some tricks, you know, so I can learn to swim faster."

Cubiak gave a noncommittal nod. "Where's your mother?" he said just as he saw Cate walking toward them.

The sheriff gave his son money for ice cream and watched him run off past his mother.

"I'm glad we came. Not that we could see anything except what was up on the screen over there." Cate pointed to the restaurant. "Some guy was streaming it live. But still, the roar of the greasepaint, the smell of the crowd, and all that."

She laughed and when he didn't join her, she got serious. "Why are you here?"

It was the question that he both anticipated and dreaded. "I need to talk to Veronica about Scott Henley."

"Oh, Dave! Why?"

"She had a thing with him for a while, and they argued the day before he disappeared. It's routine follow-up."

Cate scowled. "She's just a young girl."

"I know, and I'm giving her every benefit of the doubt—"

"Hey!" Joey yelled and waved them toward the water. "Come on, they're here!"

Veronica was the first swimmer to stagger out of the water. She was breathing hard and appeared dazed but triumphant. The two ferries moored at the pier blasted their horns, and as the crowd cheered, she pulled off her red swim cap and waved it overhead. Someone threw a towel over her shoulders, and she turned and watched as the other swimmers appeared in quick succession. They had all made it. There were more cheers and hugs and group photos.

Joey ran to the cluster of people gathered around Veronica. She smiled and shook hands, posed for pictures, and signed posters and pamphlets and whatever was shoved at her, but it seemed to Cubiak that all the while she was looking beyond the admirers for someone else, perhaps her father or mother. Eventually Joey returned, grinning and brandishing her signature on his right arm. Cubiak tousled the boy's hair, hiding his own concerns. Not for the first time, he wished his instincts were wrong.

The impromptu celebration ended quickly. As the greeters moved off to their cars, the swimmers exchanged hugs and disappeared into the thinning crowd. Veronica made her solitary way to the wooded parking lot. Cubiak followed her.

"Veronica, I need a few minutes," he said as she unlocked the door of her car.

She turned toward him. You again, her look said. "Oh God, I'm so tired. Couldn't this wait?"

He wanted to say yes but knew better. If he was right, the tarp in the Kaisers' shed was covering Henley's car. As soon as Veronica got home, her mother would tell her that he had been out and had been in the shed, and she would have reason to get rid of it quickly. A few hours' sleep and the young woman would be energized enough to drive the vehicle far from the peninsula.

"Sorry."

She slumped against the front fender. Her short blond hair had dried in the breeze, and it frizzed around her head like a halo.

"You did well today, congratulations," Cubiak said.

She ignored the comment. "I already told you everything I know about Scott."

"Actually, I wanted to ask you about his car."

Her eyes narrowed, then she caught herself and lifted a placid face toward him. "His car?"

"It was seen parked alongside the road near Jacksonport the afternoon of the storm. You drive that way from work, and I wonder if you know anything about it."

Veronica rummaged in her duffel bag and pulled out a pack of cigarettes. She took her time extracting a smoke and then lit it. Could she really have the urge or the lung capacity to smoke after completing such a grueling ordeal, or was she stalling for time?

"Want one?" she said, holding out the pack.

Cubiak hadn't had a cigarette in four years, but he still found the aroma intoxicating. He shook his head.

"It's a red Porsche. Hard to miss," he said, as if needing to jog her memory.

"I know what he drives. What he drove," she said. She took a deep drag and then another. When she was nearly to the filter, she flicked the butt away and crushed it with her foot. "Can't say that I remember seeing it. In fact, I'm not even sure I went that way. What day did you say it was?"

"Wednesday. You left work early to drive your mother to the doctor, but she said that by the time you got home, it was too late. I wonder what kept you."

Veronica looked thoughtful and moved her foot.

"There's a witness who saw a blue car like yours in Jacksonport that afternoon," he said as he bent to retrieve the butt from the forest floor.

"There are plenty of cars like mine around here," she said.

"That's true, but let's assume for the moment that it was yours. You would have seen the Porsche on your way home and known it was

Scott's. Let's also assume that you were determined to ignore the car and the unusual circumstances, so you drove past. But your curiosity got the best of you."

Her concern as well, but he didn't say that. Instead he played with the facts as he knew them. "So you parked in town and walked back. It's not that far. It wouldn't have taken more than five or ten minutes. How odd it must have been to find Scott dressed in that costume and looking so beat up. I wonder what the two of you talked about and how you got him to the water."

Veronica bit her lip. "You got it all wrong, Sheriff. Yeah, I saw the car on my way home, but there wasn't anyone in it. I stopped to look, thinking that maybe Scott had hung one on and was sleeping it off in the grass. But he wasn't there."

Cubiak pretended to be surprised. "What did you do?"

"I looked for him. I knew he wouldn't have walked back to Camelot; it was too far. And he wouldn't have left the car there if he'd called someone for a ride. That wasn't like him. He'd have made sure someone came for the car too."

"Where did you think he'd gone?"

Veronica opened the car door and plopped onto the seat. She sat sideways, with her feet on the ground and her arms pressed to her knees.

"When Scott and I were together—when I was Guinevere—we had a favorite spot near the park. Down at the end of the road. We'd meet there when I got off work and sit and talk. He called it his sanctuary, where he went to get away from the stress of running Camelot, where he could sit and think. I had a hunch that's where he'd gone. I still had plenty to say to him, so I went there to look, and I was right. He was sitting on the old log we used to share. I thought it was strange that he was dressed like that, and I thought it even stranger when I realized that he was wearing the Lancelot costume."

She scrubbed her head. "For a moment, I had this fantasy that he was there waiting for me, that he wanted to get back together. Then I noticed the welts on his face, and I knew that something had happened and that he was using our old spot as a refuge."

"You talked to him?"

"Yeah." She stared at the trees and made a harsh sound like a bark. "I asked him what the fuck he was doing there."

"What did he say?"

Veronica was quiet for a moment. "He looked at me and started crying. I'd never seen Scott cry, not until then. I didn't know what to think. Mad as I was, I sat down next to him and asked him what was going on. Part of me hoped that maybe that bitch Amy had dumped him and I was glad. I wanted him to feel what it's like to be rejected. I knew that didn't make sense, not with the bruises on his face, but I wasn't thinking straight. I was still so mad at him. I wanted him to beg me to come back to him so I could tell him to drop dead."

She stopped and blinked. "That's not true, not really. I missed him so much. If he'd asked, I'd have gone back to him, not right away but eventually."

Veronica hugged her arms to her chest. "Boy, was I off base. He never even mentioned Amy. Instead he told me this crazy story about this girl Wendy and what had happened when he was a kid and how he'd never been told and that it was his fault or maybe it wasn't, and anyway Wendy got in touch with him because of Camelot and when her father saw him talking to her, he dragged him out with a rope and started slapping him around. It was all so weird I didn't know what to think, and then I got really pissed, because I realized that there was Scott our hero ruining yet another life and I mean really ruining it, even if he didn't mean to or it was an accident. She's paralyzed, right? This Wendy woman?"

"Yes."

Veronica sprang to her feet and paced. "Fuck, I can't imagine. I can't even . . ." She shuddered, and her entire body trembled. "Scott told me that Wendy's father said it should have been him and that the old man tried to kill him. He should have, I thought. But all the time he's outside getting beat up, Wendy's inside yelling for her dad to stop. Can you believe it, what a fucking charmed life this bastard lived until now."

As she talked, Veronica clutched her hands and began to shiver. Exhaustion, cold, emotional trauma? Probably all three. Cubiak steered her toward the jeep and pulled a blanket from the back. Under the filtered shadows of the tall pines, he draped the throw over her shoulders.

When he opened the passenger door, she sat down and huddled into herself like a frightened child.

When she had calmed, Cubiak questioned her further.

"Do you remember what time it was when you found Scott by the lake?"

"Somewhere close to three thirty. I don't wear a watch so I can't say for sure."

"What happened after he told you about Wendy?"

"We just sat there for a while not saying anything. I know Scott was looking for sympathy, but the more I thought about that poor girl and what had happened to her, and how he just went on, free to do whatever he wanted, the more upset I got. I remembered how easily he'd tossed me aside and wondered how many other girls, women, I guess, that he'd hurt. It was as if I suddenly saw him for the bastard he was—the bastard my mother said he was—and decided to teach him a lesson."

Veronica pulled her feet up and tucked the blanket around them. Hunched over her knees, she seemed impossibly fragile, but her voice remained strong.

"There was an old rowboat hidden in the bushes nearby. It's been there forever. Scott was skittish around water, but when the lake was calm, we'd sometimes go out in it and drift around looking up at the sky. I dragged the boat out and convinced him to go for a quick row around the cove. I told him it would be soothing, that he could watch the changing colors in the sky and take his mind off things for a while."

"You knew the storm was coming in?"

"Yeah, I'd heard the warning on the radio and could see the sky out west getting dark. But I kept the boat turned so his back was to it. When we got to the middle of the cove, I stood up and started rocking the boat. I knew it would scare him. He yelled at me to stop, but I just kept at it. He was holding on for dear life and shouting at me, calling me all kinds of names. I let him go on for a few minutes and then I took one of the oars and swung at him."

"Did you hit him?"

"Yeah."

"Where?"

"Here." She pressed a hand to the left side of her face. "I wasn't trying to hurt him. I just wanted to stun him. He'd been leaning forward on the seat, and when I hit him, he fell backward. I remember his helmet fell off, and I stood there and looked at it for a second. Then I dove off."

"You left him on the boat?"

"Yeah. I left him there and swam to shore."

"You swam to shore in your clothes?"

"I was wearing a thin sundress, no big deal. And I'd left my shoes on the beach."

Veronica tugged the blanket tighter. "I wanted Scott to sit up and realize he was out there alone on the water with the storm blowing in. I wanted to punish him for what he did to me and Wendy, to feel desperate and scared, even if it was just for a little while. I didn't know if he'd ever rowed a boat in his life, but I figured he'd manage somehow. He was a smart guy and it wasn't that hard."

She burrowed into the seat. "Anyway, he wasn't that far from shore. I was sure he'd make it back. I didn't think he would drown."

Veronica started to cry again.

"Scott didn't drown."

It took a moment for her to take in what the sheriff had said.

She looked up, puzzled. "Then how . . . ?"

"He was killed by a blow to the head."

24 \ BLINDED BY LOVE

"Oh my God, no! No! I didn't do that. I didn't kill him! I would never do that. I couldn't!"

Veronica clutched the blanket and rocked back and forth on the seat. "I admit that I hit him, but just on the side of his face, on the cheek. He was okay. He wasn't hurt, not really. He was yelling at me when I was swimming away, calling me a bitch. When I got to shore, he was sitting up and flailing with the oars, but he was rowing toward the beach. I swear it's true. You've got to believe me. I remember the sunlight bouncing off his tunic. He was alive when I left! You've got to believe me. I didn't kill Scott. I love him."

"Did you see him reach the shore?"

"Pretty much. Yeah."

Veronica crumpled and wept uncontrollably.

Cubiak shut the door and walked to the driver's side. As he climbed in, she grabbed his arm. Her face was white and her eyes wide with fear.

"You believe me, don't you, Dave? You know me. I took care of Joey that summer. I was always good to him. You know I couldn't hurt anyone."

The sheriff loosened her grip. He wanted to believe her, not only for her sake but for Joey's. And Cate's. And his. Joey would not easily forgive him for arresting her for murder. If she had killed Scott in a fit of rage and jealousy, how could he and Cate reconcile the fact that they had hired someone so emotionally unhinged to care for their son?

Still, Veronica admitted hitting Scott with an oar. A young woman who could swim across Death's Door had the strength to deliver a solid wallop, perhaps one powerful enough to kill. A good attorney would advise her to plead self-defense, but based on what she had told Cubiak, he didn't think that argument would hold up. If she was lucky, the prosecutor would settle for a charge of manslaughter.

In the end, there would be one man dead and the life of a young woman upended. The life of another young woman.

Cubiak consoled her as best he could.

"There are still some things I have to check out," he said.

Veronica sniffled and fumbled for the door handle. "I need to go home."

"You're in no condition to drive. I'll take you back."

She sat upright. "I'm not in any trouble, am I?"

"No." Not yet.

They followed the windy road across the tip of the peninsula and then headed south. Veronica stared out the windshield in a daze, the glow of the day's triumph erased. In Sister Bay, the streets were filled with tourists and locals enjoying the afternoon sun, and Veronica slumped in the seat and burrowed down low. Either she was exhausted from the swim or she didn't want to be seen riding in the sheriff's jeep.

Sensing her discomfort, Cubiak took back roads the rest of the way, both to offer her some peace of mind and to give himself a chance to think. By the time he remembered to ask if she had hidden Scott's car under the tarp, she had fallen asleep. He let her be, her head drooping toward her shoulder, her mouth agape and the breath passing through with a whisper.

They were in Jacksonport when Veronica woke up.

"Why are we here?" She sounded scared.

"I need you to help me understand what happened that afternoon."

"How? What am I supposed to do?"

"Just walk me through everything you did after you swam back to shore. Can you do that?"

The storm surge had reduced the beach to an outcropping of sand wedged between the park and the string of cottages that ringed the shore to the north. The debris in front of the cabins had been cleared away, but on the other side, the shore remained littered with detritus.

Veronica glanced around uncertainly. "It looks so different," she said.

"Take your time."

She studied the shoreline for a minute or two. Then she slipped off her shoes and hopscotched through the debris as if propelled by mental memory.

"I was here, ankle deep in the water when I first turned around to see what Scott was doing. He was over the sandbar, so maybe fifty feet out, no farther. See it? It's where the waves are breaking."

From the shore, she moved back to a cluster of rocks. "He was probably halfway in," she said, pointing to the water.

When she reached the edge of the park, she slipped between two large trees. "I waited here until he made it in."

"You saw him on shore."

Veronica hesitated. "I saw the boat land. Then I saw Scott stand up."

"Did you see him get out?"

She hung her head. "No. But he'd made it back. All he had to do was step out of the boat. Scott was fine, I'm telling you. I didn't kill him. You've got to believe me."

Listening to her plead, the sheriff remembered what his son had told him about Veronica. Joey said he liked the stories that she had told him when she babysat. She always made up the best stuff, he had said. Was that what she was doing? Had she waited and watched Scott row back toward shore as she claimed, or had she stalked off full of vengeful anger and pride and left him to the mercy of the heaving water? Memory and conscience could play tricks. Often witnesses to a crime told different versions that each believed true. Even when faced with irrefutable evidence to the contrary, some killers clung to the belief that they were innocent. Was Veronica's story true, or a fanciful version of wishful thinking?

Even if Scott had reached shore, one or two powerful waves could have pulled the boat back out into the lake before he had a chance to climb out.

168

"You don't believe me, do you?" Veronica said.

"I'd like to find the boat," he said.

He pulled up the photo on his phone. "Is this it?"

"Oh my God, yes, that's it." She fell against one of the trees. "I don't understand any of this."

Veronica walked back to the jeep barefoot. She threw her shoes on the floor and then sat down and pulled the blanket over her lap.

"What about Scott's phone? Did he have it with him?" Cubiak asked.

"Which one?" she said as she wrapped the blanket around her legs.

The answer caught the sheriff off guard. He had never suspected that Henley had more than one phone. None of the larpers had said anything. How many did he have? Two, three?

The sheriff took his best guess. "Both of them," he said.

Veronica sniffled. "Probably. He was real anal that way."

"Did you see either one that day?"

"No."

"Maybe he didn't bring them."

"Scott? No way."

"But how would he carry them around? Medieval knights didn't have pockets, did they?"

"Scott did. He modified his costume," she said. There was a pause and she gasped. "But he wasn't wearing his outfit, was he?"

It was a short ride from the shore to the Kaiser home. When the sheriff slowed and turned into the drive, Veronica braced against the dash.

"I thought you were going to arrest me," she said.

"For now, I'm remanding you to the care of your folks. You need to get some rest. I'll be back tomorrow, and we can talk more then."

She shivered. "My parents are going to ask why you brought me home."

"I'll tell them that I didn't think it was safe for you to drive back alone after the swim. I'll remind them that you were one of the last people to see Henley alive and that I'll need to ask you a few more questions after you've rested up."

"You believe me then, that I didn't kill Scott?" she said.

Despite the evidence against her, he wanted to think she had told him the truth. "We'll talk again," he said.

Veronica nodded once more. "I understand. Thank you," she said. Then she pressed her fingers to her eyes. "I must look like shit."

At the sound of the jeep's doors slamming shut, Doris Kaiser ran up from the yard, dusting dirt from her hands. When she saw Veronica, she screamed and descended on her daughter as if she was a long-lost prodigal child. Moments later, Stan emerged in the doorway. He beamed with pride and gasped for breath from the exertion of moving from the couch to the porch.

Doris rushed Veronica up the front steps, where the two lavished her with hugs and her father peppered her with questions. He knew the specifics of the swim from the YouTube video but still he pumped her for information. What was her time? Did anyone drop out? Who was second? Was the water colder than usual because of the storm? How bad were the waves, the currents?

In the midst of their reunion, Veronica's mother looked up at the sheriff.

"What's he doing here?" she said in a voice loud enough for Cubiak to hear.

Before he could answer, she blanched and looked at her daughter. "Where's your car? What's happened to it? Oh God, did you have an accident? Are you hurt?" She began patting Veronica's arms and shoulders.

The young woman freed herself from the tangle of arms. "I'm fine, just tired. The sheriff was at the ferry landing when we came in. Joey, too, and Cate." A subtle reminder to Cubiak of her connection to his family. "He was kind enough to bring me home. I'll get the car tomorrow."

With that, Veronica opened the screen door. "I want to go in now. I need to sleep and then maybe eat something."

Her father followed her inside, his booming voice relaying the details of the grueling ordeal she had just completed. As soon as they were gone, Doris descended the stairs and marched down the short span of crumbling sidewalk to confront Cubiak.

"What's this all about? I've lived here long enough to know the sheriff doesn't provide door-to-door service to anyone."

He repeated what he had said earlier to her daughter.

Doris almost smiled. "Right, and she may remember something important," she said in a mocking tone, repeating the typical TV cop show patter.

Cubiak let her have her moment of fun before he went on.

"For now, I'm more interested in the car."

"The car? The car's still up at Northport. You know that."

"Not that one. I'm talking about the car that's under the tarp in the back of the shed."

Doris went very still.

"You told me that Veronica was storing a vehicle for a friend, but I have a feeling it's Scott Henley's car. Either Veronica lied to you about it, or you knew all along that it was his convertible. If that's the case, then you've been withholding evidence in a murder investigation."

She started. "Murder? I thought he drowned."

Cubiak continued as if she hadn't spoken. "You can either let me take a look now or wait until I come back tomorrow with a search warrant. If you insist on waiting until the morning, I will take steps to ensure that you can't tamper with the vehicle between now and then." He had no idea how he would manage that, but it was worth the gamble.

She blinked fast, and in the flicker of her eyes he imagined her running through her options. "You can look," she said finally.

The sheriff grabbed a flashlight from the jeep, and for the second time that day, he followed her to the metal building.

"The car is not to move. It's not to be touched," Cubiak said as he lowered the canvas over the gleaming hood of the red sports car.

Then he retraced his steps to the doorway and motioned her outside.

"What time was it when Veronica showed up with it?"

Doris raised a hand against the sun's glare. "She didn't."

"What do you mean?" As he spoke, he understood his mistake. "It was you who drove Henley's car here." He tried to keep the surprise from his voice.

She nodded, and in the late afternoon sun, the lines in her face deepened, making her look older than her years.

"Why?" he asked.

"Veronica told me he'd parked his car by the road and that she'd found him at the lake feeling sorry for himself because of what had happened to that Tinsel girl. I knew the story, and when she said she'd left him stranded there, dressed in his ridiculous costume, I was glad. She said that he was too proud to call one of his larping friends for help and that without his car, he'd have to walk or hitch a ride back to Door Camelot. I imagined him stumbling along the road like the tin man, and the absurdity of it appealed to me. The knight in shining armor without his horse. To be honest, I was hoping he'd be struck by lightning along the way. It would serve him right."

"And when you heard that he was dead?"

She pinched her mouth tight.

"You got scared, didn't you? You thought that Veronica had something to do with his death, so you lied to protect her."

Doris Kaiser drew herself up. She was a tall woman, and standing erect she came close to looking Cubiak straight in the eye. "Wouldn't you, Sheriff? Wouldn't you do anything to help your kid?"

25 | A REASON TO KILL

Cubiak was on his way to the justice center when Rowe texted with news about Bill Fury, the worker Henley had unjustly fired. Fury had been injured on a construction job in Green Bay ten days ago and has been in traction since.

Cross him off the list of suspects, the sheriff thought.

When he got to his office, he was surprised to find his deputy waiting there.

"I got your message. Is there more on Fury?" he said.

"No, it's something else."

Before Cubiak could say anything, Lisa walked in and the two of them approached his desk.

"Is there a problem?" the sheriff said.

They responded together.

"Veronica Kaiser," Rowe said.

"Fish," was Lisa's contribution.

"And?" The sheriff had a good idea what was coming.

"There's no way she killed Scott Henley," the deputy said.

"How could you even think it?" Lisa added, her tone accusatory. She put her hands on her hips, clearly ready to defend her former schoolmate as she had her uncle.

"Where's this coming from?"

They didn't answer. But by now Cubiak knew that news traveled fast on the peninsula, with speculation hard on its heels.

He pulled out his chair, sat down, and considered the two young staffers. They meant well, and he hoped that they were right. He had his own reasons for wanting Veronica to be innocent, but he had been in the business longer than either his deputy or his assistant and had seen a number of cases, too many in fact, where the person who appeared the least capable of committing a crime was the one ultimately charged and found guilty.

"You both know her," he said.

"I was in scouts with her younger brother. He was killed in a boating accident senior year of high school," Rowe said.

"What happened?"

"He fell water skiing on the bay, and some drunk idiot in a powerboat ran into him. Veronica saw the whole thing. A bunch of us jumped in and tried to save him, but we were all too late."

Her brother's fatal accident explained Veronica's determination to conquer the water and her mother's aversion to it, as well as her refusal to watch her daughter take on the treacherous Porte des Morts strait.

The sheriff looked at Lisa. "You already told me about being in school with Veronica," he said. He went on quickly. "I understand how you feel, but you have to realize that she was the last person known to see Henley alive."

"That doesn't mean she killed him."

"She argued with him the day before and again on the afternoon that he went missing. She also admitted that she hit him with an oar."

"That's no proof of murder," Rowe said.

"That's true, and I haven't charged her. But I can't ignore the circumstances. Also there's her mother to consider."

"Mrs. Kaiser?" Lisa said.

"She claims that she's the one who drove Scott's car to the farm and hid it in a shed."

"Are you saying that Mrs. Kaiser might have killed Henley?" Lisa slipped into a chair. "I can't believe that. She used to make brownies for us."

Cubiak took his time answering. "To be honest, I don't know what to make of matters. There was no love lost between anyone in that family and Scott Henley. But the same is true for George Tinsel and, sorry, Lisa, but for your godfather too. With the videographer, that makes five suspects with motive and opportunity."

"What about old man Kaiser, Veronica's father? Why not throw him in the mix?" Rowe said.

Cubiak figured his deputy deserved to be upset and ignored the sarcasm in his query. "Stan Kaiser can't drive, or so it appears. But maybe that's an act," he said.

Around midmorning, the report on the fibers that the sheriff had found on the boat came back. The threads were from the tunic Henley was wearing. While the information proved nothing, it strengthened the argument that the victim either had been killed in Jacksonport or had died out on the lake and not on the beach where his body was found.

Then the evidence team got back from the Kaisers with the report that they'd found prints on both the inside and outside of Henley's car. They had his from the morgue, and both Kaiser women's prints were on file as well, Doris's from her former job as a childcare worker and Veronica's from a DUI. The prints from the vehicle's exterior belonged to all three: Scott Henley, Veronica Kaiser, and Doris Kaiser. There were numerous prints inside, but the only two on the steering wheel were Henley's and Mrs. Kaiser's.

Through the afternoon, Cubiak mulled over the case. No matter how he looked at it, he came up with holes that couldn't easily be filled. When he left, he went to see Bathard. He was anxious to check on his friend, but he also wanted to use him as a sounding board.

When they sat down in the doctor's library, the sheriff was ready for the ritual glass of sherry that Bathard offered.

"The woman is either stupid or very clever," Cubiak said after he had gone over the evidence teams' report on the car.

"To which woman are you referring, the mother or the daughter?"

"The mother, Doris Kaiser." Cubiak lowered his glass to the table.

"It's impossible to wipe off one set of prints and leave any other prints intact, so the evidence proves that Doris and not Veronica drove the car to the farm.

"Doris is a volatile, angry woman, and if Veronica is telling the truth that Henley was still alive when she left the beach, it means that her mother could have gone there and confronted him. It wouldn't have taken much for her to whack Henley with an oar. Not lightly on the side of the face like Veronica said she did, but hard, across the back of the head, hard enough to kill him. Then all she had to do was dump his body into the boat and push it back into the water. With the storm coming in, she could assume that the boat would capsize, and the weight of the armor would drag him to the bottom."

Bathard leaned forward. "But if she killed him, wouldn't she have wiped the steering wheel clean?"

"That would be her first instinct. But by leaving her prints in place, she makes it appear that she has nothing to hide. If asked, she could say she drove the car to the house as a favor to her daughter, nothing more."

"Where does that leave you?"

Cubiak sank into the chair. "Right where I started, with one victim and five suspects, each of whom had reason to hate Henley and each of whom had the opportunity to attack him on the day he died."

"Did any one of them despise him enough to kill him or to want him dead?"

"Isn't that always the question?"

The sheriff retrieved his drink and cupped his hands around it.

"The videographer Nick Youngman had motive enough, given what Henley had done to his father. The same holds true for Tinsel, although after hearing him describe his confrontation with Henley, I'm inclined to believe that he had a change of heart. Urbanski could have struck out in a fit of rage, but the timing is off, given his need to shelter the animals before the storm hit. Veronica fills the bill as the classic scorned woman. And as for her mother? I don't think she would hesitate to kill if it meant helping her daughter."

Bathard was silent for a moment. "Do you really think it is possible that a parent would murder a man because he broke off a relationship with their daughter, a relationship of which they disapproved?" He spoke slowly, giving the question the weight it deserved.

"It's more complicated than that. Mrs. Kaiser is fanatically protective of her Veronica. But more than that, she's boiling with anger and guilt over the death of her son. She was one of those who tried to rescue him and failed. That's a heavy burden to carry. Unable to save the boy, she'd do anything to safeguard her only remaining child. She probably realized that Veronica still loved Henley or that she was still susceptible to him. The only way to avenge her and keep her from getting hurt again was to get rid of Scott. She may have even rationalized that she was avenging Wendy Tinsel as well. Remember, Doris lived here when Wendy was injured. She told me that she knew the story, so she understood what the family had endured. She may have imagined herself as justified in trying to right past wrongs. Not just those committed against her daughter but against others as well."

"You are speculating," the coroner said.

"I'm thinking out loud. Events get clouded in people's minds. Doris Kaiser may have struck out at Henley in a blind rage and only afterward realized what she'd done. Whatever transpired on that beach happened in a flash."

Cubiak took another swallow of the sweet wine. "All that aside, Veronica remains the most likely suspect. One minute she told me that she despised Henley because he cheated on her and then jilted her, and the next she said that she still loved him. Unfortunately, love wouldn't prevent her from killing him whether by accident or in a fit of passion."

"Is there any chance of testing the oars for fingerprints?"

The sheriff shook his head. "There was only one oar on the boat, and it was clean. God only knows what happened to the other one. There are pieces of driftwood up and down the shore and more still floating in the lake. There's little to no chance of finding the missing oar, if it's even still in one piece. And even less chance of finding and identifying pieces from it."

"There is another possible explanation to events," Bathard said. "As you pointed out, Henley may have reached shore, but one large wave could easily have pulled the boat back out into the lake. If that happened and he didn't make it back a second time, it means that he was out on the water during the storm, and that raises the possibility that he took a fatal fall then."

"It's an unlikely scenario."

"Not any more unlikely than Veronica or her mother killing him."

Cubiak suppressed a smile. "Were the Kaisers your patients when you were still practicing?"

"Yes, but that is not relevant."

"Of course, although human nature being what it is . . ." Cubiak let the thought trail off. "But let's assume both that Henley was alive when Veronica left and that her mother had nothing to do with his death. Let's also assume he got out of the boat and pulled it up on the beach. If that's what happened, it means that someone else showed up and killed Henley."

"You mean George Tinsel or the filmmaker? Or Florian Urbanski, as unlikely as that appears to be?" Bathard said.

"No, I mean someone else. A sixth suspect, someone we haven't even considered yet."

26 \ A DESPERATE CALL

Thursday morning, Cubiak was in a foul humor on the drive to Irma Zubek's store. If his deputies fumbled during an investigation, he assured them that mistakes happened. The thing to do was catch the error and correct it. But he expected more from himself—much more, and he was annoyed that he had forgotten to ask Veronica an important question.

He got there are ten thirty but Veronica wasn't in yet.

"Late as usual," Irma said, with a sassy chirp.

The sheriff accepted a cup of coffee from the proprietor and listened to her tales about local history for half an hour. When Veronice still hadn't reported for work by eleven, he was even more annoyed with himself. Had he made another mistake allowing her to spend the night with her parents? If she had slipped away before dawn, she would be hundreds of miles from the peninsula by now. But why run if she had done nothing wrong, as she claimed?

Cubiak was on his way to the jeep when Veronica's blue compact car appeared around the bend. She was coming from Northport, which meant she had wangled a ride up to the ferry dock to retrieve it. She parked on the other side of the store and, with the boundless energy of youth, seemingly unfazed by the arduous swim she had completed less than twenty hours earlier, she hurried toward the shop.

As soon as she saw the sheriff, she skidded to a halt.

"Oh no, I knew it. You're arresting me," she said.

"I need to clarify something, that's all."

"I'm late for work."

"This will only take a minute," Cubiak said, and waved to Irma, who stared out the window from her station by the register.

Veronica fidgeted. "What?"

"It's about Scott's phone. You said he had two."

"Yeah, I already told you that."

"I know, but I need the number for the second one. Not the one for Door Camelot but the one you used when you called him."

She frowned. "I don't know it. It's on autodial. Let me look," she said as she pulled out her cell. She tapped the screen and then handed the device to the sheriff.

Door Camelot's number, the number Cubiak had been told that Henley used for all his calls, had a 414 area code, the code for Milwaukee. Henley's private number started with 715, the area code for much of the northern half of the state.

"Is that it? Can I go now?" Veronica raised her sad eyes to his. "Please?"

Earlier that morning, the sheriff had requested a search warrant for Henley's private phone. Now that he had the number, he texted it to Lisa. By the time he got back, she had compiled the records for all calls made from and to the device for the previous sixty days.

"Scott Henley was a chatty guy," she said, holding up the report as the sheriff approached her desk.

Cubiak took the handful of pages and flipped to the last one. The list of phone numbers ran three-quarters of the way down. Unremarkable on their own, the trail of digits documented the final hours of the man's existence.

According to the official record, Henley made his last phone call fifteen minutes after Veronica said she had left the Jacksonport beach. If she was telling the truth, Henley was alive when she last saw him.

The sheriff felt a wave of relief. While the phone records didn't completely exonerate Veronica—Henley could have lost the phone earlier and someone else could have made the last few calls—they at least lightened the shadow that hung over her. Unless she lied about when she left.

Not until Cubiak was at his desk did he realize that Henley had called the last number eight times within the space of a few minutes. Who was he so desperate to reach? The first seven attempts went unanswered, but the last one had gone through. Someone had answered.

The records showed that over the previous two months, Henley had used his private phone to text or call fifteen different numbers more than 150 times. Lisa had highlighted the phone numbers with yellow marker the first time each appeared. Cubiak compared them with those of the larpers at Door Camelot. There were no matches. Henley must have used the official business phone to contact his inner circle.

Three numbers with the local 920 area code accounted for a dozen or so of the entries. The rest started with the 608 code linked to Madison, the 414 code for Milwaukee, or several others that the sheriff didn't recognize. But that didn't mean much. Most of the numbers on the list were probably for cell phones. In the era of landlines, people got new phone numbers when they moved. Now they simply carried their cell phone numbers with them. Henley's private contacts could have been in Door County or anywhere in the country.

Cubiak buzzed Lisa. "You know the numbers you highlighted in yellow?" Before he could go on, she interrupted.

"I figured you'd want the names of the people they're registered to so I went ahead and got them. I'll be there in a second."

When the sheriff's assistant came through the door, she was triumphant. "Fifteen numbers and fifteen names, in alphabetical order," she said as she handed the list to Cubiak. Then she frowned. "As you can see, they're all women. Who was this Henley, some kind of lothario?"

Lisa leaned over the desk. "The last call went to her," she said, pointing to a name in the middle.

"Angela Fielding."

"Married to Zachary Fielding." Lisa gave him a knowing look.

"That Fielding?" he said.

"One and the same."

If there was a list of the top ten financially well-heeled residents on the peninsula, Zachary Fielding would be on it and near the top.

"Do you have an address?"

"They're on Rosemary Lane. I already texted the number to you."

"Lisa, where would I ever be without you?" Cubiak said.

"No doubt fumbling around in the dark somewhere."

"I'm sure." The sheriff stood. "You hold up more than your share, don't you?" he said.

"Of what?"

"The sky."

27 \ ANGEL OF MERCY

Cubiak crossed the highway bridge and headed north along the water. As he drove, he glimpsed the lake between the trees and buildings that lined the shore and felt his earlier gloom dissipate. After the many false starts in the case, he sensed that matters were finally about to turn.

Stranded on the shore, Henley had made a desperate attempt to reach Angela Fielding. Seven, eight calls one after the other in a matter of minutes. With storm clouds blotting the sun and lightning slashing the sky, he had reached out for help from an angel of mercy.

The homes along Rosemary Lane were as majestic as the lake they bordered. Cubiak crested the last in a series of soft rolling hills and arrived at the Fieldings' home. The turreted, three-story stone house was tucked behind an arbor of tall pines and guarded by two stone lions that flanked the driveway entrance. By the North Shore standards of Milwaukee and Chicago, it was a rather modest structure, but along Rosemary Lane it was one of the grander residences to make a recent appearance on the peninsula. The homes on either side were the original 1950s one-story frame ranches. Compared to the Fieldings' behemoth, they appeared quaint and insignificant.

In Cubiak's experience, people with money thought they deserved special treatment from the law. And it didn't matter how they had come by their wealth. Waiting at the door, the sheriff wondered if Zachary had been to the manor born or if he had clawed his way to success. And what of his wife, Angela? The couple's money could be hers.

Perhaps she had signed the checks for the pricey waterfront property and the extravagant home with the pretentious lions out front. Or the two were on equal footing and theirs was a marriage made in financial nirvana. More likely, especially if she was considerably younger, she was a decorative feature, like the lion statues, the kind of ambitious woman whose good looks unlocked the door to the heart and wallet of an older wealthy man eager to impress. The kind of woman whose physical beauty could never quite overcome the layer of desperation it was meant to hide. The kind who would tempt a purported womanizer like Scott Henley.

Cubiak pressed the buzzer again, and a moment later, the door sprang open. A tall, trim woman in late middle age glared at him. She had coifed hair and dark, arched eyebrows that failed to distract from the wrinkles that radiated from her almond-shaped eyes. She stood rigidly, with her shoulders back and her clenched fists at her sides. In denim capris and a flowered top, she looked dowdy enough to be a rich eccentric.

"Angela Fielding?" Cubiak said.

"No. Who are you?"

Cubiak identified himself. There was a flash of bright pink as the woman grabbed the brass knob and started to close the door.

"Is Mrs. Fielding home?" he asked.

"I have to check."

"You don't know?"

The woman turned and glanced at the hall that led off the foyer. The passageway ran through the house to an open door on the other side.

"It's a big house. Give me a minute," she said.

Just then, a tall, slender figure in a long white robe appeared in the patch of bright sun at the end of the passageway. The robe shimmered in the light, and it took a moment before Cubiak realized that the apparition was both real and a woman.

"Geez Louise, Lulu, let the man in." The woman had an underlying hint of a twang foreign to Door County. She advanced toward the foyer with a youthful stride and the carriage of one bred to poise and manners.

Lulu grimaced and yanked the door wide open. "As you say," she said, stepping aside to let the other woman pass.

The woman in white tossed a magazine onto a marble side table. "I'm Angela Fielding. Angela is sufficient. May I help you?"

Her tone was suddenly bored and affected. She was not as young as she had first seemed, but to the sheriff the hint of maturity added to her attractiveness. In a touch of reverse modesty, the sleeves of the robe covered her hands, while the front opened far enough to reveal the red bathing suit she wore underneath. She was blond, barefoot, and tan. A tasteful pink lipstick accentuated her full mouth, and oversized tortoise sunglasses perched on the end of her slim nose.

Angela took her time assessing her visitor. Then she motioned at Lulu. "Go make yourself useful," she said, speaking sharply.

Cubiak identified himself again.

"The sheriff," Angela said. She tensed and peered at him over the top of her glasses. "What is it? What do you want?"

"Is there somewhere we can talk?"

Angela moistened her lips and then turned away. "Let's sit by the pool," she said as she moved toward the long hall.

The house stretched along four hundred feet of prime lakefront and it had a pool? Had he misunderstood? Perhaps she had said "pond," one stocked with goldfish or koi. She walked quickly, leading him past bright abstract paintings and then two rooms filled with figurines and heavy dark furniture that seemed more appropriate for a manor house on a moor than a home on a Lake Michigan beach. Another hall opened off the second room, and as he passed, the sheriff caught a whiff of a familiar smell from his past.

Bleach.

Cubiak detested the odor. It was the aroma of his childhood, his mother's signature perfume. Every week, she had scrubbed their meager kitchen and bathroom with a sudsy solution of hot water, soap, and bleach. She embraced the smell, convinced that it cleansed the air and made the apartment feel larger. But to the young Cubiak, it meant that they couldn't afford the more expensive pine-scented cleaners used by the other women in the neighborhood. It meant that they were poor.

The sharp odor seemed out of place in the grand house on the beach. Surely, Angela of the provocative red bikini and luxurious, thick robe hadn't recently dipped her hands into a solution of chloride. That left Lulu. Maybe she was as old school as she looked. Or maybe the pool had been treated with a disinfectant product after the storm. What did he know about swimming pool maintenance? Nothing.

At the end of the hall, Cubiak followed Angela onto a sprawling stone terrace and inhaled deeply. The terrace was three steps down from the house and a full flight of stairs up from the sand beach. Cushioned chairs surrounded two glass-topped tables at one end of the patio, but most of the space was taken up by an oval pool with water as blue as that in the lake beyond. Both the terrace and the beach were pristine, as if a supernatural force had intervened to spare the grounds from the terrible force of the storm, akin to Moses holding out his hand to divide the Red Sea. More realistically, a sizable crew of locals had been hired to do a quick and thorough cleanup.

Angela led him across the patio to a shaded area away from the door. She motioned him toward a chair, then she plopped a wide-brimmed straw hat on her head and settled into a pink-and-white striped chaise.

"A visit from the sheriff—what's going on? Has anything happened to my husband?" she said.

Her face was in shadow and nearly impossible to read. She tried to sound worried, but to Cubiak she seemed more hopeful than concerned.

"Nothing like that," he said as he sat.

"What is it then? Fundraising for a new jail or something?"

"Nothing like that either. Our jail is more than adequate."

He wanted to see her reaction to what he had to say, but there was no way to ask her to remove her glasses and hat. "I'm here to ask you about Scott Henley."

"Who?" The response had a ring of innocence, but Angela had waited a moment too long to answer. "I'm afraid I don't know anyone by that name."

"You are Angela Fielding?"

"Yes." She wet her mouth a second time, and when she spoke, she was on the offense. "I don't understand why you're here. Why are you questioning me about this Scott person?"

Could she really not know what had happened?

Cubiak read a phone number off a slip of paper. "That's your cell number, isn't it?"

Angela shifted in her chair and ran her hands over her lap as if she had discovered a sudden need to smooth the robe.

"I can't really say. Who calls themselves?" She smiled. "Why do you ask?"

"Because it's one of the numbers Henley called numerous times over the past two months."

"It must have been a mistake. I'm always dialing wrong numbers."

"I doubt you call the same wrong number repeatedly."

Angela looked away. "I get all kinds of calls all the time. Usually they're from people looking for donations for one organization or another. Why does it matter if this man called me?" she said finally.

"Because it was the last phone number Scott Henley called."

"What do you mean? I don't understand. Has something happened to him?" This time the concern sounded sincere.

"Scott Henley is dead. His body was found several miles north of here on—"

"No." Angela drew her knees to her chest and grabbed her ankles. "No," she said twice more.

"The report's been on the news. I thought you'd have heard."

Her head shuddered back and forth. "I don't listen to the radio. We never watch—oh my God, I'm going to be sick."

Angela stumbled to the edge of the patio and bent over a row of low hedges. By the time Cubiak reached her side, she had finished retching. As he lifted her shoulders, he noticed a blur of discoloration beneath her right eye. The color told him that the bruise was a few days' old and the huge sunglasses that she was trying to hide it.

"Okay?" he said.

She nodded.

He resettled her on the chaise and filled a glass with water from a pitcher on the table. Her hands shook when she took it, but she managed a sip.

"You knew Scott Henley?"

She nodded again. "Yes," she said, her voice low and hoarse. She gulped more water and clutched the glass to her chest. "What happened?"

Cubiak told her what he could about the discovery of the body on the beach, uncertain how much she was taking in. When he finished, she leaned back in the chaise.

"You said he called me when, last Wednesday?"

"That's right. The calls were made as the storm was coming in."

"He called my number?"

"According to the records, yes."

Angela glanced down at the ground where her phone lay alongside her chair. It was a gaudy thing, pink with a rhinestone border. "That has to be wrong. I didn't get a call from Scott. It's a mistake. You need to check that number."

"I can do that right now."

Cubiak tapped the digits into his phone. After a moment's delay, the pink phone began to chime. The ringtone was vaguely familiar, one of those catchy pop beats that all sounded the same to him.

Angela snatched the device off the stone and silenced it.

"Oh my God," she said. "What do you want? Why are you here?"

"I'm investigating the death of Scott Henley, which means talking with people who knew him and who may have had contact with him before he died, hoping they can shed light on the circumstances."

Angela pulled her robe tight. "What do you mean 'the circumstances'? You said his body was found on the shore. Didn't he drown?"

"It looked that way initially, but the medical examiner found a number of suspicious injuries on the body."

She gasped. "Someone hit him?"

"He would have been banged around in the boat if he was out in the storm."

"But you think someone hit him. You think someone killed Scott, don't you? You think I did it." Angela looked at the phone and made a disparaging sound. Then she hurled the device to the ground.

"Why would I want to hurt Scott? I . . ." She hesitated. "I was in love with him once. I would never do anything to harm him."

"His last call was to you," Cubiak said.

"That's impossible." Angela sat up straight, and he imagined her glaring at him from behind the dark lenses. "I keep telling you I never got a call from him. I was at the spa all afternoon. I go every week. I have standing appointments for a massage, body scrub, and manicure. You can check. Three hours of peace and quiet. No phones allowed. I didn't talk to Scott or anyone that afternoon."

"Did you have your cell with you?"

She shook her head. "Electronic devices aren't allowed in the spa— no phones, tablets, notebooks, whatever. If you forget and bring one in, you have to give it to the receptionist. She keeps them behind the front counter."

"If you didn't have it, where was it?"

"I don't know. I was running late. I guess I could have left it in my car or at home." She frowned. "To be honest, I don't remember seeing it that day."

"Think about it, please. And try to remember. It's important."

"Why?"

"Because the call went through."

"Someone answered my phone?" Angela frowned. "If I left it here, then it was Lulu, who else? That bitch, she knows not to touch my things. But if it was in the car, it's impossible that anyone answered it. Unless . . ." She put her hand to her mouth.

"Unless what?"

"Once last year, Zachary took my phone with him when he went away. We'd had a disagreement, and he was angry with me. After that, I made him promise he wouldn't do it again."

"Are you sure he didn't have your phone with him last week?"

"He shouldn't have had it. He gave me his word," she said, but she answered in a way that tainted the response with doubt.

"But you're positive you didn't have it with you at the spa?"

Angela threw her hands up. "I'm so confused now, I'm not sure about anything."

Over the lake, a gull screamed and plunged headfirst into the water. Moments later, the bird resurfaced, holding a small silver fish in its beak.

Cubiak poured another glass of water for her. "How long did you know Scott?" he asked.

"I'm not sure. Ten years, twelve maybe. I used to work for him."

"How did you meet?"

"I was working at a restaurant. In Chicago. That was the first place I went when I finally got away from that pissant town I grew up in. I'd been voted prom queen my senior year in high school and prettiest coed freshman year at the community college. I knew I'd get a break someday if I waited long enough. Then I got an email from a modeling agency in Chicago describing all the opportunities I could have if I signed on with them and went through their training program. I jumped at it, and why not, what did I have to lose? Hell, I was still living at home with my parents. Anyways, I had some money saved so I moved to Chi-town, signed on with the agency, and waited for my big break. Like that ever happened."

She reached for the glass of water and seemed surprised to find it refilled. She took a sip and then set the glass back down. "Meanwhile I worked part time, waitressing at an Italian restaurant in the west Loop that turned out to be Scottie's favorite joint. He used to ask for me when he came in for dinner, and before I knew it, we were dating. Scottie said modeling would put me in a box, and that I had too much personality for that.

"He said I should pursue an acting career, and then he told me about larping. He said it would be good practice, a way for me to find out if I had the talent to be on the stage or in movies. There were larping events every other weekend, and I was welcome to participate in as many as I wanted. Well, I thought, that was just about the best advice I'd ever got because becoming an actress was my secret desire—modeling was just a way to get me there."

As Angela talked, her sophisticated veneer cracked, and Cubiak watched as she devolved into a small-town girl with big ambitions and no means of attaining them beyond wishful thinking.

"You became a larper?"

"Yeah. For three years and Scott was right, it was good practice. I played dozens of different roles, and no matter what part I was assigned or took on, I really had a chance to act. Sometimes everything was spontaneous—ad libbing and such—but more often we used scripts that Scott had written, so there were lines to memorize as well. The only problem was that no one saw me except the other larpers, and most of them were a bunch of losers. So there I was, acting but still stuck in a rut."

Cubiak glanced around the patio. "Something changed your life," he said.

Angela smiled generously. "My lucky day. I met Zachary."

"At the restaurant?"

"Oh God, no, not there. Ironically, I met him through Scottie." The smile vanished and she turned away.

"It's okay. Take your time," Cubiak said.

Angela nodded and took a deep breath. "There was an article about Mythweavers Productions in the paper. Zachary read it and decided to host a larp for his employees—he was always very innovative that way. He asked Scott to write a script just for them. Something fun that would give his staff a way to connect and allow them to challenge each other outside the workplace. Scott was torn; he didn't really want to do it, but he needed corporate clients to help pay the bills. This was his first big chance, and he knew that if it went well, he could leverage it to bring in more business. All together there were three day-long events spread out over a period of a month."

"And you helped?"

"Of course. At the time I was living part time with Scott and assisting him with the larping business as well. After the first event, Zachary gave Scott a bonus for a job well done and sent me flowers to thank me for my work. After the second larp, he sent me candy and a bottle of champagne. At the end of the month, a messenger showed up at my door with a diamond tennis bracelet and a plane ticket to Cabo. The ticket was in an envelope with a key and a note saying it opened the door to Zachary's condo and that I was welcome to stay there over the weekend, no strings attached."

"Did you tell Scott?"

"No, of course not."

"But you went."

"Yeah, I went. I needed a break and told myself it was just a lark. By then Scott was completely consumed with his new venture. It was larping twenty-four-seven. We hadn't gone anywhere together in ages, and I figured I deserved a vacation. The next Friday morning, I flew to Mexico and spent two days sitting in the sun by the pool, just like here. On Sunday afternoon, Zachary showed up and I thought, uh-oh, here goes, but he was the perfect gentleman. It was his condo and he didn't even come in. He stood in the hall and asked if I'd care to join him for dinner that evening."

"I assume you said yes?"

"Well, yeah. It would have been rude not to. Over dessert, he went on about how he'd given me a taste of his lifestyle and said that if I wanted more, it was mine for the taking. He gave me two days to decide. Yes or no—as simple as that, he said. It was winter in Chicago, and all I had waiting for me was a lousy job, a dingy apartment, and a boyfriend with a crazy dream. I liked what Zachary was offering. I knew I could get used to it." Angela motioned at the pool and the patio. "Obviously you know my answer."

"What happened with Scott?"

"I broke up with him. It wasn't easy and at first I felt like a heel, but that was the only condition Zachary insisted on while we were dating and again when we got married. For five years, I had no contact with Scott. In the meantime, Zachary sold his business and built this house, our paradise retreat, he called it. Everything was fine until about eighteen months ago."

"That's when you reconnected with Scott."

"Yeah, and all by accident, too. I was in town buying wine and I saw him. I hadn't thought about him in ages and thought I was hallucinating, but when I got home, I googled his name and found the Door Camelot website. Somehow our names got on his mailing list because a couple of weeks later, we got an invitation to a fundraiser at the center. I threw it out before Zach saw it. Eventually, though, Scott called and asked me to meet for coffee. In a weak moment, I said yes, and before long we were getting together regularly. At first everything was strictly business. All he talked about was Mythweavers and his plans for Door Camelot. When he asked for a donation, I gave him one, and this, too, became part of the routine. I didn't want Zachary to find out, so I always gave him cash. I never wrote a check."

She hesitated. "I'm sure that sounds weird, but I was never short on money. As I said, my husband was very generous. But who did I think I was kidding? Door County is like a small town where everyone knows everybody's business. Before long, Zachary heard about Door Camelot. One night at dinner, he brought it up and asked if I was in touch with Scott. I lied and said no. But he must have suspected something because he had me followed."

Angela looked at Cubiak. "He had photographs of the two of us together. We weren't drinking coffee."

"When did all this happen?"

"About a year ago. Zachary gave me an ultimatum, and I told Scott that was it, we were through."

"But you started seeing him again?"

Angela pulled off her sunglasses and looked directly at him. "No!"

"Do the letters or initials *ALE* mean anything to you?"

She didn't flinch. "No. Nothing."

"But your husband thought you were cheating on him with Henley, didn't he?" Cubiak said.

Angela glanced down and shuddered. "How did you . . ."

"The bruise under your eye," he said.

28  RHINESTONE COLLAR

As Angela fell back into the chair, the door from the house banged open and a large white dog bounded across the patio. The animal ran straight to Angela and prodded her hands with its massive head. She shrank back even farther.

"Go, go away," she whispered fiercely, trying to fend it off.

A tall man followed the dog. He had a regal shock of silver hair and wore a silky black T-shirt that showed off his trim torso and muscular arms.

"Jasper loves you!" he said as he strode across the terrace, announcing himself in an imperious tone.

"Zachary Fielding," he said as he extended one hand to Cubiak and grabbed Jasper's rhinestone collar with the other, yanking the dog away from Angela.

"Sit," he said.

The beast dropped to its haunches.

Fielding kissed Angela's forehead and smoothed her hair. He hooked his foot around a nearby chair and dragged it into their circle. After he sat, he took his took time arranging the creases of his pressed khakis over his knees before he spoke again.

"To what do we owe the pleasure of the sheriff's company?"

The question seemed directed at both his wife and their visitor.

Angela whimpered and kept her faced turned toward Cubiak. Beneath her tan, she had gone pale. Even with her eyes hidden by the glasses, the sheriff sensed her pleading gaze on him.

"We've met?" Cubiak asked.

"No, but Lulu told me you were here."

"Of course, Lulu." The housekeeper who had been eager to stop the sheriff from entering the house. "We had a recent report of a break-in down the beach. The owners were away during the storm, and the neighbors said they'd seen strangers prowling around the deck the following morning. I was just checking to see if you'd had any trouble or if you or your wife had noticed anything out of the ordinary either during or right after the storm."

"Sorry, Sheriff. We were cooped up here for days. First it was the weather and then it was work, a spate of international calls that I couldn't miss and such. Believe it or not, yesterday was my first time out of the house."

Cubiak looked at the dog sprawled out on the warm bricks near Fielding's tasseled loafers. Tom Johansson had seen a big white dog on the beach the morning he had found Henley's body.

"What about Jasper? Doesn't he need to go out?"

"We have a dog run alongside the house that we use when we need to."

Cubiak held out his hand for Jasper to smell, but the dog ignored him. The sheriff's knowledge about canines didn't extend much beyond collies, Labs, and retrievers.

"I'll bet there aren't many like this around here. What kind is it?" he said.

"Great Pyrenees."

"Really? My son's a dog lover. He'd be crazy about your pooch. Do you mind if I take a picture?"

Before Fielding could object, Cubiak snapped a photo with his phone. "How about one of him standing?"

Not hiding his annoyance, Fielding ordered Jasper to get up. Cubiak stood and clicked off two more pictures, one with both man and dog in the frame.

When Cubiak remained on his feet, Fielding rose as well. The sheriff was nearly six feet tall, but the other man had at least two inches on him.

"Lulu said you asked specifically for my wife."

"Did I?" Cubiak tried to sound confused.

"Any particular reason?"

"Not really. One of the neighbors must have mentioned Angela by name." He offered a contrite smile. "The department's been quite overworked these last few days, as you can imagine. We're all operating on too little sleep and too much caffeine."

"I know what you mean. I think the storm's been hard on everyone. My little darling here seemed to think it was the end of the world."

In a gesture of affection, Fielding reached for Angela's hand, which was still sheathed by the sleeve of her robe. For a moment she resisted, but he won out, and in a courtly gesture, he brought it to his lips for a kiss. That done, he straightened and scrutinized her fingers.

"What happened to your manicure?" he said.

Angela flushed and snatched her hand away. "I didn't get one—again. The manicurist has been off sick," she said.

"More's the pity." Fielding stepped behind her chair. "But lovely nonetheless," he said as he clamped his hands on her shoulders, like a man staking a claim.

With that, the visit ended, and Fielding escorted Cubiak to the foyer. Jasper trailed behind, his nails clicking impatiently on the hardwood floor. In the hall, the sheriff smelled bleach again, although this time the odor mingled with the aroma of frying onions and garlic.

"Lulu must be a good cook," he said as his host opened the front door.

Fielding shot out a hand as Jasper tried to sneak past. "Pure gourmet. Now I'm sure you have a busy day. Don't let us keep you," he said, holding the dog by the collar.

Cubiak was in no hurry. He surveyed the grounds. "You're lucky you didn't sustain any serious damage in the storm. How long did it take to shore things up?"

"I wouldn't know actually. The landscapers had the place buttoned down before the weather turned."

"You weren't here that day?"

"No, I was in Green Bay. Coming home, I had to go like hell to try to outrun the storm. I made it to Brussels before it hit."

"That's still a good distance away. It must have taken you some time to get here."

"Little over an hour, why do you ask?"

"Just curious."

The sheriff handed Fielding his card. "Call me if you think of anything. About the break-ins?"

"Sure thing." Fielding smiled but his eyes were hard.

From the base of the stairs, Cubiak glanced up at the house. Fielding was still in the doorway with Jasper at his side. A tall figure, and a white dog. Just like the duo that the sculptor Tom Johansson had described.

The sheriff found the artist alongside his house. He was feeding corn to a brood of red-feathered chickens in a small pen.

"The wife's idea." Johansson nodded toward the clucking hens. "She grew up on a farm and missed the fresh eggs. Unfortunately, the ladies aren't cooperating," he said as he tossed a handful of kernels over the fence. "No eggs for two weeks. First it was the foxes that scared them and then it was the storm. I don't know why I bother, except to please the little lady."

Johansson set the bucket on the ground. "But I don't imagine that you're here to talk about chickens."

"I have something to show you," Cubiak said.

"It's about the body then?" the sculptor said. He started toward the house. "I've been following the news about Scott Henley and this Door Camelot place of his. I never heard of either one before, but I guess that explains the costume."

Cubiak scrolled to the picture of Jasper that he took on the Fieldings' terrace.

"Do you recognize this dog?" he said.

Johansson peered over the top of his glasses. "It sure looks like the fancy mutt I saw on the beach that morning, but there's got to be more than one big white dog on the peninsula."

"This one's a Great Pyrenees. Not a very common breed."

Johansson pushed his glasses up the ridge of his nose and looked at the picture again. "Maybe not, but there could still be a few around, especially during the summer with the tourists here. Some of them have really unusual dogs."

Cubiak swiped to the next screen. "How about him?" he said as he held out the picture of Zachary Fielding.

The sculptor shrugged. "I told you I never saw the guy up close. He was on the dune the whole time and in the fog. Who knows? It could have been anyone standing up there. All I can say for certain is that he was tall and slender."

As he talked, he leaned over and rubbed his knee. "Damn arthritis is acting up again." He eased down into a chair and continued massaging his leg. "Now the dog, that's a different story. The dog was right in my face for a couple of minutes. Let me see the picture of that mutt again. A close-up of its face if you can, and make it bigger too."

His mouth pinched in concentration, Johansson studied the enlarged image.

"Hmm. I'll be damned, but that's the same dog all right," he said finally.

"Are you sure?"

"Well, you asked me and I'm telling you. That's the dog that came running at me that morning. I can be sure because of the collar. I'd forgotten all about it until now. The dog on the beach had a collar studded with big, white stones, like diamonds. Probably rhinestones or glass but they looked real enough to me. The corner of one stone was cracked off, just like in the picture. Here, look, you can see for yourself."

Johansson handed the phone back to Cubiak.

"The dog jumped up, with its paws on my chest, and I remember thinking how things can go along with nothing happening for years and then all of a sudden, bam, it's one thing after another. One night a storm mows down the two century-old trees in front of my house—pulls them up by the roots and drops them inches from the porch. The next morning, I go for a walk on the beach and find a dead man lying under a boat, and then I meet a Lucy with diamonds. You know, like in the song, only the Lucy I meet isn't a young girl, she's a big white dog and she's not in the sky but on the beach. And the diamonds aren't real. They're glass."

Johansson tilted toward the sheriff and tapped the screen. "I don't know about the man, but I recognize the collar. This here's the same dog I saw that day. No question."

29 THE MYSTERY LETTERS

The next morning, Lisa walked into Cubiak's office with a stack of mail and yellow folders piled precariously on her outstretched hands.

"What's all that?" he asked.

"The reports you wanted on Fielding, Angela, and the housekeeper, Lulu, and then a bunch of magazines and today's mail," Lisa said, as she tipped her hands down and let the pile slide off on the desk.

"Shoot," she said as the material fanned out across the polished surface.

Flashing her blood red fingernails in front of the sheriff, she tried to corral things back into a neat pile.

"Sorry, I should have waited for the polish to dry before I did this," she said.

"That's fine, just leave it," Cubiak said.

Lisa fluttered her hands in the air.

"Sorry," she said apologizing again. "I know I shouldn't be doing my nails on the job, but they were chipped and needed a quick touch-up. The bummer is that I went to the Woodland Spa as a special treat and even paid extra for no-chip polish. Just goes to show that you don't always get what you pay for."

She sighed and then gingerly tapped one of the folders. "You might want to read the reports first, especially the one on Lulu." Lisa gave

Cubiak a knowing look. "Remember the three letters you told me about, the ones that kept showing up on Henley's calendar?"

"Of course I do. A. L. E. You've figured them out, haven't you?"

The assistant grinned. "It's amazing what you can discover with a little digging. Lulu's been married twice. She's Gardner now, but her first husband was Horace Ecker, and the two of them had a daughter they named Angela."

"I'll be damned," Cubiak said, templing his hands on his chest. "Lulu is Angela's mother. I thought there was something odd going on between those two, but I couldn't put my finger on it. Good job," he said.

"There's more. Angela's middle name is Lynn."

"Angela Lynn Ecker. A. L. E. The letters sprinkled across Henley's calendar."

The previous evening, Rowe had presented Cubiak with several different scenarios involving Henley's last phone call. But there was one neither of them had considered. What if Lulu answered the phone but didn't tell anyone? She had to know about Angela's ongoing affair with Henley and would realize the danger it posed to her daughter's marriage. Fielding had already threatened to divorce Angela once before. Learning of her continued infidelity could push him over the edge.

Without Fielding, there was no money, no upscale lifestyle in the grand house on the lake. Lulu was no dummy. She knew that the only way to keep Angela in line—the only way to keep her daughter in diamonds and to guarantee a comfortable old age for herself—was to get rid of Henley.

The morning when Tom Johansson stumbled on Henley's body on the beach, someone with a large white dog had been watching from the dune. Johansson had identified the dog as Jasper and described the onlooker as tall and slender. Fielding matched that vague description, but so did Lulu.

Both of them had reasons for wanting Henley dead. Either one—perhaps Lulu more readily than Fielding, if his alibi held up—had the opportunity to confront the larper on the beach. There would have been an argument and a fight. A vicious swing with an oar followed by a sickening thud as the long wooden board cracked Henley's skull. Then a struggle to maneuver his body into the boat. After that, the rest was easy. The high waves lapping around the hull helped lift the vessel off the sand and float it back out into the lake. The killer would assume that the boat would capsize and the body, weighed down with the armor, would sink to the bottom of the lake.

What then?

Fielding was accustomed to taking control and getting his way. If he had killed Henley, he would come home and go about his business unruffled. It wouldn't occur to him to stalk the lakefront searching for signs that the plan had gone awry.

Not so Lulu. She was an anxious, skittish woman, the type who would be haunted by the vision of Henley's body resurfacing on the shore. She would need to check to make sure it hadn't, and what better reason to get out than taking the dog for a walk. Fielding said they had been cooped up in the house, but he also said that he had spent most of Friday morning in his home office on a series of international business calls, giving Lulu the opportunity to slip out with Jasper unnoticed.

Armed with the information Lisa had uncovered, Cubiak returned to the beach where Scott Henley had washed up. Piles of storm debris remained scattered across the sand, but all evidence of the crime was gone. The body had been taken to the county morgue. The *Wahoo*, still unclaimed by its owner, had been trucked to a warehouse outside Sturgeon Bay where it was being kept as evidence. Even the yellow caution tape had been rolled up and discarded.

There were eight houses within reasonable walking distance of the beach. Johansson and five of his closest neighbors lived on the lake side of Rosemary Lane. The other two families were on the wooded sites across the road. Rowe had asked the residents if they had seen a man and a dog.

Cubiak retraced the deputy's route and rephrased the question.

One couple had just returned from a week in the Pacific Northwest and were of no help. The other families had weathered the storm but hadn't ventured out until the next day. And no, they told the sheriff, they hadn't looked out the window toward the road. They hadn't seen anyone. He showed them pictures of Jasper and they shook their heads.

"That's all you have to go on?" one man said. He was a hefty middle age, and both surly and incredulous. "We got a dead body on the beach and you're out looking for a woman walking a white dog? God help us all."

30 | TRACES OF BLOOD

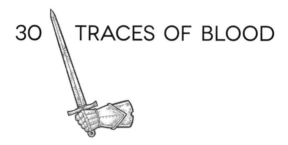

From the crime scene, it was a quick drive down Rosemary Lane to Zachary Fielding's home. The front yard was quiet, the only sound the muted shush of the waves lapping the shore on the other side of the house.

Cubiak mounted the stairs slowly. When he pressed the bell, Lulu opened the door almost immediately and moved aside to let him enter. The first time they met, she had eyed Cubiak with suspicion, but today her gaze was easy and confident.

"Hello, Sheriff," she said, almost cheerfully, as if enjoying a private joke. Without being asked, she beckoned toward the long hall and led the way to the terrace where Angela and Zachary Fielding lingered over the remnants of breakfast. Coffee and croissant, a bowl of fresh strawberries, and champagne flutes filled with orange juice, probably mixed with vodka.

They were a handsome couple. With the stately home as a backdrop, they presented the epitome of casual elegance. He in a distressed shirt and khaki shorts, his arm draped across the back of his wife's chair, and on his head a faded blue baseball cap, despite the heavy cloud cover. She in a straw Panama hat and a yellow beach dress with a modest V-neck that managed to look seductive. The familiar oversize sunglasses propped on her tanned face. Jasper sprawled on the warm stones in front of them.

"You again," Fieldling said, not bothering to get up. "What is it this time? Still in hot pursuit of phantom burglars?"

"I came about the body that washed up onshore last week, a few miles from here."

Fielding raised an eyebrow. "You mean that son-of-a-bitch Scott Henley? I don't hesitate to speak ill of the dead, Sheriff, not when they deserve it. An accident, surely."

"There are indications that Henley was murdered."

Fielding scrambled to his feet, kicking Jasper aside. "And?" he said.

"You were both acquainted with him."

Fielding's face clouded. "You think we had something to do with it," he said, pointing first to his wife and then to himself.

"Angela used to work for Henley, so what? She was romantically involved with him at one point, so what again? I hired him for a job once, what does that prove? Nothing. That's why you were here the other day, isn't it? You were on a fishing expedition."

"Not entirely." Cubiak dropped the search warrant between an empty cup and a plate of pastry crumbs.

Fielding threw his arms up. "Oh, sweet Jesus, where the hell do you people come from? Look, Mister Kubak, I don't know how you got a judge to issue that or what you think you're going to find here, but what I see is a sheriff out of his league, a sheriff who has nothing better to do than to harass me."

"The name's Cubiak."

"Whatever." Fielding scoffed and then waved a hand at the patio and house. "Go ahead, look all you want. We have nothing to hide." He sat and took Angela's hand. "But just out of curiosity, what exactly do you expect to find?"

"Traces of Henley's blood. A few specks will be sufficient. Specifically, particles of blood on the soles of the shoes that were worn by the person who killed him."

Fielding forced a laugh. "As I said, search all you want, Sheriff. You won't find anything here." He glanced around the terrace again. "Where'd you stash the bloodhounds?"

"I've got what I need right here," Cubiak said, holding up a spray bottle.

Fielding's eyes narrowed. "What's that?"

"Luminol. What you might call a chemical bloodhound. When it mixes with hemoglobin, it alters the molecular structure of the blood, turning the black-red color to a luminescent bluish-green."

Angela gasped and pulled the top of her dress tight around her neck, but her husband sneered.

"Well, good luck with your witch hunt. Just know this, when this farce is over, I'm going to sue your ass off. You, your department, and what passes for a justice system in this county."

"I'd like Lulu to be out here with us," Cubiak said, ignoring the threat.

The request seemed to surprise Fielding. "Lulu? The housekeeper? What the hell do you want with—"

The sheriff cut him off. "As I said, I'd like Lulu, your mother-in-law, to join us."

For a moment, Cubiak thought Fielding was going to leap up again and take a swing at him.

"How the hell . . ." He swallowed the rest of the question and stalked to the doorway, where he bellowed her name down the hall.

Lulu appeared almost instantly, as if she had been nearby and eavesdropping. Unruffled by what she had undoubtedly overheard, Angela's mother strode out onto the terrace looking as sanguine as when she had first greeted the sheriff.

For Lulu's sake, the sheriff repeated what he had said earlier about using luminol to find traces of blood on the premises. But this time he elaborated. Henley had died from a blow to the back of the head. According to the medical examiner, the wound would have bled profusely, making it nearly impossible for the killer to avoid stepping into the victim's blood while dragging the body to the boat. Given the storm breaking overhead and the real if unlikely possibility of a witness arriving at the scene, the murderer had to get away quickly. There would be no time to consider incriminating details. No time for the killer to wipe traces of blood from the shoes. The time for that would come later.

While Cubiak expounded, Lulu smirked, which was the reaction he expected. The ersatz housekeeper was an old-fashioned kind of woman, like his mother, one who relied on bleach for the most stubborn cleaning jobs: A grass stain on a pair of pants or an ink stain on a shirt. Or blood on the bottom of a shoe. In her worldview, bleach was a miracle worker. Combined with diligent scrubbing, it would erase all evidence of wrongdoing.

The sheriff would bet money that Lulu hadn't bothered to check out her theory. Even if the notion had occurred to her, she wouldn't have known how. Chances were that Lulu didn't know how to use library references and resources or how to conduct an internet search on the subject. Cubiak wanted to tell her to wipe the smirk from her face but realized it would disappear soon enough. He almost felt sorry for her; she had tried so hard to do everything correctly but had got it all wrong.

While Cubiak talked, Fielding feigned boredom and Angela played with her empty champagne glass. Though she never looked at her mother, she quickly assumed the older woman's brash attitude.

"Aren't you worried that one of us—the guilty party, surely—will run off while you're puttering around inside," she said as she gestured to the open terrace and the long expanses of beach that stretched out on either side of the house.

Cubiak refused to be baited. "My deputy is waiting on the road. He'll be here as soon as he gets my signal."

The sheriff palmed his phone. "I'm texting him now," he said.

With Rowe stationed on the patio under orders to keep the trio in place, the sheriff retreated inside. Passing the collection of abstract art, he wondered what the paintings were worth—probably more than he could earn in several decades or even a lifetime. Add in the house, jewelry, and the stocks and bonds hidden in the safe—Cubiak was sure there was a safe in the manse—he figured he was breathing the rarefied air that the 10 percent took as their birthright. How ironic that this fortress of wealth and the power that it represented was about to be undone by a cheap bottle of bleach.

If he was right.

He started at the opposite end of the building. The kitchen was upscale, like everything else he had seen. A breakfast nook at the back opened to the lake; from the side there was another short hall and the door to the garage. There was a symmetry to the structure: three steps down to the terrace and three down to the large garage, which provided ample space for the three vehicles inside. Fielding's SUV was parked nearest the entrance door. A two-seater yellow convertible, the kind of sporty car Angela would drive, was next. The third was a beige compact registered to Lulu.

The floor had been swept clean and doubtless washed as well. To the naked eye, the concrete appeared pristine. Cubiak shut the door and switched off the overhead fluorescent bulbs. The room dimmed immediately.

If there was any blood in or around any of the three vhehicles—even minute amounts remaining after a thorough scrubbing with plain water, soap, and even bleach—the luminol would find it.

Starting with the SUV, the sheriff sprayed the chemical on the floor and on the brake, gas pedal, and floor mat in front of the driver's seat. Then he waited for the telltale glow to appear.

Nothing happened.

Had the bastard driven a rental that day and been astute enough to walk into the house in his stocking feet? Grudgingly, Cubiak acknowledged the possibility.

He found no traces of blood in Angela's car either.

Finally, the sheriff repeated the procedure with Lulu's vehicle. Within seconds, splotches of the revelatory glow emerged inside the car. He sprayed luminol on the garage floor alongside the car and watched as a ragged trail of luminescent pinpricks emerged. As he worked his way toward the house and the kitchen door, the trail lengthened. Each bright fleck on the narrow path identified a telltale speck of blood left by the killer.

Cubiak called the state crime lab and requested priority assistance at the scene. The forensic imaging unit would photograph the evidence, and further testing would show if the DNA in the blood matched

Henley's DNA, but for now, for his purposes, this was enough.

He had found blood. Cubiak had expected as much; what he didn't expect was that the evidence would point to Lulu as the killer.

From the garage, Cubiak went into the house to test the shoes. There were shoes by the inside rear door and in the front hall. Shoes kicked off in the office and media room. Shoes in the bedroom closets and under the dressers. Fielding's footwear came away squeaky clean. The same was true for Angela's cornucopia of stylish footwear.

Lulu's shoe collection was far more modest than her daughter's and tended toward thick-soled sensible oxfords that closed with laces or Velcro. One by one, Cubiak sprayed luminol on the soles of the shoes but he found nothing. Given that he had discovered traces of blood in Lulu's car and on the garage floor leading away from it, he should find corroborating stains on a pair of her shoes.

The sheriff cursed under his breath. But shoes were easily disposed of. Lulu could have thrown out or destroyed the ones she had worn that day.

On the terrace, the household trio waited in sullen silence. The clouds had thickened and a cool wind had come up from the lake. Mother and daughter sat bundled in matching pink-and-white striped beach towels, while Fielding appeared oblivious to the drop in temperature and lounged with his bare legs extended on the terrace, his bony feet crossed at the ankles.

Cubiak glanced at his watch. He had been inside for more than an hour, far longer than he had realized.

As soon as Fielding spied the sheriff, he spoke up. "It's about time you got back. We're sitting out here freezing, and that guy over there"—he gestured toward Rowe—"wouldn't let us go in and change. What the hell did you find anyway? Nothing, I'll bet," he said.

Ignoring him, the sheriff approached Rowe.

"Everything okay?" he asked.

The deputy nodded.

"I'll take over then. And while I'm out here, I want you to secure the garage." Cubiak spoke quietly so the others couldn't hear.

Rowe nodded again. No questions asked.

"Now what? Where's he going?" Fielding said as the deputy headed toward the door.

"You'll find out soon enough," Cubiak said.

He set the luminol on the table.

"Lulu, have you . . ." The sheriff was about to ask the housekeeper if she had loaned her car to anyone lately when a whiff of a familiar aroma stopped him.

"Are you wearing shoes?" he asked.

Lulu looked down. "Yes," she said in a whisper.

"May I see them, please?"

"Oh, for God's sake," Fielding said, unwinding his limbs and making as if to stand.

Cubiak didn't bother to turn around.

"Sit down and be quiet," he said. Then he added, "Lulu?"

The housekeeper vibrated with fear. She wet her lips and threw anxious glances at her companions. Then she lowered her eyes and slowly peeled away the striped towel, revealing her feet on the stone patio. Unlike Angela and Fielding, who were barefoot, Lulu wore red canvas slip-ons. The shoes were faded and scuffed, the kind of old favorites a woman would slip on when she was in a hurry. They were the one pair Cubiak had yet to test.

"Please, give me your shoes," he said.

Lulu stared straight ahead as if she hadn't heard.

"If you don't mind . . . ," Cubiak said.

Reluctantly she pressed the toe of one foot against the heel of the other and pushed off one shoe and then the other.

"These are your shoes?" Cubiak said.

"Yes," Lulu said, and then she started to cry.

The sheriff turned the shoes over and set them on the table.

Fielding stood and stared at the thin soles. "What are you doing?" he said.

"Finishing what I started," Cubiak said as he pulled the coffee urn alongside the shoes. Then he arranged a stack of plates and cups on the opposite side. Finally he draped a beach towel over the two short towers.

"This should keep out enough light," he said as he looked inside the makeshift tent.

"You're crazy, you know that? Wait until my lawyer gets done with you," Fielding said.

Brushing aside the taunts, Cubiak reached inside and sprayed the luminol on the soles of Lulu's red shoes.

31 \ INVISIBLE PROOF

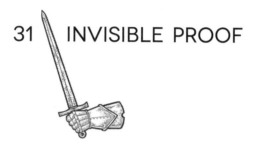

After a few seconds, Cubiak peered under the towel. Fielding leaned over his shoulder. The man was so close, the sheriff felt his hot breath on his ear.

"Well, what's there? What do you see? Anything?"

"There are traces of blood on both shoes. More on the right one than the left."

Fielding shoved Cubiak aside.

"Let me look," he said.

A moment later, he straightened and let out a laugh. "There's nothing on those shoes." His tone was smug and taunting. But as he stepped back it became angry. "What the hell kind of stunt are you trying to pull?"

"You didn't see anything because the luminescence disappears in about thirty seconds. You weren't quick enough," the sheriff said. He sprayed the shoes a second time. "Now look."

Fielding sneered and leaned down. When he finished looking at the shoes, the sneer was gone, but he remained stubbornly defiant.

"So, there's a little blood on the shoes. So what? It could be from a dead squirrel or deer. We're surrounded by woods. Hell, half the peninsula is forest. Lulu could have picked up traces of blood walking anywhere and not known it."

"Then why wash the shoes?"

Cubiak directed the question to Lulu, who remained frozen in place, with her head bowed and her hands clasped in her lap.

"You don't have to answer that," Fielding said.

Lulu wet her lips and squeezed her hands tighter.

Cubiak continued to talk to her. "The other day, when I walked through the hallway and smelled bleach, I was puzzled. Who'd use that kind of cleaner in this posh setting? And why? You would, wouldn't you, Lulu? It's what you know from your past. It's what you always used to clean your house, isn't it? Bleach is strong and cheap. Living here, you didn't worry about cost, but you needed something strong, something you could rely on.

"What were you so desperate to clean? Grease stains, rust, or maybe blood? You used bleach to wipe off the soles of the shoes you wore when you killed Henley, and you washed the garage floor with it too. You thought that it would take care of everything, didn't you?"

Lulu yelped and grabbed for her daughter's hand, but Angela reared back and swatted her away.

"Don't touch me," she said in a low growl.

Cubiak ignored the histrionics and went on addressing the housekeeper.

"Ironically, you were right but only partially. The bleach eliminated the visible signs of blood, so you were certain the evidence had been washed away. But it wasn't. The bleach didn't get it all; it can't. There are always minuscule specks left. They were too small for you to see but not too small for the luminol to detect."

A solitary tear trickled down Lulu's face. She groped for Angela's hand again and this time she latched on. Watching her, Cubiak remembered Lulu grabbing for the doorknob on his first visit and the flash of bright pink he had noticed as her hand darted past him. At the time, the splash of color had seemed inconsequential. But if it wasn't . . . ?

"Please," Lulu said, pleading with her daughter.

Angela's face contorted in horror. She tore loose and leapt to her feet. Clutching her hands to her chest, she looked around wildly and then screamed at her mother. "Oh my God, you're a murderer. I've been living under the same roof as a killer."

"No, no," Lulu sobbed.

"What a fool I've been. I trusted you. I should have known better. You're insane. You've always been a crazy bitch."

Angela snatched a glass from the table and raised it to hurl at her mother.

"Stop it," Cubiak said, grabbing her wrist.

Angela shrieked. The glass fell and smashed against the brick, shattering into dozens of pieces. She stared at the shards.

Then her arm went limp. As her fury drained away, Angela assumed a helpless innocence and turned a cherubic face toward him.

"I'm okay now," she said quietly.

The shift in her manner was instantaneous, almost magical.

Cubiak released his grip but kept his attention focused on her. Not only did her demeanor and appearance change, even her voice was different as she called out to her husband for help.

Fielding swept her into his arms. "My darling girl," he said.

Cubiak was tempted to applaud. He had witnessed a similar swift metamorphosis when watching the video of his son on stage. Like Joey's mutation into his character, Angela's makeover was a performance. An aspiring actress who had had years of practice playing Guinevere, she knew all the tricks. Suddenly Cubiak started to realize that she might even have fooled him.

While Fielding held his wife, the sheriff reached under the towel for the red shoes and slid them into an evidence bag. Then he picked up Lulu's cup and put it into a second bag.

"What do you need that for? You've got her shoes. Isn't that proof enough that she killed the son of a bitch?" Fielding said.

"Is it?" Cubiak held the man's gaze. "I was inside your house for nearly an hour looking at shoes. Did you know that Angela and her mother wore the same size?"

"So what?" Fielding said, tightening his grip on his wife.

The sheriff held up the evidence bag with the shoes. "There's little doubt that the killer wore these on the beach where Henley died. It's also a given that forensics will find dead skin cells with Lulu's DNA inside them. The issue is whether they will find Angela's as well. Because if they do, that changes everything."

Then Cubiak picked up a chunk of glass from the terrace. He chose a piece from the rim of the stemware that Angela had deliberately dropped, the same flute she had been drinking from earlier. He put the shard in a third bag.

Fielding pulled his wife closer, but his outcries sputtered into silence.

Cubiak displayed the three evidence bags.

"Both Angela and Lulu had a motive to murder Scott Henley. Lulu also had the means, and I'm beginning to think that Angela may have as well. The question is: which of the two is the killer?"

32 \ A LITANY OF HORRORS

Saturday morning dawned bright and clear. A hopeful sign, Cubiak thought as he drove to the justice center. On his way, he made three calls.

The first was to his assistant. "What day did you say you were at the Woodland Spa for that manicure?" he asked.

"I didn't, but it was the day the storm hit." Lisa's tone betrayed her curiosity, but he ended the call before she could question him.

Wednesday. Angela's day at the spa. The day Henley was killed.

Next the sheriff called the spa and asked the manager if Angela had missed her manicure the previous week. No, she said. According to the schedule, Angela had kept the appointment.

"You're sure?"

The manager hesitated. "Well, someone kept the appointment. Who else would it have been?"

Finally he contacted the jail and told the matron he was coming in to talk to Lulu and was stopping for coffee on the way. He would pick up something for the suspect as well, if he knew what she wanted.

By the time Cubiak arrived, Lulu was seated in one of the interview rooms. The sheriff placed a cup of Earl Grey in front of her and then he took his place on the other side of the metal table. She ignored the tea, but he took a sip of his coffee and began recording the session.

"I have a theory about manicures and how you got your nails done in

216

place of your daughter on the day Scott Henley was killed," Cubiak said.

Lulu flushed.

"Unless you tell me everything that happened that day, the day the storm hit, you will be charged with killing him," he continued.

Lulu stared past him at the white wall. Her face was inscrutable; her hands were neatly folded into a fist and planted on the table.

"If you cooperate, if you tell me the whole story, it will work in your favor."

Lulu squeezed her eyes shut and breathed in heavily. She hadn't slept well since the storm, and the fatigue showed in the dark circles under her eyes.

"You want me to snitch on my daughter," she said, finally.

"I want you to tell the truth."

"The truth?" she said, as if she had been asked to defend an obscure, existential doctrine. "Does anyone really know the truth?"

"Maybe not about everything, but we all know the truth about something," the sheriff said.

Lulu conjured up a wan smile. "I have nothing to say."

"Then I have no reason to be here." Cubiak stood and picked up his cup of coffee. "I'll be back this afternoon. You have until then to decide."

He gave her five hours to brood over the situation. He was sure she hadn't killed Scott Henley, but he couldn't prove that she was innocent without her help. Even if forensics found traces of Angela's DNA in the red shoes, that was not proof she had worn them the day Henley was killed. She could have slipped them on anytime. Even a mediocre lawyer would pick up on that possibility and use it to advantage.

At two o'clock, Cubiak faced Lulu across the same table in the same windowless interview room. He set a thick folder on the table and slid another cup of Earl Grey toward her. When she reached for the tea, he took it as a sign that she meant to cooperate.

The sheriff was anxious to pin down the specifics of the past week: Why had Lulu answered Angela's phone? What had she heard? How had she snuck into the spa and passed Henley's message to her daughter? Most critically: what happened afterward?

Lulu ignored the questions.

"You want the truth? I'll give it to you—all of it. Otherwise you won't understand why I did what I did and why Angela is the way she is," she said finally.

For the sheriff to know the truth, Lulu needed to reconstruct an Angela that existed only in her memory, an Angela he would never know. She needed to talk about the years when her daughter was a blessing and life was good before she could describe the descent into hell.

"I'd had problems with my health, the kind that made it hard to have a baby. Angela was a miracle child, and after she was born, we wondered what we'd done to deserve such an angel. She was a sweet, darling little girl. Unless you've had a daughter, you can't imagine the joy she brought us."

Cubiak had and he could, but he didn't share that with Lulu.

"We did everything to make her happy, gave her everything we could, and when she looked at us with those beautiful blue eyes, we did more, anything she asked. She was a good child. Every night before she went to bed, she knelt and said her prayers, and do you know what she asked for? She asked God to make her daddy and mommy happy."

Lulu swiped at her eyes.

"Now it all seems like a dream, something I imagined. I don't know when things started to change. It happened so slowly that we didn't notice. But by sixth grade, Angela stopped being sweet and started acting mean. Some of it was natural. Children rebel, don't they? Some of it was our fault. We couldn't afford to buy her the things the other kids had and that made her mad. When she was in eighth grade, one of the girls got a fancy video game player for Christmas, and Angela wanted one too. When we said we couldn't afford it, she didn't talk to us for days. Things got worse after she started high school. She called us her white-trash parents and said she hated us. She started to wear makeup, lots of it, and she had things that we didn't buy for her. Expensive clothes and jewelry. One day she came home with a cell phone. When I asked her how she got it, she said she found it."

Lulu toyed with the half-empty cup of tea. "Angela found lots of things. We were decent churchgoing people, and she broke our hearts.

If I didn't give in to her and let her do what she wanted, she'd pinch my arm black and blue. Once she slapped me."

The litany of horrors went on: the litter of kittens they found strangled in the garage after they refused to buy a car for Angela; the time she ran off and stayed away for three days when they said she couldn't attend a coed sleepover, and then lied and said she had been home and they had been too drunk to notice. An endless stream of lies. Things gone missing from the house.

"Did you talk to anyone about this?"

Lulu shook her head. "We were afraid that people would think we were unfit parents and that someone from the state would take her away and put her in one of those horrible foster homes."

The air-conditioning kicked in, and Lulu pulled her green sweater tight across her chest.

"We kept asking ourselves why. Her daddy drank, probably too much, and I used to, too, not so much when I was pregnant, but some. So I thought maybe it was my fault, that something I did twisted her around when she was inside me. Could that be it, Sheriff?"

Cubiak didn't know how to answer. How could he tell Lulu that the characteristics and behavior she had ascribed to her daughter fit the profile of a sociopath. Had she ever heard the term? Would she know what it meant?

He cleared his throat. "I don't think so," he said.

She gave him a small smile. "Thank you. You're being very kind."

Lulu reached for her tea, and he waited for her to finish.

"What about school? Did her teachers say anything?" Cubiak asked.

"School?" Lulu sniggered. "Everyone at school loved Angela. She was their pride and joy—always the best student, the first to volunteer for any project. Captain of the cheerleading squad and star of the school play. Class president junior year. Prom queen senior year."

Lulu picked at the rim of the paper cup. "Well, maybe not everyone. Angela had enemies too. She said a couple of the girls were jealous, so they spread lies about her cheating on tests and stealing their boyfriends. She couldn't help it that she was so pretty and that the boys all liked her. It didn't take her long to learn how to use her looks."

Cubiak stopped himself from nodding. Angela's red bikini under the white robe and the soft mound of her breasts over the top of the bra: she had made sure he would see what she wanted him to see.

"My daughter liked nice things. She craved money and what she could buy with it. That's why she wanted to be a model. She thought she'd be one of those women who were paid thousands of dollars an hour for pouting at a camera. Instead she ended up being a waitress, like me. Only I worked at a truck stop, and she was at a fancy Chicago restaurant. That's how she met Scott. He seemed like a nice guy."

"You knew him?"

"Not really. I went to Chicago one time to see her, and he was there at her apartment. She was furious that I hadn't called first, but I knew if I did, she'd make an excuse—she always did. I wanted to tell her that her father had left me. We'd been fighting a lot, and he said he'd finally had enough. Of her, of me, of everything."

Lulu stopped abruptly and waved a hand dismissively. "Doesn't matter now. But that's the day I met Scott. Such a handsome young man, I said to her. I hoped they'd get married and that she'd change back to the way she'd been before. But he was a lot like Angela, never satisfied with what he had, always dreaming and wanting more."

Lulu sighed. "It didn't take long before Angela got caught up in that ridiculous larping business and the fantasy of being an actress and all that bullcrap."

"Did she love Scott?"

"She loved what she thought she'd get from him, that's all. When the larping business didn't deliver, she looked for a better catch, someone with money."

"Zachary Fielding."

"Mister Money Bags himself—that's what Angela called him. There were a few others before him, but eventually she settled on him."

"Why did she take up with Scott again?"

Lulu rubbed her chin. "For the excitement. Her married life was posh but dull. Why do you think she convinced Zach to let me move in with them? By then I'd remarried and divorced again, and she pretended that she wanted to help me out, but really she wanted me there to be her spy. She needed me to keep track of where her husband went and what he did, so she could go off and be with her old boyfriend. I warned her that it would come to no good, but she didn't listen. She never listened. 'It's just a fling. It doesn't mean anything,' she said."

"Did Fielding ask you to spy on her for him as well?"

"Not as such, but he wasn't stupid. I don't know if he ever trusted her completely, but about a year ago, he started watching her like a hawk. Whenever she went out, he'd ask where she'd been and who she'd seen. It wasn't a marriage based on love, Sheriff. It was an arrangement, and when Zachary suspected that Angela wasn't keeping her part of the bargain, he wanted to know what was going on."

"Did you ever see signs of abuse?"

Lulu shifted in her chair. "Physical abuse, no. Zachary was a hard man to please. He knew what he wanted—what he'd paid for—and he went after it, but I never saw him raise a hand to Angela."

"It wasn't Fielding who gave her the black eye?" As Cubiak was convinced Angela had wanted him to believe.

Lulu shook her head.

"It was fake, a trick with makeup?" Angela putting her stage knowledge to work?

Lulu looked away, pained. "The black eye was real. I gave it to her."

"You?"

"She made me. I didn't want to. I told her I couldn't. We argued about it for days. She said it was important, that it would help. Help what? What do you mean? I asked, but she wouldn't say. She just kept pushing me until I did what she wanted. Like always."

"She pushed you how? Emotionally? Physically?"

"Both. I tried to stand up to her, but I couldn't. When Angela wanted something, she wouldn't let up, and I could take only so much before I gave in. But this time I absolutely refused. I wasn't going to hit my own child."

Lulu looked stricken. "One morning when Zachary was out, she shoved me against the bathroom wall and started jabbing me with her fingers. Like this—" Lulu opened her hand and punched the air over the table.

"You hit her?"

"I pushed her away, but she kept coming back and poking at me. Really hard, with those long nails of hers. Over and over. When I pleaded with her to stop, she sneered and slapped me across the face. I didn't know what to do, so I made a fist and started swinging."

Cubiak nudged a box of tissues across the table. The kind of family fights where insults were screamed and punches thrown weren't unheard of in his old working-class neighborhood. He had grown up thinking that people who lived in expensive lakefront apartments or mansions were different, better. But he had come to learn that meanness was pandemic.

"Did she try to get away from you?"

"Get away? She was practically on top of me. She wanted me to hurt her. Later she even made me take pictures of the bruise. She said she was going to keep it in case she needed proof that Zachary had hit her in one of his jealous rages. They had a prenuptial agreement. If Angela was unfaithful, he could divorce her, and she'd be left with the clothes on her back and whatever she could fit in one suitcase. If she could prove that he'd cheated on her or abused her in any way, she'd walk away with a million dollars."

"She was setting him up?"

"She was up to something, that's for sure. Angela liked to plan ahead. Think about it, Sheriff. If she could pull it off, she'd have her fancy boyfriend and a million bucks to boot."

Then why murder Scott? It didn't make sense unless he was disposable. If she killed her boyfriend and framed her husband for the crime, she would be rich and free.

"Were you in the habit of answering Angela's phone when she wasn't home?"

"Are you kidding? I wasn't supposed to go anywhere near it."

"Why did you answer it that day?"

"Because it wouldn't stop ringing, one call after another. It rang so many times I figured it must be an emergency."

She closed her eyes and inhaled. "I wish I'd left it alone."

"It was Scott, wasn't it?"

Lulu nodded. "He thought I was Angela! He sounded so desperate, babbling on about how much he loved her and how he'd seen the light. He said that money didn't matter, that they needed to be together and that he would come clean with Zachary and tell him everything. He said he was stranded and hurt and begged her to come get him. 'Help me, please,' he said."

"Did you say anything to him?"

She shook her head. "The line went dead. I didn't know what else to do but go and tell Angela."

"How'd you get into the spa without being seen?"

"I parked around back and went in through the rear door."

"It wasn't locked?"

"It's never locked. Angela said the receptionist and a couple of the employees kept it open so they could slip out back to smoke. I'd come in that way before to sneak messages to her."

"What happened after you told Angela about the call?"

"She was furious. She called Scott a fool and said she wasn't going to let him ruin everything. Then she dragged me into the ladies' room and made me switch clothes with her. 'I have to talk to him before he does something stupid,' she said. She told me to stay at the spa in her place—that she'd be back as soon as she could. She wrapped a towel around my head and told me to sit in the sauna until I was called for a manicure. 'It's a new girl, she won't know you're not me,' she said. Then she left."

"You gave her your shoes?"

"I had to. She couldn't go barefoot or wearing those flimsy spa slippers."

"Whose car did she take?"

"Mine. Hers was parked on the street so it was just easier that way."

"How long was she gone?"

"I don't know. I don't wear a watch and there weren't any clocks on the walls. I laid down in the sauna with my face to the wall, pretending to rest. You're right about the manicure. After a while, a young woman—probably one of them college kids working there for the summer—opened the door and said, 'Angela, you need to get up. It's time for your manicure.' I kept my head down and followed her to the room where the

the woman was setting things up. She never really looked at me. She just worked on my nails."

Lulu sighed and spread her hands on the table. Her fingers were red and swollen. Her nails were bare. "I'd never had anyone fuss over my me like that before. It was nice."

"You chose pink polish, didn't you?"

She nodded. "Angela made me take it off. But that's okay, it was chipping."

"No one else at the spa saw you?"

"No. Everything there is very private so it was just the two of us in the booth. When my nails were finished, the manicurist started tidying up and I went back to the sauna. A few minutes later, Angela showed up. I tried to talk to her, but she said I had to go, that she'd tell me everything later at home. We changed clothes again and I left."

"What about Fielding?"

"I wasn't supposed to say anything to him. I knew that without Angela even telling me. She was home by the time he got back. The storm was already so bad we didn't pay attention to much else. Around ten, the power went out and the generator kicked in. When Zachary went into the basement to reset the breakers, I got a chance to ask Angela what had happened with Scott. 'What do you mean? Nothing happened. He was already gone when I got there. Don't worry about him, he's probably sitting around somewhere having a glass of wine right now.'"

Lulu started shredding a tissue. "I wanted to believe her. I didn't have any reason not to, not until later."

"What made you change your mind?"

"I told you I couldn't sleep—first it was the storm and then it was worrying about her and Scott. I got up around one and walked around the house, trying to tire myself out. I must have fallen asleep for a little while because when I woke up again, it was just after three. I don't know if I'd heard something—the wind was howling like mad—or what. I got up and sat in the living room, as far from the windows as I could get. I smelled bleach, just like you said you did, and I thought I was imagining it or that maybe it was something from the storm. Doesn't lightning make things smell weird? Then I saw Angela coming out of the laundry room. She was barefoot and wearing an old T-shirt and shorts."

"Did she see you?"

"No."

Cubiak folded his arms and sat back. "You didn't wash the shoes, did you?" he said.

Lulu shook her head.

"Why didn't you say something yesterday, when I accused you at the house?"

She shuddered and started to cry.

Watching her, the sheriff understood that Lulu hadn't been obstinate when she had refused to answer his question about the shoes; she had been naive, trusting that her daughter would do the right thing.

"You were waiting for Angela to speak up, weren't you? You didn't think she'd let you take the blame."

Lulu clamped a hand over her mouth and began rocking back and forth.

"By the time you realized that she wasn't going to say anything, it was too late. You knew that if you started to deny doing it, it would look like you were trying to shift suspicion to your daughter. Is that it?"

Lulu bobbed her head.

"When you saw her that night, did you say anything?"

A moment passed. Lulu stopped swaying and settled her hands in her lap. "No, I didn't want to risk waking Zachary, and I didn't know what to say. The next morning, when I found my red shoes in the laundry room, I could tell the bottoms had been scrubbed clean, and I got scared. I didn't know what was going on. I couldn't go anywhere or do anything that day because of the storm. But on Friday I got up early. The mister was in his study making his calls and Angela was still sleeping, so I put Jasper in the SUV—it's the only thing he fits in—and drove to the beach at Jacksonport. I don't know what I thought I'd find. I guess I was looking for Scott, but there wasn't anyone there, just a big mess on the beach. I headed back, stopping at every beach along the way. In some places, there was hardly any sand left. After a while, I told myself I was being silly, and that Angela was right. Scott was fine and everything was okay. Then I climbed that dune and saw the boat turned over on the sand. A man called up to me and said there was someone trapped underneath. He asked me to help him lift the boat."

Lulu went on as if in a trance. Her voice steady, she described how Jasper got away from her and ran toward the man on the beach. How she understood in a way she couldn't explain that the person under the boat was Scott, that he was dead.

"I couldn't go down there. I stayed on the dune and whistled for Jasper to come back. Then I put him in the car and drove home. When I got here, Zachary was still in his study and Angela was in the bedroom, sorting through her sweaters. She had a pile on the bed of the ones she wanted to keep. The rest were on the floor. They'd be mine to give away or wear, hand-me-downs from my rich daughter. 'Where were you?' she said. I told her what I'd done and what I'd seen, but she wouldn't look at me. When I finished, she turned toward the window and stood there just staring out. She got real quiet for a minute. Then she turned back toward me. 'Well, maybe it's not him. Maybe it's just some dumb fisherman who got caught in the storm,' she said.

"That's when I told her that I'd seen her that first night and that I'd found the bottle of bleach and my shoes in the laundry room. She said she'd washed them off because she'd accidentally stepped on a dead fish on the beach. She said she'd even wiped up the car and the garage floor as best she could but that I should do it again just to make sure everything was squeaky clean and didn't start to stink."

"So you did."

"Of course."

"And the fire at Door Camelot? Were you involved with that as well?"

Lulu tugged at her sleeves. "That was her big idea, after we'd heard on the news that it was Scott under the boat. She said that whatever had happened was probably an accident, but that in case it wasn't, there were lots of people who didn't like him and that if there was a fire at the center, there'd be plenty of suspects. One of the neighbors, an old farmer, had threatened him in front of the other larpers. Maybe he'd get blamed. We wouldn't hurt anyone, she said, just damage a couple of the buildings. She called it a diversion."

With little prompting, Lulu walked Cubiak through the steps they had taken. The rendition she gave matched the scenario that the fire chief had outlined the morning of the blaze.

"How did you get away without Zachary seeing you?"

"Angela gave me a sedative to put in his tea. He always had a cup of chamomile before going to bed so he could sleep better."

"You didn't think to say no to any of this?" Cubiak said.

"Of course, I did. I didn't want to believe that my daughter had anything to do with Scott's death, but I had to help her." Lulu gave a sad smile. "Besides, I knew it wouldn't do any good to refuse. Angela always got her way."

In the shadow of the opulent home on Rosemary Lane, the sheriff arrested Angela Fielding for the murder of Scott Henley. Her husband raged at Cubiak, but Angela remained mute in response to the charge. Later, at the justice center, she remained silent throughout the formal interrogation, refusing to answer any questions, even when her lawyer nodded his approval.

"Your evidence is circumstantial at best," the attorney said as he scribbled furiously in a hand-tooled leather-bound notebook.

Cubiak pulled several pieces of paper from a plain white folder and pretended to review them. Finally, he tapped the pages on the table, and when the edges were aligned he slipped them back into the folder.

"Is it?" he said.

The sheriff regarded the suspect. "It was all very clever, and you might have gotten away with it, if it hadn't been for the lie you told your husband, about what happened at the spa."

The attorney's scratching stopped midsentence.

"I was there. I heard it."

Angela's right eye twitched.

She knows I've got her, Cubiak thought. He switched off the recorder, picked up the folder, and pushed back from the table.

The session was over.

33 THE COLOR OF HOPE

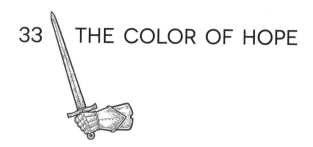

Two weeks later, the larpers held a memorial service for Scott Henley at Door Camelot. A wooden stage had been erected in the meadow behind the horse paddock, and rows of chairs were arranged in a half circle before it. The King Arthur costume hung on a tall T-frame in the middle of the platform, as if waiting for Henley's ghost to appear. A trio of madrigal singers gathered near the entrance gate and serenaded the guests as they entered. Even the horses took part. Standing along the fence, they nickered softly and kept careful watch over the crowd.

Cubiak and Bathard found seats in the rear.

"What made you suspect Angela?" the former coroner asked.

"I didn't at first. She had me duped until I remembered that she fancied herself an actor. When I watched her go from hot to cold and back instantly, I realized she'd scripted the whole thing and was putting on a performance. And when I finally caught on that she had lied about the manicurist, I knew she was guilty."

Bathard frowned and looked at the sheriff. "The manicurist?"

"Angela had a standing Wednesday appointment at the Woodland Spa that included a manicure. She was there the Wednesday that Henley disappeared, but she didn't get her nails done. She said the manicurist was absent, but that wasn't true because Lisa got a manicure at the spa that afternoon. Angela made Lulu keep the appointment, while she slipped away to Jacksonport where Henley was waiting to be rescued. But instead of saving him, she killed him."

"Money before love," Bathard said.

Cubiak nodded and stood to let a young couple slip past. As the seats filled around them, the two friends fell into companionable silence. While Bathard studied the program, the sheriff surveyed the crowd. Most of the people filing in were strangers, but not all.

Near the front, Lisa and Veronica Kaiser sat with their heads together. Pardy was across the aisle. There was no sign of George Tinsel, but Cubiak didn't expect him to come. The sheriff was surprised to see Florian Urbanski standing off to the side.

The old farmer glanced around wide eyed and lost. Cubiak got up, ready to intercept him before he disrupted the program, but as he started forward, he realized that Urbanski had donned his Sunday best. He looked like a man headed to weekly services, not one on his way to stir up trouble. The seat next to the sheriff was empty and Cubiak waved him over.

Moments after Urbanski settled in, Isabelle Redding took the stage. She wore black leggings and the red-and-gold striped tunic of a medieval lad, and she carried a long brass trumpet. With a dramatic flourish, she raised the instrument to her mouth and sent a heralding blast out over the assemblage.

At the signal, the Knights of the Round Table appeared in full costume. As the music continued, Travis came down the aisle, followed by the squires and Amy Baxter dressed in the billowing Guinevere gown. With one hand, she clutched a bridal bouquet of white lilies to her breast, and in the other, she held the reins of a majestic black steed, which trailed obediently in her steps.

When they had reached the front, Guinevere and the knights ascended the stage and formed a semicircle around the King Arthur icon. At a final trumpet blast, the men raised their swords and the fair lady knelt and laid the flowers down in tribute. She remained kneeling while Isabelle sang a lyrical medieval song. Cubiak couldn't catch the words, but the melody was sad and sweet.

Urbanski cleared his throat. "This is almost as good as church," he said.

A long litany of eulogies followed. Praise for Scott Henley and his dedication to larping. Praise for his dream of Door Camelot. The speeches droned on. Travis spoke last and announced his intention to keep the center open. Larping groups around the country were sending financial aid and messages of support, he said, and the audience stood and cheered. Then with a final trill from the trumpet, the ceremony ended.

As the mourners headed to the lunch buffet, Cubiak exchanged handshakes and sympathetic words with both those in costume and those in street clothes. No one mentioned Angela Fielding, but several thanked him for apprehending Henley's killer.

Nick Youngman trolled the sidelines, filming.

"I didn't expect to find you still around here," Cubiak said.

"Trav asked me to record the service. He's going to use it as part of the fundraising campaign."

"What about you? What will you do with all the footage you've got?"

Nick toed the grass. "I don't know yet. I guess I'll keep it until I decide. The plan was to destroy Scott's reputation, but I don't really see the point now."

They talked a few minutes more, and then Cubiak caught up with Bathard at the buffet table. Urbanski lurked close by and followed them to a cluster of chairs in the shade. He eased down just as one of the knights walked past.

The old farmer laughed. "Lucky bastard. When I was his age, I got my dreams knocked out of my head with a quick slap and an order to get back to work."

Bathard patted his arm. "What did you want to be, Florian?" he asked.

Urbanski looked into the trees. "I thought I'd be another Mickey Mantle and play for the New York Yankees!" He colored, but for the first time since Cubiak had met him, he seemed happy.

"What about you, Doc? Did you grow up wanting to stick people with needles?"

Bathard chuckled. "Not at all. I envisioned myself as the next Edmund Hillary. I intended to climb Mount Everest first and then to conquer the rest of the world's towering peaks."

"And you, Sheriff?" Urbanski seemed to enjoy his role as grand inquisitor of dreams.

"Nothing special," Cubiak said. Emulating real-life heroes like Mickey Mantle and Sir Edmund Hillary sounded noble, unlike his childish fantasy of riding the range as Cowboy Cinnamon George, a notion he would rather keep to himself.

Urbanski looked at Cubiak. There was a sparkle in his eye. "I don't believe it," he said. "Not for a minute. I'd peg you for another Wyatt Earp."

Driving home, Cubiak was in an oddly melancholy mood. He took his time crossing the peninsula. As he meandered along the narrow back roads, he thought about the unhappy story Lulu had told and the youthful aspirations that Bathard and Urbanski had shared. He thought of his own life as well. So much loss, so much sorrow, so many dreams vanquished.

In the midst of his reverie, the sheriff crested the dune behind his house.

The lake came up suddenly. After the miles of thick forest he had gone through, the unfettered expanse of water was shocking. All that beautiful, vivid blue. The color of hope.

The beach below was pristine. His wife and son were on the deck. Against a backdrop of red azaleas, Cate sat in a high-back wicker chair. With their pet dog sprawled at her feet, she listened to Joey recite his lines for the play.

As he watched, Cubiak touched a hand to his heart. Camelot, he thought. Then he hurried down to join them.

ACKNOWLEDGMENTS

On rare occasions, a novel emerges from a single golden idea. More often, the plot develops from interesting threads of information that collect over time, simmer in the imagination, and then coalesce into a storyline that begs to be written.

That's how *Death Washes Ashore* came to be.

The book evolved from two ideas that were presented to me by different people at different times. The first tidbit arrived in the wake of a harsh storm on the Door County peninsula when my beach neighbor Bill Schultz sent an email about a boat that had washed up on the sand. "Wouldn't it be interesting if there was a body under it?" he said. The suggestion was facetious, and I took it that way, but the more I considered the possibility, I thought, well, why not?

Sometime later, my daughter Carla told me about larping or live-action role-playing. I knew a little about Civil War reenactments, but larping was different and grander in scope. The more I learned about this form of fantasy game playing, the more I realized that a fictional larping center in Door County was the ideal backdrop for a Dave Cubiak mystery.

There were many details to work out, but when I combined the elements—a devastating storm, a body washed ashore, and larping—I knew that I had the framework for the sixth book in the series. My thanks to Bill and Carla for getting me started.

Ultimately, many people helped shape the story and move the manuscript from the initial rough draft to the final, polished form. My deepest appreciation to my early readers: Barbara Bolsen, B. E. Pinkham, Norm Rowland, Jeanne Mellet, Julia Padvoiskis, Esther Spodek, and Carla Walkis. As with the previous volumes, additional thanks to my daughter Julia for the original map used in the book and for her continuing technical support.

By the time the manuscript was submitted to the publisher, the coronavirus had stamped its ugly mark on the world. Despite the uncertainty and challenges imposed by the subsequent pandemic, the staff at the University of Wisconsin Press proceeded to work apace and miraculously maintain a semblance of normalcy.

For this and for their unwavering support, I would like to express my gratitude to Director Dennis Lloyd, Senior Project Editor Sheila McMahon, Managing Editor Adam Mehring, Publicity Manager Kaitlin Svabek, and Sales and Marketing Manager Casey LaVela as well as to copyeditor Diana Cook. To Sara DeHaan, kudos for another magnificent cover.

Finally, a salute to the nation's independent booksellers who kept their doors open and stalwartly supplied books to readers during this challenging time. You deserve our ongoing gratitude and support.